Prussian Blue

Prussian Blue

An Alaric von Trelow Mystery

Book 1

Jason Collings

BEROLINA
BOOKS

ISBN-978-1-9191962-0-6

To Kath
All my love

Chapter 1

"Tannhäuser," whispered the night.

The young sentry's heavy eyes snapped wide, fatigue falling from his shoulders like a shed cloak. His throat tightened, the cold that gnawed his bones forgotten. He turned his head, straining to hear over his pounding heart. Silence. Had there been a voice at all? Had he dreamt it? The cautious rim of his helmet rose above the lip of the observation slit. Nothing. Black October fog had devoured the cratered ground and tangled wire. Even the gaunt giants of the shattered Argonne had vanished. He blinked and drew a chill breath, shivering his unease.

"Tannhäuser," the darkness breathed again.

Bloodless fingers gripped his rifle, clutching it to his mist-damp chest. He swallowed the childish instinct to cry out. The countersign, what was the countersign? Breathe... And again, breathe...

"Elizabeth," he hissed. Was it too soft? Had they heard? Best to say it again. "Elizabeth."

My God! Movement—a dark, formless shape, cresting the sandbags barely an arm's length away. Strangling a cry, stumbling backwards out of the plank-lined sentry post. Breaths coming too fast, heartbeat almost choking. Boots slipping and slithering on the mud-slick duckboards of the trench. The rifle's barrel leaping unsteadily, tracking his gaze. Why couldn't he feel the trigger?

The thing on the parapet teetered for a moment, as if caught by indecision, then tumbled awkwardly into the trench, landing with a thump and a heavy gasp. It lay there unmoving, then it groaned. A man.

Hartman fumbled an angular, brass torch from his tunic pocket. Its dim, unsteady glow revealed an American, an officer, a major—bare-headed, caked in mud, hands bound, cords cutting into the soft flesh of his wrists.

Mud-caked boots struck the duckboards beside the major's head. Christ! The torchlight leapt with Hartman's own nerves. The weak beam washed over a colossal, shapeless form, grown from the mud of the Champagne. Panic, cold and prickling, swallowed his thoughts. He almost crossed himself but couldn't move his hand from his rifle stock. Words from childhood hung on his lips.

Into Your hands I commend myself: my body and soul and all things.

Let Your holy angel be with me,

That the evil foe may have no power over me.

Yet it was a man—only a man—shrouded head to knee in a mud-spattered rain cape.

My God, though, he was huge. At least half a head taller than Hartman, a guardsman chosen for his height. Taller even than the Yank, a burly 'six-footer' bred on endless corn and beef. The figure's whole being bore menace, something primeval—a spirit of the deep old German forests.

Duty clawed reluctant words from Hartman's throat.

"Identify yourself." His voice wavering as much as the barrel of his weapon, leaving his cheeks washed with burning shame.

In reply the hooded individual threw the bulky cape over one shoulder revealing a filth-stained uniform of German field grey. One of their own. A rush of relief. But... Mein Gott... an officer... a Guard's officer... God in heaven! A lieutenant-colonel with the Iron Cross on his breast and, nestled at his throat between the flashes of his collar, a bright blue cross with fine gold lettering—'Pour le Mérite'. The Blue Max.

"God in heaven." The whispered words were in the cold air before he could trap them.

"Oberstleutnant von Trelow und Ehlinger," said the officer, each word deliberate. "First Prussian Foot Guards. Divisional Intelligence Officer, First Guards Infantry Division." His voice as deep, even, and cold as January snow upon the northern plains.

Hartman's breathless lips quivered wordlessly, his throat tight as a vice. His pulse pounded behind his staring eyes. The blessed sound of the sergeant's heavy steps along the duckboards. A rope for a drowning man.

"What is it, Hartman? What's going on?"

"Feldwebel..." Hartman croaked, but the sergeant's savage glare silenced him. Released from the crushing weight of responsibility, Hartman noticed the officer's incongruous load: Luger and trench knife, wire cutters, stick grenades, and over it all an American officer's brown leather pistol belt draped about him like a sash.

Hartman saw the sergeant snap off a salute sharp enough for the Potsdam parade ground and matched him without thinking. The lieutenant-colonel pushed back his hood and returned it. The face revealed in the flashlight glow was streaked with boot black and mud, but the features beneath belonged to a man not yet thirty—dirty blond hair cut regulation short and glacial eyes.

"Herr Oberstleutnant, we had no idea..." said the NCO. He got no further.

"I require immediate escort to my car at Marta/6," the lieutenant-colonel demanded.

The sergeant saluted again. "Of course, sir." Surely that wasn't a quaver in his voice.

Hartman prayed he wouldn't choose him. His watch was almost over, and this apparition from no-man's land…

The sergeant—thank God—lunged into one of the shallow shelters carved into the back wall of the trench and hauled out a sleeping man.

"Niedermann, you're to escort the Herr Oberstleutnant and his prisoner to Sector Marta/6, at once," snapped the sergeant, adding under his breath, "And for Christ's sake, don't get lost."

Hartman watched Niedermann struggle from exhausted sleep. He saw sleep-fogged eyes blink, searching for explanation for the abrupt awakening. They found the figure in the torchlight, and the colour drained from the guardsman's cheeks.

Niedermann's back snapped straight. He mumbled his understanding, saluted the sergeant, the colonel, and began to salute the prisoner—catching himself with his arm half-raised. He lurched back into the scrape for his rifle, moved it to port, and stumbled towards the communications trench, casting a nervous glance towards the mud-caked colonel who'd appeared from no-man's land.

The imposing officer, evidently satisfied with their response, laid a large and proprietorial hand upon the American's shoulder, and steered him after the guide, gracing them with a silent nod of thanks.

Hartman joined the sergeant and watched them out of sight, exhaling a grateful, ragged breath.

"An Oberst… Coming in from no-man's land," he whispered.

The sergeant replied with a grim nod. "And with an American staff officer, Hartman."

The sergeant's words carried hidden weight, but the young soldier didn't understand. He looked at his superior with blank incomprehension. His naivety earned him an exasperated frown.

"Staff majors don't go into forward positions, boy, the closest they get to the Front is a headquarters dugout in a second- or third-line support trench." The sergeant paused for a moment to allow his meaning to sink in. "Which means, that oberstleutnant went in there and dragged him out."

"God in heaven!" said Hartman once more, finally understanding.

"Something like that," agreed the sergeant.

*

Oberstleutnant Alaric von Trelow und Ehlinger swallowed bitter bile. The adrenaline drained away with the gall of fear, leaving the familiar, hollow nausea—the twisted knot in the belly he'd learned to cherish. It meant he'd survived.

He stared past the American's shoulder, breath steady, posture firm despite the turmoil inside, watching every step of the young guardsman as he led them along slippery boards, around ammunition boxes, discarded ration tins, abandoned water cans, and the huddled forms of slumbering soldiers. He envied them, but his night's task remained incomplete. The dangers of no-man's land lay behind him but he couldn't relax, could not lose focus; not yet.

His hand lay heavy and firm on the prisoner's shoulder, steering him the weaving dog-leg course of the stinking communication trench. He felt an anxious shudder in the major's heavy shoulder. A good sign. Fear opened doors and the man had secrets locked away—vital secrets. Twenty thousand men were depending on him to tell them what they were facing, where and when it was coming. He needed those doors to open.

Each twisting turn of the trenches told the character of those who dwelt there; a jovial signpost marking the distance to Paris, Vienna, and Berlin, a small shrine with a carved Madonna, and the inevitable truly macabre trophy. Von Trelow kept his eyes open for a suitable example, eventually spotting one ideal for his purpose cut into the left side of the trench ahead. A wire party approached, spooling out field telephone line. He stopped to let them pass. The courtesy, remarkable from a senior officer, confused and surprised them. The wiremen exchanged silent, bewildered glances with Niedermann, before offering a salute and continuing their slow progress. All the while von Trelow waited, deliberately holding his prisoner toward the candle-lit niche in the opposite wall: Six skulls stared blankly back from a pile, one bullet-pierced through the forehead. The top-most wore the flat, soup-bowl helmet of the British and Americans. The major's breath quickened beneath his hand. A shiver shook him core deep. He was almost ready.

They moved on, further to the rear, trudging into the support lines, passing beneath the fractured tail of a crashed French Nieuport, its torn canvas hanging from its frame like withered skin on the bones of a slaughtered beast.

Hollow-cheeked faces stared from behind the glow of cigarettes, yet for every pair of curious eyes, von Trelow counted four too exhausted or sick to care. The guardsmen went quietly about their duties, still impressive, their backs straight, weapons clean, their discipline still good, but their patched and threadbare uniforms, often mismatched or missing pieces altogether, hung too loose upon their tall frames. The Americans he'd seen on the far side of no-man's land were well-fed, well-equipped, eager. They were winning and they knew it, and the men here knew it too. Once again, he felt sick.

His little group continued past hurrying messengers, pioneers carrying stakes and barbed wire, supply troops with crates of ammunition, and cooks at their stoves busily dicing turnips, carrots, and bullet-hard potatoes into huge pots. If fortune smiled there might be enough stringy pork or horsemeat to give a trace of flavour. A few kilometres to the west the Americans were eating tinned salmon, corned beef, and chocolate, and drinking real coffee. He forced the thought aside—Duty, first and always. His grip on the prisoner's shoulder tightened unconsciously, hard enough to make the American wince.

Ten minutes further on they passed beyond the tortuous, overcrowded filth of the trench lines, away from the ever-present sickly stench of decaying flesh, illness, effluence, explosives, and poison gas. They emerged into open country where they could breathe cold, clean air, though the ground still lay scarred, pockmarked by craters, and dotted with the occasional resilient ruin or scorched tree. Here the fields and woods had been torn open to make way for looming artillery positions. Sturdy howitzers and monstrous heavy mortars, stinking of nitrocellulose, their wide muzzles gaping ravenously at the sky, each stood arrayed behind their own protective earthworks, huddled beneath sheltering nets.

Beyond them came the ammunition dumps, rest areas, hospitals, and the supply depots—bustling like hives whilst darkness protected them from remorseless airborne eyes.

Finally, and after only a momentary hint of being misplaced, Niedermann led them to the sector marked by a listing, drunken sign. Marta/6, an undistinguished railhead spur surrounded by stacks of hastily camouflaged crates, barrels, boxes, and bundles. Squatting between them, beyond the hissing wheeze of a shunting engine shuffling wagons, lay a mud-dappled grey staff car.

Von Trelow yanked open the rear door and thrust the unresisting American major into the well-worn back seat. He dismissed Niedermann with a salute and climbed into one of the jump seats, facing his slumped captive and with his back to the driver.

The squealing jolt of the door had woken Gefreiter Max Becker, and the old soldier stifled a yawn as he scrubbed sleep from his eyes. Von Trelow dropped something cold, heavy, and cylindrical onto the seat beside him. There were the soft sounds of exploration, the click of a lighter, and the flicker of a flame-lit glance. Priceless treasure was being revealed, a fresh tin of American coffee beans. Becker grabbed it up and held it like a sacred relic.

"Coffee!" he said with reverent delight. Von Trelow made an affirmative sound and hid a smile, pleased to have brought a moment of joy amid such madness.

"Headquarters, Max."

Hastening to comply, Becker quickly stuffed the coffee can out of sight and set about starting the car.

In the back, von Trelow examined the remaining contents of the satchel by the light of his torch: Notes, orders, schedules, communication protocols and, most importantly, maps. He selected one he liked the look of. The car burst into clattering life, and he carefully folded the map to the section he wanted.

The brakes shrieked their release, and the car jolted forwards, jostling and bounding its way along the pitted track as von Trelow's mind mechanically registered the layered zig-zag lines of the Front in the leaping light. He found strongpoints he knew, noted the different Allied names, and made sense of the units, symbols, and numbers marked in coloured pencils. It took him a little while before he understood all it showed. The stark reality of what faced them across the mud and wire brought back the nausea that had begun to fade. No time for that. He breathed deep and turned the map to the major, stabbing at one of the symbols with a dirt caked fingernail.

"This unit is tanks, correct? British or French type? Heavy or light?" His English was perfect, with the slight trace of the southern counties.

The American looked both surprised and scared, precisely as von Trelow had expected and built towards, but the prisoner still began with:

"Major William Sadler, 164th Infantry Brigade..."

Von Trelow curtly cut him off. “Major, I already have your identity disc. I did not drag you across no-man’s land for information that I could have taken from your corpse. What tanks are in this unit?” He stabbed again at the mark on the map.

He watched as Sadler chewed his lip, took a breath, and summoned his reserves of courage.

“Major William Sadler, 164th…”

Von Trelow’s trench knife, gleaming sharp in the light of the torch, appeared at the American’s pale neck. The man flinched, his Adam’s apple bobbing as his wide eyes tried to fix on the blade, and von Trelow felt the usual mixture of professional satisfaction and personal unease.

“Major,” he began coldly, “if you will not tell me what I need to know you are of no use to me. I slit the throats of four men to reach you. Do you truly believe I would hesitate to do the same to you?” He paused to allow the weight of his words to sink in.

The American’s frightened brown eyes sought in his own cold blue-green for some sign of whether he was telling the truth and found nothing. Sharp steel stung tight flesh as the car jogged along the rutted road. The major shrank into the upholstery, as if the seat might open and offer him escape.

Von Trelow pressed a little harder.

“All right!” gasped the desperate American. “I’ll talk. For God’s sake, don’t kill me.”

The German nodded with professional satisfaction and replaced the knife in its sheath.

“Good.” He once again pointed to the map. “What type of tanks are these?”

Chapter 2

Sapphire ghosted the eastern sky as Becker eased the car to a halt before the pretty French chateau—the latest headquarters of First Guards Infantry Division. A guardsman, hunched in his greatcoat at the foot of the sweeping front steps, flicked away a cigarette and snapped to attention at sight of the car. He stepped forward, opened the rear door, and offered a smart salute. Von Trelow stepped out, rain cape draped over one arm, satchel and the American's pistol belt slung over one shoulder, and responded in kind.

"See that the prisoner is taken for interrogation." He jerked his head towards the slumped figure in the back seat. The major passed the point of no return; he'd talk easily now.

"Yes, Herr Oberstleutnant," snapped the sentry.

Von Trelow took the stone steps two at a time, pushed open the front doors and crossed the marble hallway leaving a trail of muddy boot prints behind him. An anxious orderly attempted to catch his attention. He ignored him, barely making it upstairs, to the chill bathroom with its rattling plumbing, before dropping to his knees and violently purging the night's tension into the porcelain.

Ten minutes later, with his belly emptied of fear and the *Ode to Joy* on the gramophone, he sank into a hot bath and cleansed himself of the external signs of his exertions. Another ten brisk minutes and, scrubbed, shaved, and mostly dressed, he took an army mug of freshly brewed American coffee from Becker and spent a moment to savour the rich smell before taking a grateful sip. Bitter, black, and scalding to his tongue, but it tasted of being alive.

"Max, I am growing tired of playing the bully. I really thought the American was going to weep."

Max had been his Bursche for over two years, maintaining his kit, preparing his meals, acting as his driver, servant, bodyguard, and confidante. He nodded as he finished putting a high-gloss on von Trelow's tall black boots.

"Yes, sir. The American gentleman didn't seem to make much of a fight of it. He certainly became much more talkative once you told him you'd cut your way through half a dozen men to get to him."

"Unfortunately, fear is a fine motivator," yawned von Trelow, rubbing his eyes.

"I assume there was no contact, sir?"

"No, of course not," confirmed von Trelow. "You know the rule, Max, blood is messy, and conflict is loud; best to avoid both. At least he came bearing gifts." He raised the coffee in a mock toast and drank, scalding himself a little more in his enthusiasm.

"Yes, sir," agreed Max with what for him, was close to a smile.

"Have you had some yourself? Do."

"Not yet, but I will. Thank you, sir."

Max finished his polishing and presented his colonel with the now gleaming footwear.

"Thank you, Max. You know, I feel rather sorry for the fellow," admitted von Trelow. "I doubt he's been on the Front for more than a week. He was a schoolteacher from Idaho before all this."

"Where's Idaho?"

“I’ve no idea,” admitted von Trelow and sat down to pull on the boots. “Probably somewhere in the middle.”

“He won’t be seeing it for a while,” said Max grimly.

“I’m not so sure, Max,” admitted von Trelow. “He wasn’t a coward, just green. They’re learning fast and they have everything we don’t and plenty of it. Our friend the teacher may be out of the cage inside the month.”

“You can’t mean that, sir,” said Max sceptically. “After all that’s happened?”

Von Trelow shrugged and climbed to his feet.

“I follow where the intelligence leads, Max. It’s who I am.”

The two men said nothing, each lost in their own memories of missing friends and prices paid for futures that would likely never be.

“He had a nice pistol though; I may keep it.” Von Trelow nodded to the big Colt still in the brown leather holster on the table and sipped a little more coffee. The cobwebs began to clear; it was working.

“By the way, did I hear a knock when I was in the bath?”

“Not that I noticed, sir. But I took a moment parking the car in the motor pool.”

Von Trelow nodded as he took a final gulp, too much and still too hot, and put the empty mug on the ornate marble mantle.

“If it’s important it will find me.”

Max, knowing the form, helped him into his grey Waffenrock tunic, watched as he fixed the Blue Max in place over the top button, passed him his leather map case, now containing all the papers taken from the American, and then handed him his cap.

“Thank you, Max.” Von Trelow seated the cap upon his head and studied his reflection in the gilded mirror above fireplace. “God in heaven, I look ridiculous." He flicked the gleaming line of decorations across his chest. "Like the portraits of the old warhorses on the walls at Potsdam."

"Less moustaches, sir," Max reassured him.

"Perhaps that's something to aim for," said von Trelow with a smile. "You know, Max. I used to admire them. They were all I wanted to be. Now I feel absurd, like a character in an operetta. Sometimes I hope I'll never wear the uniform again."

*

The divisional staff was still assembling when von Trelow arrived in what had once been the chateau's ballroom. Familiarity and ill use had eroded the room's once opulent grandeur. Its mirrors and paintings had been replaced by pin covered maps and overlapping sheets of reconnaissance photographs. A stately dining table occupied the centre of the room, groaning beneath carefully sorted stacks of reports, schedules, and communiques. Trestle tables, deep in more of the same, stood where revellers had once danced. The parquet floor, scarred and gouged, would never host a waltz again, but the gilded chandeliers still glittered and dazzled.

"Good morning, sir," said von Trelow, exchanging polite nods with von Hellekant, the rapier-thin and meticulous Chief of Staff. Von Hellekant returned to his murmured conversation with the chain-smoking operations officer, Major Bechmann. The latter barely seemed to notice von Trelow, absorbed in a haphazard pile of maps. Further along the table, Major Klemper from logistics, his belly testing the buttons of his waffenrock, yawned wide enough to swallow his coffee cup.

"Missed your beauty sleep?" asked von Trelow. "What's her name?" Klemper grunted a laugh. Major Ollendorf's monocle flashed as he turned, lips taut in disapproval as they hovered over a tiny coffee cup, held with an extended little finger.

"Ollendorf."

"Oberstleutnant."

At the table's end, old 'Uncle' Gewold, representing the divisional artillery, was relating a ribald story to bespectacled, Mahler, from signals, and the Divisional Medical Officer, Colonel-Doctor Schacht. It had been 'Uncle's' birthday a few days previously and he was still in good spirits. He paused in his tale to exchange 'Good morning's' as von Trelow passed.

The liaison officers from the battalions, the cavalry brigade, and the pioneers—all minor players in the headquarters theatre—had huddled against the far wall, smoking and drinking ersatz-coffee. Von Trelow made his way past them to the corner that was his own. Leutnant Lessing stood waiting. Von Trelow liked the young subaltern, even if he had been assigned him rather than chosen him.

"What do you have?" he asked as cheerfully as his exhaustion would allow and dropped the bulging map case on the table. The junior officer cleared his throat and adjusted his spectacles, as he did every morning, before commencing to present the morning update.

Overnight he'd collated every unit report within the division: observations, changes, captives, information. He now read them back at remarkable, practiced speed, his delivery ice crisp. Nothing missed, not a second wasted. Von Trelow stood motionless, eyes closed, hands clasped at his back, absorbing each word, as if it were Beethoven or Bach. His only response was an occasional slight nod of satisfaction. Next came the reports from Corps, information from other divisions, and from Army General Headquarters, the Oberste-Heeresleitung or OHL. Von Trelow listened to them all, and when Lessing finished, continued to stand, still and silent, the wheels and cogs of his meticulous mind whirring as he considered all that he'd heard.

"The Canal du Nord fallen?"

"Yes, sir," confirmed Lessing with a wince, as if the officer might blame him.

"Men and guns lost?"

"Thirty thousand men and three hundred and fifty guns, sir," answered Lessing with a glance at the notes in his hand.

"Now the British First and Third Armies threaten Cambrai," noted von Trelow.

Lessing said nothing. They both knew the answer.

"The Lys?" asked von Trelow.

"The British crossed yesterday, sir. A counter-attack is planned."

With what? In the east the Bulgarians had already surrendered, the Turks and the Austro-Hungarians were both, by all accounts, near collapse. Here in the Argonne the Americans and the French continued to press their attacks, with more men, more guns, more ammunition, more tanks, and more planes, than the defending German armies could dream of mustering. The situation was clear, if not encouraging.

"Well at least it's not raining," said von Trelow with a smile.

He wasn't sure Lessing ever laughed, and this was no exception. "No, sir," said the young subaltern. "Was your evening successful, sir?"

Von Trelow nodded, faking another smile. "Yes, Lessing, I believe so. The American attack has largely stalled. There will be only limited local offensive operations today. Their 35th Division, facing Fifth Guards, has been almost entirely destroyed as a fighting unit."

"Excellent news, sir."

"It is, except that in two days Pershing plans to launch his reserves into a second wave of attacks, and they have substantial tank support. I have the full dispositions for the General." He tapped the map case and Lessing stared in quiet appreciation.

"Remarkable work, sir." In most men he might have thought it sycophantic, but not in Lessing.

Von Trelow shook his head. "Thank you, Lessing, but really, good intelligence is simply a matter of calm and methodical analysis. You gain the maximum available information and then even an average mind cannot fail to draw the correct conclusions."

"Yes, sir, of course, but to gain such information..." von Trelow waved the protestation aside with a tired shrug.

"That does sometimes require a little extra effort, I agree, but isn't that supposed to be the oath and duty of an officer, to do their utmost?" Did he still believe that? He certainly had, once. He still behaved as if he did, but was it simply habit, reflexes, a train upon rails?

The assembled officers suddenly stopped whatever they were doing at the sound of swift approaching footsteps. They turned towards the door and came to attention as one, saluting, as their immaculately uniformed commanding officer, Major-General Prince Eitel Friedrich von Preußen, marched into the ballroom, followed closely by his adjutant, Hauptmann von Mansfeld.

"At ease," said the Prince, throwing off a casual salute in reply. All moved to parade ease. "Stand easy, gentlemen." Everyone relaxed, gathering their briefing papers and approaching the large central table, as they did every morning. Yet today, instead of taking his usual position at the centre of the long far side of the table, the Prince walked around it, his eyes unmistakably on von Trelow. A dark emotion shadowed his face, held in check beneath the military discipline.

"Oberst von Trelow, if you would?" The Prince-General gestured towards the end of the room and led the way. Von Trelow followed, leaving the other officers awkwardly waiting at the table.

A small fire flickered and cracked in the grand fireplace and the Prince stopped before it, turning to meet his officer. Still, that look; eyes not quite meeting his, moustache twitching at one side. Von Trelow sought to grasp its meaning.

The Prince had one hand tucked behind his back, his dress gloves held in the other, swishing them several times from side to side, a known tic that betrayed anxiety, or anger.

Von Trelow, curious and cautious, waited at ease. What was going on? Was this about last night? Another unapproved lone reconnaissance, the latest of many. Admittedly against regulations and despite the concerns of superiors, but he'd always been successful. Last night had been no exception. He'd taken the rote complaints as tacit, if unofficial, approval. Now he stood unsure and quickly began to gather his defence.

The Prince-General hadn't yet spoken. Kaiser Wilhelm's second son seemed uncharacteristically lost for words.

"General?" asked von Trelow finally, wincing at the breach of strict decorum, but unable to stand the uncertainty.

Spurred by his voice the Prince seemed to reach a decision, drew the flimsy yellow paper of a telegram from inside his tunic and thrust it towards him.

"I'm very sorry, von Trelow."

What was this? He'd called him 'von Trelow', not his full name, not his rank, it was unheard of. He hesitated—for once uncertain—then took the telegram, looked at his General and, having received a nod of grim encouragement, unfolded it.

The Brandenburg address stopped the breath in his chest before he'd read a word.

FRAU OBSTLT VON TRELOW UND EHLINGER

WIFE OF OBSTLT ALARIC VON TRELOW UND EHLINGER

DIED 19 40 HOURS OCTOBER 1 1918

That was all.

He read it, then again. Turned it over, grasping for hope. Nothing. He looked up, searching the Prince's face for explanation—for denial, for a lie. Nothing. Cold, empty incomprehension washed over him like a Baltic wave.

"I'm sorry," repeated the Prince. "You must, of course, go at once. Take leave."

Von Trelow shook his head. "It must be a mistake," he said breathlessly.

The Prince didn't deny it. "You must go," he simply repeated.

The room tipped. Thoughts scattered, papers in a storm. He crushed the telegram until his fist ached, then he grasped at duty.

"General, there's obviously been a mistake," he said with brittle confidence. "The Americans—I can't leave. I have new intelligence..."

The Prince waved him to silence and shook his head firmly.

"I hope you're right, but you must go, nonetheless. I am certain the intelligence is, as always, of the highest quality. We shall review it in your absence."

Von Trelow attempted to protest but could not bring himself to interrupt a Prince of the Imperial house.

"We will deal with the Americans. You have done enough, more than enough. Now go to your family, von Trelow, to your son. Report back on the morning of the tenth, not before. That is an order, Oberstleutnant."

Chapter 3

The compartment door had opened twice since Düsseldorf, each time to noisy knots of rear-echelon soldiers in search of seats. Both times they'd fallen swiftly silent, muttered apologies, and backed away upon finding the lone Guards officer staring at the floor. Since then, no one had disturbed him and the blinds had remained down, as the train in the blue livery of the Royal Prussian State Railway rattled towards Berlin—swift, efficient, inexorable. The Front might be on the verge of collapse, the economy failing, people starving, and the state teetering towards revolution, but the trains still ran strictly to time.

There had been a mistake, certainly, yet the more he repeated it, the weaker it sounded—a thread unravelling in his mind. He sat, trying to grasp the misunderstanding. Perhaps his mother? But no, then the telegram would have come from Tangdau, his family home, not Retzen. So, Frau Buhler perhaps, his wife's mother? Yet either possibility seemed almost as unlikely, both still in their fifties, fit and hale. He considered his sisters, even his elder brother's wife, searching for the truth the telegram concealed—but each imagining was no more likely than the last. He stared at the shuddering floor, as creeping doubt clutched his heart, leaving him unable to breathe.

Eventually, he could stand it no longer. He lifted down his travel case, somehow packed in neat order despite his confused haste, and found the carefully oilcloth-wrapped bundle of letters stowed in one corner. For a moment he simply stared at them, fearful of what he might find, what he may have missed. He steeled himself. Even pain would be better than this fog of doubt.

The knots of the strings yielded to his fingers, and he tenderly unfolded the waterproof oilcloth and removed the topmost letter, her last letter, and set the others carefully aside. The thin, cheap wartime paper slipped easily from the envelope, releasing the faintest scent of rose otto. He stopped. He lifted it to his face, closed his eyes, and breathed her in. The sharp clatter of points snatched him back and he straightened, hands unsteady, as he unfolded the letter with reverent care.

Dearest Alaric,

I saw seven geese today, that's something lucky, I'm sure of it. They are all flying south. Many have already left, and it is impossible for me not to wonder if I will see you before they return. That's rather melancholy and perhaps it's wrong of me to say, but it feels such a dreadfully long time since July. I am praying that you'll be here for Christmas, our first real Christmas together as a family. I won't raise my hopes, but Father Christmas can work miracles and it would be wonderful.

Paul is very well, although he seems to be constantly leading his grandmother a dance. You will remember how much I worried when Frau Rentz left us, that I would not be able to cope, well you were quite right, all has been fine. I am simply being a full-time Mother and spending much more time with him, which is always a delight. He is truly getting to enjoy being read to, often we have story after story for hours before he gets tired. He is speaking more, even the odd sentence, although sometimes they make no sense to anyone but him. A favourite is 'Mutti is cat', many times a day! He even says it to passing strangers, visitors, and the people of the town, I'm not sure why, but it does make him laugh to proclaim it! He's walking further too, going from here to the lake most days, usually to look for ducks or geese, hence my delight to see some still with us.

In other news Mother and Father are well, although Father is busy with the business as always. He has taken to asking me all the time about what you intend to do once the war is over. It's an absurd question, if I'm being honest, isn't it? I tell him I don't know. He says I'm keeping secrets! Absurd, as it is hardly being secretive to say that none of us can judge when that will be or how things will be at the end of it. So, I have simply told him lots of delicious lies about you planning on doing nothing but travelling to the coast and to spa resorts and otherwise lounging on the terrace, playing with Paul and feeding me sweetmeats as I lie beside you. You can imagine his reaction! I said it only in jest, of course, but he has quite swallowed the hook, so you are warned and can prepare an answer for when he inevitably asks you, although if I'm honest I do prefer my idea!

We have had a number of visitors here over the past few weeks, the Heigls last weekend and before that a business associate of father's named Gephart with his charming young wife. Even Friedrich appeared, unannounced of course, telegrams sent in advance having gone astray, or so he claimed, not that any of us believed that old line. How he manages to get leave, and twice in a month to boot, when I haven't seen you in half a year, I have no idea. It is positively unfair. Although they hardly seem like leaves. He was constantly receiving or making telephone-calls or getting telegrams. Most strange. Anyway, he has insisted that I send you his love and regards. Also, that I must enquire after your health, as if I wouldn't ask for myself. Isn't it odd how much his opinion of you has inflated since you won your big medal? Which is the blue one? The one that you always wear on the chest or the one at the neck. Whichever it is, that one. I know, I shouldn't say such things of my brother, but it is true. Anyway, he sends his regards.

I must go now; Paul and I are taking our walk to the lake. I'm hoping we'll see the geese. I'm perhaps expecting too much though. They've probably all flown south already (am I too absurd to imagine that they fly over you?) Perhaps best, geese always leave him worried, they are rather too large and noisy, better that we hope for ducks. He does love ducks.

Be safe and well my dearest love. Write soon, I shall devour whatever you send me, but I would adore a long letter, best of all one telling me that you have leave!

Fondest wishes and most constant love,

Jana

He laid it in his lap and stared, dazed. No answers there. Only more shadows.

After a while he lifted the pages again. This time he read the other message, the hidden message only they knew, the one she'd written only for him. As always, the key lay in the opening line: 'seven geese'—the seventh word of each sentence:

Something is wrong. Father seems worried. Mother being odd. Many strangers here. Are all being secretive. Lots of visitors, telegrams, and telephone-calls. Send your opinion on things. I am worried. Love you, Jana

"And I love you," he murmured quietly.

Even to read it wracked his heart. It was part of her—clever, playful, alive. She adored word games, codes, and other puzzles. It was the place they could be alone together even whilst apart, where the quiet, thoughtful, often shy girl could be herself, away from the invasive eyes of parents, servants, and the army censors. Von Trelow's mind drifted to her witty, incisive, and often very intimate messages, concealed in codes it had sometimes taken him delightful, frustrating weeks to crack. His mouth twisted—a pained echo of a smile. This letter, her most recent letter, had used a simple code—she'd been in a hurry.

Something is wrong… I am worried.

"Worried about what?"

What if the telegram was not a mistake? The idea took hold—choking fingers about his throat. He shook his head in hollow disbelief. It couldn't be. She was so vital. He tried again to find an answer, but the whirling of his brain had no intelligence on which to work and failed at its task. His eyes fell again upon the letter in his hands. The paper felt suddenly brittle, as if it might crumble to ashes between his fingertips, stealing her last words to him. He wanted to place it between sheets of glass, seal it away from time, preserved forever. Instead, he read it again, drawing out every phrase. She was alive in those words, simply at the other end of a pen. His fingers caressed each line over and again, trying to reach her.

*

His eyes rose, lifting his face from the thick, cloying pale mud that sucked at his body and soaked his clothes to the skin.

A pregnant pinprick of light raced, fizzing and hissing, into the cold midnight sky to burst like a photographer's flash, flooding the landscape with harsh magnesium brightness. Lingering illumination hung, sputtering in a drifting pall, setting the twisted nightmare scene into sharp relief. Where the light fell, all lay flattened and whitewashed by the brightness, where anything blocked its sight sat the blackest of impenetrable shadows.

Von Trelow froze at the flare's spitting rise, clamping one eye shut to preserve his night sight. The remaining eye, squinting against the spluttering glare, scanned the hellish terrain. Torn earth lay heaped and turned, great, black-mouthed pits of shell craters gaped and overlapped, holes torn from their lolling lips by further shells until the ground became an intersecting mass of hollows and ridges. The ridges treacherous, mud slick and exposed, strewn with bent and shattered steel stakes and spiked wooden gates, twisted hedgerows of impenetrable barbed wire, layered upon layer until two or even three metres tall and ten times as deep. Here and there a festering, grinning corpse-thing hung inseparably bound amongst the knots and spirals, staring. The yawning craters, between and betwixt, offered shelter like a sweet-scented dew, and like flies, any who succumbed to their promise would find cloying, smothering death, slithering and sliding hopelessly in the mud choked depths, struggling desperately until exhaustion overcame them, and they slipped inexorably into the fetid, poisonous slime.

Von Trelow's single open eye, pupil pin sharp in the glare, scanned for movement, for unfamiliar shapes, for anything not as it should have been in that incarnate madness. He found it as it found him. Across the rim of a shell hole, six metres away, no more, a muddy curve a little too even, slightly too smooth, a hollow darkness beneath its edge, and the merest twin gleams of flare-light on glass. His attention fixed upon the binocular lenses beneath the muddied blanket and sought from there, the scantest suggestion of a shape behind, a face, eyes watching, having seen him even as he saw them.

Neither man dared to move, to risk a sound that might call down the mortars and machine guns waiting with eager malice on either side of the line. The flare hissed and sputtered on its descent, leaving a drifting trail of spectral grey smoke in its wake. Von Trelow calculated the seconds left. His hand sliding slowly and silently beneath the long, hooded cape and easing the trench knife from its scabbard. He shifted his weight, drawing in legs, arms, and feet, ready to rise and rush. The faintest of answering movements responded.

The flare-born shadows lengthened as it sank, reaching out clawing fingers across the churned mud, their shifts sowing deception, implying obstacles where there had been none and swallowing lethal impediments into treacherous blackness. Von Trelow calmed his breathing, stared across the deepening dark gap, fixing it in his mind. And then the light fizzled and died.

He switched eyes in an instant, rising like a sprinter, moving fast from memory, and reaching the enemy whilst the Englishman was still on his knees. Von Trelow slammed into him, sending them both plunging in the mire. Each frantically sought the others' knife hand, grasping at twisting wrists and struggling, chest to chest for purchase, rolling over and over, exchanging position, one on top and then the other, until von Trelow's strength and size prevailed, leaving him pressing down on the smaller man.

Hot gasps, rank with stewed beef and cigarettes, swept his face as both struggled to free their knives. A harsh movement beneath him. White pain flashed as the Englishman smashed his forehead into von Trelow's cheek. He kept his grip and tucked his head low, leaving the flailing head rasping against his own. The other man fought with wild desperation, his grip like a steel band. Von Trelow felt his own breaths coming harder and deeper, stars still flickering across his sight.

The Britisher's knife hand yanked sideways. He almost broke free. Von Trelow snatched it back across their bodies as he lifted his great barrel chest and slammed it back down, pinning the other man's hand between them.

His own left hand now free, he scrabbled for his enemy's face. He pressed his palm tight over nose and mouth. He felt the knife hand between them jerk and pull, but the fist wrapped tight about the hilt was trapped like a monkey's paw in a bottle. The Englishman would not release the knife, and until he did, could not pull clear. He struggled and thrashed, kicking out in the slathering mud.

Von Trelow held on, pressing down his chest, stopping up nose and mouth until finally the need to breathe overcame all other instincts. Von Trelow felt the grip on his own wrist suddenly release and desperate fingers claw at his smothering hand, even as he plunged his knife in between the other man's ribs.

The English soldier twitched and uttered a muffled groan. He struggled still, tearing the hand away from his face with frantic strength. Von Trelow stabbed again, hilt deep. The man beneath him gurgled and gasped, a soft, wet sigh of pierced lungs. A free hand scratched at his hooded head. Von Trelow plunged in the knife again and again, blood hot on his hand. He seized the grasping arm and pinned it back into the mud as he stabbed and stabbed. Coughs of warm bubbling blood splattered his face, the trapped body beneath him twitched and jerked. Still struggling. Still not dying. A falling shell's rushing shriek…

*

Von Trelow snapped awake as an express train screamed its passing. His heart hammered in his ears, skin damp despite the autumn chill. He lay curled tightly like a child, reflexively making himself small against the mortar's steel rain. Except, no mortar had fallen that night. The Englishman had died with barely a sound, despite the ferocity of their fight. Von Trelow had crawled away, he'd completed his reconnaissance and made it back unscathed, two years ago on the Somme. Yet still he could taste the blood in his mouth, smell the lingering stench of death and gas. He rubbed his dry fingers together to rid them of the cloying touch of cold mud, sat up and raised the window blind, then stared at the passing fields and fleeting towns until the visions of trenches and wire faded slowly away.

Jana's bundle of letters, half wrapped in oilcloth, remained on the seat beside him. Her latest—final—letter lay forlorn on the floor where it had fallen from his nerveless hand. He snatched it up, chest tight with guilt, and gently brushed and blew away the dust until he was sure it was unharmed. Only then did he return it to its envelope, the envelope to the bundle, and the bundle to the safety of his travelling case. He considered returning the case to the luggage rack. But he was still tired and liable to fall asleep. He wouldn't risk a thief. He wedged it behind his long legs and settled back. He need not have worried, sleep wouldn't come.

Chapter 4

He hated to be back in Berlin. A city tragic, wasting. He'd last seen it in July, bright in sunlight, with Jana on his arm in her pale summer dress. They had walked beneath the whispering trees of the Tiergarten and along the Unter den Linden. They had made love in a room at the Adlon Hotel.

As he took a horse-drawn cab along Budapester Strasse, from Potsdamer Bahnhof north towards the river, he passed the Tiergarten again. Now the trees stood dark and bare, shedding their leaves like desolate tears. The Brandenburg Gate loomed grey. The Adlon's windows gaped, empty and black.

He closed his eyes and for a moment it was July once more. The heady successes of the Spring Offensive still echoing through the streets. Russia had been forced to make peace. France and Britain were reeling.

"One more push and it's Paris!" cried a boy in a soft cap, waving newspapers from a corner. The board at his side said the same, quoting a general von Trelow had never heard of.

"Well done, lad," said a passing old man with the 1871 campaign ribbon on his chest. Von Trelow smiled and nodded, but his smile was really for Jana. Her fingers stroked his arm, making promises.

"Will it really be over by autumn?" she asked.

He shrugged and placed his right hand over hers.

"Perhaps by Christmas," he said.

She pouted, like a child denied a treat.

They crossed Budapester Strasse, darting between the cabs and carriages. No one seemed to mind. The people on the streets were thin, hungry, and tired after four years of war, but they were smiling again, believing, toasting the soldiers, the Kaiser, and the Reich.

"Shall we have tea when we get back to the hotel?" he asked her. It was a game, of course, and she played along.

"Or ersatz-coffee?"

He wrinkled his nose at the idea, making her laugh.

"Or we could just... wait in our room... until dinner," she suggested coyly. It was barely four o'clock. What would they do with the hours in between? They exchanged playful, excited smiles; their lovemaking too rare to have lost any of its delight. Their hands clutched at each other and their paces quickened as they turned the corner towards the hotel.

Von Trelow brushed away the memory with his errant tears. It was autumn now and the faces on the street, even on the Unter den Linden, were grey, their cheekbones sharp as knives and their eyes listless and dull. They stared blankly as angry gangs bearing red banners marched towards Königsplatz and the Reichstag, demanding strikes and revolution. The cab slowed and tried to pick a way through the crowd. Many of the marchers were starved-looking women, but here and there soldiers marched with them.

"Peace and bread!" they cried. He could hardly blame them for that. Most of the shops he saw were closed, their windows whitewashed or boarded up. The ones that were open had signs warning that they had no bread, no potatoes, no meat, no flour, yet ghostly thin people queued anyway, presumably for whatever they did have, no matter what it was.

At least those in the queues had money. It made them better off than those who huddled in almost every doorway, ragged bundles, some of them battledress grey with an old soldier at their heart, missing an arm, a leg or half a face. Others held women whose men were lost, often clutching children listless beyond tears. All begged hopelessly from those who had little more.

Someone spotted him in the back of the cab, his gleaming uniform and the Blue Max at his throat.

“Why won’t you end the war?” they screamed at him. As if he had the power, as if anyone did.

The driver flicked the horse and drove on, away from the trouble. In any case the mob had seen another focus for their desperation. A motor car rattling away from the rear of the Reichstag, escorted by a pair of mounted police. The whole street, protestors and passersby, suddenly seemed to surge and lift as one, to raise arms, fists, voices, and banners, baying wordlessly after the unknown official who was undoubtedly as powerless as they.

The cab left Königsplatz, crossing onto the red-brick span of the Moltke Bridge. Von Trelow was grateful to be leaving the city and its ghosts. They swung right, alongside the Stadtbahn. The raised tracks leading them to the Lehrter Bahnhoff, from where the express trains headed west to Hamburg and Bremen, and the local trains serviced the little towns to the west of the city. Von Trelow paid the driver without a word and drifted inside.

The connecting train to Brandenburg, and all the small towns between, departed just as promptly as the Dusseldorf train had arrived. It would take a little over an hour to reach the small industrial town of Retzen where Johanna’s family had their home. Most carriages stood deserted. It was easy to find a compartment to himself. He climbed aboard and sat upright and rigid, staring at the floor, until the train shuddered like a child wracked by weeping, and rolled out towards Charlottenburg and the west, chasing the dying light.

*

He stared out of the window at the hotel's immaculate lawn, words flickering and dying before they reached his lips. He'd tried horses—she barely rode, mentioned dogs—her family kept none. He spoke of the army—she hated it, and the war; less to disagree with there. His people held land and worked the soil; hers owned factories and chased profits. They both read, but he preferred histories or the English classics, she preferred German novels and papers on mathematics. Both knew only Goethe—rough ground for a first conversation. He enjoyed Beethoven and Brahms—she preferred operettas by Lehar and Kalman.

He looked about for help, but there was no one he knew nearby. Why had he agreed to come? Because he had leave and spending it alone in a hotel was almost as bad as going home. At least she was pretty.

"Do you like puzzles?" she asked. His heart sank. Visions of jigsaws of Neuschwanstein or Koln Cathedral—hours lost to forced politeness and painted cardboard.

"Some puzzles."

Perhaps he could make an excuse to slip away. Hardly gallant, but then he only had another two days of leave.

"Do you prefer word squares, rebuses, or acrostics?" she asked. "Or are you a crossword man?"

He felt a slight jolt, like static electricity.

"Word squares," he said with an arched brow, "although a complex acrostic can be intriguing."

She smiled—the first he'd seen. A good smile. A little colour flushing her cheeks.

"I agree. My mother is devoted to crosswords. She always takes several newspapers, mainly to clip the puzzles from them."

"And you have followed her example?"

She nodded, a delicate inclination of her golden tressed head. "It's our hobby. I sometimes design puzzles for her or send her messages to decipher."

"Codes?" he asked, forgetting the room about him, the chatter, and the music.

"And ciphers. I find them fascinating."

"So do I," he admitted. Another smile, broader this time. "I'm an intelligence officer in my regiment."

"How thrilling," she said, and unusually in his experience, seemed to mean it. "What do you use? Playfair?"

"Usually," he said. They leant together; heads close to hear each other's words. "Or double transposition. Sometimes a book code. Although for simple messages at the Front we usually just use a substitution code." They were both smiling now. "Do you break codes too?"

"Isn't that the fun part?" she grinned.

"Yes. I'm brought papers and documents taken in trench raids and from prisoners. I determine if there's anything of use in them. A lot of the time they're in code, just as ours are."

They spoke about the codes he'd broken, the ones he'd failed. Few enough, and he was proud of that. She saw that as a challenge.

"Would you write to me?" she asked, colour rising in her cheeks. "In code?"

"Would you like me to?" His heart was beating faster.

"I would."

"Then I shall." Her eyes caught the light—bright, dazzling blue. Her skin glowed flawlessly pale, other than the rose sheen of her cheeks and the rouge of her lips. He wondered about those lips, about how they might taste. “What code should we use?”

“Don’t say,” she insisted, “we should have to work it out.”

The idea was slightly mad, delightfully so. “We’d have to hide the code in a letter. The censors wouldn’t like it if we were sending pages of ciphered text.”

“Of course not,” she agreed. “But that would make it more fun.”

She was right, it would.

*

A sixty horsepower Mercedes stood outside Retzen station, its polished black body catching the flicker of the gaslight like a lacquered beetle. How had they known? The uniformed chauffeur stood tall and rail-thin, his pale skin wrinkled as linden bark. The two men recognised each other at once.

“Klosel.”

“Herr von Trelow und Ehlinger. Welcome. Please allow me to take your case.” The old man reached for von Trelow’s bag, but he wasn’t ready to give it up.

“Klosel, is it true?” he asked simply and realised at once how absurd it was. Jana was fine, what he’d asked would make no sense, the poor old man would be bewildered and embarrassed by not understanding what he was asking…

“I’m sorry, sir, most dreadfully sorry.” The chauffeur’s voice was leaden with grief. The words fell like a hammer blow. He’d felt it coming and been unable to step aside. Life drained from his limbs, leaving him shaking and cold.

“How?” was all he could manage to say.

“Perhaps Frau Buhler should explain,” said the old man, his voice thick with emotion and almost breaking, but of course he’d known Johanna since she was a child. “I’m so sorry, sir.”

Von Trelow held his breath and clenched his jaw, forcing his hands to still their shaking.

“Thank you, Klosel. It is a terrible shock.” He was about to ask more, all the vital questions that the telegram had failed to answer, but there was the tread of someone else approaching from the station, someone Klosel seemed to recognise.

“Herr Braun, a pleasure to see you again. May I take your bag?”

Von Trelow turned to blankly observe the new arrival, a fleshy man of middling height and middling years, with a pale oval, undistinguished face behind round glasses. His broad moustache was of the fashion at Court several years ago and somehow managed to be less impressive than the bristling pair of bushy dark eyebrows glowering from beneath the brim of his hat. He handed across a well-worn weekend bag and Klosel took it whilst making introductions.

“Herr Braun; Oberstleutnant von Trelow und Ehlinger. Herr von Trelow und Ehlinger; Herr Braun.”

Von Trelow straightened reflexively, clicking his heels and offering a slight bow.

The smaller man seemed surprised. He half extended a hand, then seemed uncertain and withdrew it, settling for an awkward nod instead.

“Oberstleutnant,” he responded rather stiffly, “are you also visiting Herr Buhler?”

Von Trelow struggled with a storm of swirling emotions and swallowed a curt reply.

“I am. My wife is... was... Herr Buhler’s daughter,” he croaked. At another time, in a different situation the look of sudden realisation and acute discomfort on the face of the other man might have been funny. Now he waited, dreading the inevitable platitudes. They arrived as promptly as a Prussian train.

"Oh, of course. Please forgive me, my profound condolences, a terrible loss…" He ran out of things to say and von Trelow allowed himself to sink into the silence.

"Gentlemen, if you please." Klosel gestured to the rear of the car as he held open the door with the other hand. Herr Braun tried not to catch von Trelow's eye and climbed in with a murmur of thanks, then von Trelow joined him, squeezing his tall frame into the back seat.

The drive to the house was mercifully short—you could walk it in less than a quarter of an hour—but uncomfortable, nonetheless. Herr Braun, awkward and abashed, forced himself to the far side of the car for the entire journey. He said nothing, only glancing nervously from behind his spectacles at von Trelow's still, upright profile. Von Trelow for his part sat with his case between his feet and his hands gripping his knees, spine rigid and upright. As close to attention as it was possible to be in the back of a moving vehicle. He too said nothing, he simply stared ahead and wrestled with his new reality.

Chapter 5

The house emerged as little more than a shadowed form, swathed in the dark mass of the trees behind. Even in daylight, von Trelow would hardly have noticed it—his mind consumed by a maelstrom of grief. But three years earlier, when first he saw it, he'd thought it an abomination.

Built in the 1880s by his wife's grandfather—who had taken a modest, local brickworks and transformed it into the great Brandenburg Cement company—the house stood testament to his prodigious new wealth and grand pretensions. It was large, grey, and sprawling, appearing even more so against the flat open country of the North German Plain. In style it had fully embraced the eclecticism of a then-current and peculiar architectural oeuvre.

An off-centre portico stood flanked by Corinthian pillars; baroque windows crowded the façade, and one heavy Gothic turret brooded ponderously at the western end of the house, whilst a smaller turret huddled awkwardly towards the rear. Soaring chimneys rose from a tangled geometry of intersecting rooflines, whilst fanciful flourishes—more Hans Christian Andersen than any accepted architectural style—scattered the walls like decorations on a gingerbread house.

Formed almost entirely of concrete, it had also served as a useful advertisement for the versatility of the company's product.

Having been educated in the traditional formality of his class, von Trelow's aesthetic tastes rebelled against it on sight. He'd found the interior little better—all dark Victorian panelling and dour, heavy furniture. Its boorish pomposity was carved into every surface – oversized crests above the entrances, suspect Latin mottoes on the lintels, and the founder's own initials worked into the very walls. That von Trelow had come to love the place spoke only to his feelings for Jana. For three years he'd explored the house in memory—recalling every corner, every crack—to stand there now, without her, felt incomprehensible and quite unbearable.

He entered the familiar house without a word, allowing the maid to attend to Braun while he followed in silence, his eyes drifting to doorways and the staircase, as if expecting Jana to appear. The maid led them to the drawing room and withdrew. Braun drifted uneasily, feigning interest in the expensive but unremarkable landscapes upon the walls.

After a few minutes, the awkward silence broke as the dining room door opened across the hall and voices spilled out—voluble, animated, softened by wine. A small party entered the drawing room—evening gowns, white ties and tailcoats—red cheeked and well-fed. Herr and Frau Buhler, Jana's parents, led the group, looking as though they'd just come from the opera at Bayreuth. Following them, but leading the conversation, came Friedrich, their son, resplendent in the uniform of a major of the General Staff with its scarlet piping and trouser stripe. Finally, came a couple von Trelow had never met before: a balding barrel of a man of late middle age, sporting a turned-up moustache just like the Kaiser's, and on his arm, a woman close to half his age—strawberry blonde, striking, and dazzlingly dressed.

"Alaric," said Friedrich, blinking in surprise.

The conversation faltered and died. It was Frau Buhler who stepped forward, coming to him, taking his arm, speaking gently. He couldn't hear her words. The mad incongruity of being there without Jana had set a drumming in his mind. Herr Buhler and Friedrich hung back, their mouths forming words, perhaps sympathies, he couldn't hear. The strangers remained apart, awkward, and uncertain, drifting toward Braun like leaves to the edge of a pond.

The pounding in his head hammered at his skull, their incoherent voices thumping like the clattering of a Maxim gun. He found it hard to catch his breath. Someone asked Braun about his journey—as if this were any other day. Something broke.

"My wife is dead!" he bellowed, silencing them instantly. "She is dead—and you have dressed for dinner?" He grasped at the lapel of the fat man's coat, startling him. The man recoiled. "What is going on here?" demanded von Trelow.

Friedrich stepped forward and reached for his hand where he still held the now considerably frightened gentlemen.

"Alaric, let Herr Gephart go," pleaded the young man.

Von Trelow felt the pull on his wrist and grasped at it like a striking snake. In an instant he had Friedrich by the arm, his fist raised like a hammer. Then a firm, gentle and insistent touch took it and held it. He whipped around, breath caught in his chest, fully expecting to see Jana. For an aching moment he thought it was—those same bright blue eyes, reproving and concerned. But the face, though strikingly similar, was lined, and her hair had begun to turn from gold to silver.

"Come," said Frau Buhler simply and, taking his compliant hand in hers, led him from the room.

"I think you rather badly frightened Herr Gephart, Alaric," she said as they made their way down the hall.

His breath came slower now; the angry pounding in his head fading, replaced by hollow shame.

"I'm sorry, I shall apologise."

She nodded. "Good. Let us go in here."

She opened the last door along the hall and led him inside. It had been someone's idea of an English gentleman's library, but they had clearly never seen one. It had too little light, made worse by the blackness of the furniture and massive shelves of dull, heavy, leather-bound books that no one could ever bear to read. She led him to a pair of armchairs near to the fireplace and sat down, gesturing for him to do likewise. He did as he was bidden.

"How are you feeling?" she asked calmly.

For a moment, hot anger surged—the question absurd. He mastered it, forced it back.

"I don't know," he eventually admitted. "Empty, lost. What happened?"

Frau Buhler shook her head, as if she didn't understand herself.

"Influenza. She didn't come down to dinner on Tuesday night. When we checked on her... she was gone."

Von Trelow screwed his eyes painfully shut. Had it only been two days? How could it have been something so mundane?

He'd seen plenty of cases of influenza at the front, especially in the last year, men choking their last breaths as their fevers drove them to babbling. He didn't want to imagine his Jana like that.

"How long was she ill?" he asked, "What did the doctor say?" He'd met the young doctor from the town at dinner about a year earlier. He'd seemed capable and smart.

Frau Buhler sighed heavily and pressed her palms together as if praying.

"It was quick, Alaric, very quick. She was quite well at breakfast. Doctor Meissner said that there was nothing that could have been done. She didn't suffer. Thank God."

Von Trelow swallowed a bitter, blasphemous reply. Four years of war had shattered what illusions he'd had of a benevolent God, but saying so now wouldn't help anyone. He simply nodded.

"I am sorry that you arrived precisely when you did; we hadn't expected you to get here so promptly."

"I had fortunate connections—no delays," replied von Trelow dully.

"I see. But, in any case we had to eat, and dressing for dinner, going about all our daily habits is what allows us to carry on. You must understand that."

He did. It was like order and discipline at the Front. Men continued even as their comrades were cut down because it was drilled habit. The household too were grasping routine like a shield. He felt like a fool.

"I'm sorry. It was a stupid overreaction. Of course I understand. It's just all been such a dreadful shock, for all of us, I'm sure. I never imagined... I still can't imagine that she's gone. It seems impossible."

"I know," agreed Frau Buhler, her fingers tightening about the black-beaded crucifix at her neck. "She was my dear girl. I sometimes still imagined her as that little blonde child, even though she had a child of her own. How can she have been taken from us? I don't know. But we must mourn her and then carry on, for those who are left; for Paul."

Von Trelow looked up and found her eyes firmly upon him, expectant and demanding.

"Yes, of course. He must be..." He faltered, realising he had no idea how the boy felt. He'd hardly thought about him since he'd received the news, had only seen him twice since he'd been born. Even then the child had been mostly in the charge of the nanny. He knew him only through Jana's letters. The boy was what—something over two years old? Could he even grasp what death meant?

"How is he?" he finally asked.

"He is very upset, naturally. His mother is gone, and he doesn't know why. He's asleep now, but you must see him in the morning. I know you haven't spent much time with him…"

"The war…" von Trelow protested, and she held up her hand placatingly.

"Of course. No one expected anything else. But now, he needs you."

He felt a flash of something akin to panic. What did that mean? What was he supposed to do? He took a deep breath and slowly exhaled.

"Yes. I will see him in the morning."

They sat in silence for a few minutes as his rigidly controlled anger and frustration gave way to grief.

Finally, he found his voice. "Where is Johanna now?"

She looked surprised.

"The doctor arranged for her to be taken and held until the funeral. The body had to be quarantined, because of the infection," she explained.

The body. The word struck hard, deep in the belly. He wouldn't even be able to see her, to say goodbye. All he would have of her were a few posed photographs, not one of which really caught the essence of her. He didn't even have a lock of her hair; she'd thought it bad luck.

Feeling desperate for some connection, he pulled out his old pocket watch and flicked open her portrait inside the lid. The watch had stopped working almost a year ago, and the well-made and reliable modern wristwatch he'd taken from an English officer back in the spring kept much better time than the pocket-watch ever had, but he'd kept it anyway, for the photograph.

Von Trelow lay in the soft, cold bed, as the steady tick of the English wristwatch measured out the night, waiting in vain for sleep to come. A few dream-wracked hours had been snatched on the trains, but otherwise he hadn't slept in days; yet still he lay awake, staring into the dark.

Footsteps faded one by one—family and guests behind their doors, the servants climbing to the attic rooms above. At last, silence settled across the house, thick and heavy. Yet he remained stubbornly wakeful. Finally, when a glance at the softly glowing watch dial showed ten minutes past two, he slipped from between the cotton sheets, pulled on his greatcoat in lieu of a dressing gown and crept from the room.

Moonlight slanted through tall windows, dappling the hushed and empty hallway. Von Trelow moved carefully towards the heart of the house, testing each step for the boards he already knew would betray him. He had done this before—newly engaged, home from the east for the first time. They had been desperate for each other, though he'd clearly expected to have to observe honourable restraint. She'd had no such reservations and had told him so. So, he'd snuck the length of the house, from the most distant guest room that Frau Buhler could assign, finding and avoiding every treacherous floorboard, and easing each reluctant door, until he reached Johanna's room.

Lying in her bed, they'd been so nervous—of being found out, and of each other—that they'd simply lain together and kissed. He smiled into the dark. They hadn't been so chaste the following night, nor the one after that; time had been too precious. Abruptly the appalling weight of her loss crashed like surf over stone. He stopped, shoulders trembling, breath knotted in his throat. When it passed—after an age—all that remained was a gulf of emptiness.

Eventually he stood outside her door, since their marriage, their door. He placed his hand upon the cold brass doorknob and steeled himself to what he must do next, feeling much like a man about to go over the top. He rested his forehead on the dark wood, drawing deep breaths and listening to his heart pounding, and then he turned the handle and pushed.

Heavy curtains sealed the room, leaving not a chink of light. Moonlight filtering in from the hall made no impression past the threshold. He stepped inside and eased the door shut behind him. For a moment he stood in the deep dark, then reached out and flicked the light switch. Three brass-hung bulbs flickered overhead, then began to glow—building in strength until their warm light suffused the room.

It was just as he remembered it. It even smelled the same, of soap and rose otto, and her.

He stood, stunned, eyes roaming across familiar object: the washstand with the water jug painted with roses, where she'd washed her face each night and morning; the dressing table where she'd sat and brushed her hair; the wardrobe and screen, heavy and dark, where she'd dressed.

And the bed, where she'd slept. Where they'd slept. Where they'd loved.

Where she'd died.

He swallowed something bitter rising in his throat, then walked to the bed, his legs weak.

He paused, steeling himself, then raised the corner of the quilted eiderdown. The mattress lay bare beneath—no sheets, no sign, no mark of her passing.

He'd seen so many dead—so much blood, and filth, and decay, marking each lost life. But here there was nothing.

As if she'd merely stepped away. Soon she'd return. Tell him what a fool he'd been. Wrap her arms about his neck and pull him down to kiss her.

He had only to wait.

He savoured the agony of the illusion for as long as he could, then let it fade, like mist in the morning. At last weariness found him—sudden and heavy—and he sank onto the bed, staring at the wall. An idle hand reached out and opened the cupboard of the nightstand. He froze. There were his letters, tied in a length of blue ribbon. He studied them, imagining her reading each word. Then, carefully, he placed them in his coat pocket. They were theirs, no one else's, he refused to leave them for others to paw over.

Her fountain pen lay atop a stack of books, alongside them her silver wristwatch. She always took it off before sleeping. Von Trelow reached in and lifted out the books, expecting a Bible and some novels of the more substantial sort. Instead, a thick book on economics by someone called Sombart, a private binding of lectures by Max Weber, a copy of the Reichsbank monetary policy by its president, and a heavily annotated copy of Wicksell's *Interest and Prices*. All seemed to be about business. He had no interest in them—only in the book atop the pile: bright blue leather, her initials in gold. Her journal. He turned it in his hands, surprised. It was her confessional, her comfort, her devoted diary in which she wrote every day. Yet he'd never known her to keep it in the nightstand. There was a hiding place—one she'd never revealed, a secret since childhood. He'd guessed at a loose floorboard or wall panel, but out of respect, had never looked.

She had written: '*I am worried.*' Now she was gone. He asked her quietly to forgive him and opened it. Some pages used a complex numerical cipher, most a far simpler code—alternating words, one from each line. Easy to read, once you knew the trick.

The final entry was dated the last day of September, the day before she died. It ended mid-sentence at the bottom of a page.

He frowned, exhausted and confused, and read it again. It still made no sense. Standing up he lifted the journal to the light. Along the inside of the spine, he could see the jagged, torn fragments of two missing pages. He strode to the empty fireplace and squatted down, moving aside the grate. He stared at the white ashes, some of them still in curled sheets; burned, torn paper—two pages at most. The fire had done its work. Nothing remained.

Von Trelow replaced the grate, brushed off his fingertips and stood. Thoughts turned like the toothed wheels of an inexorable machine. He had questions, increasingly he had questions, but he needed sleep desperately and they would have to wait for morning.

He considered returning to the guest room, but his heart rebelled at the idea. Instead, he switched off the light and returned to the bed. If there was a risk, so be it. He lay there, silent and still, breathing her in, feeling the ghost of her beside him, until sleep finally came.

Chapter 6

It was the habit of the house to breakfast early, and by the time von Trelow descended everyone else had already eaten and begun the business of the day. He entered the echoing, deserted dining room, took a plate from the black oak sideboard and loaded it with a pair of fat rye rolls, thick sliced ham, and rich smoked cheese. Clearly, if one had as much money as the Buhlers, rationing was not a great concern. He poured himself a cup of coffee from the pot, tried it and winced. That, at least, remained the terrible ersatz-coffee everyone else had to endure.

He had barely sat down to eat alone when the door opened. Frau Buhler entered—slim, sharp-eyed, clothed in mourning black. He rose and offered a precise bow.

“Good morning, Frau Buhler.”

“Good morning, Alaric. Please sit down and eat,” she said with a tired smile.

He resumed his seat whilst she poured herself a cup of the same appalling brew.

“Did you sleep well?” she asked.

“Yes, thank you.” Not entirely a lie. Once sleep found him, it held him. As always, when in their bed, he dreamt only of Jana. The nightmares remained at bay. No, it wasn’t sleep he’d had to endure—it was the waking.

Frau Buhler took the seat opposite him, set aside her notebook—bookmarked with puzzles clipped from the morning papers—and watched him as he ate.

"I neglected to ask you last night. How long is your leave?" she asked.

He was so tired it took a moment for him to calculate.

"Until Tuesday night, at the latest. I need to be back at headquarters by Thursday morning. If I'm fortunate and the trains all run to time, I should manage it."

"Five days?"

"Yes." The longest leave he'd had since he'd been married. What irony.

"I'll make sure the funeral is arranged before you have to return," she promised.

He wasn't sure what to say. Eventually he settled on, "Thank you."

"Paul is in the nursery. You should go and see him after you finish breakfast."

He nodded. "Yes, of course." He took another mouthful of bread and ham then washed it down with coffee—and grimaced.

Frau Buhler noticed. "Real coffee cannot be found," she noted with a sigh. "No matter what the price. The tea isn't bad though, perhaps try that instead."

He smiled politely but remained in his seat. Raised on tea with milk by an English mother, he now disliked it any other way. The Buhlers in contrast rebelled at the idea of adding milk, whether to coffee or tea, and so it was never made available. It had always been a minor point, an idiosyncrasy, now it was yet another comfort denied and missing. Somehow it brought Jana's absence into sharper relief. His chest felt tight. He knew he needed to say something, to distract himself, and since Frau Buhler seemed to be expecting it, he took up the offer.

"I went to Johanna's room," he said. She didn't seem surprised. "Her diary was in the nightstand. That's odd, isn't it? I thought she always hid it away."

"Really?" she said without apparent interest. "Well, I suppose she must have been writing whilst she was sick. She was probably too tired to put it back in the usual place."

"Yes. I expect so. Do you know where she usually kept it?" asked von Trelow.

"No," said Frau Buhler simply.

"Strange that she wasn't able to return it to its hiding place," von Trelow said quietly, "yet she managed to tear out the last two pages and burn them." He ate bread and cheese without noticing their taste and left her to fill the ensuing silence.

She took a sip of coffee before replying.

"Perhaps she did that earlier. If she wrote something when she had a fever, realised that it was incoherent and wanted to get rid of it." She looked at him as if expecting his agreement. When he merely continued to chew, she seemed to feel the need to say more. "Or perhaps she was so feverish she tore it out without thought." A slight frown had appeared on her otherwise flawless complexion.

Alaric nodded, apparently accepting it at face value.

"That does make sense, you're probably correct. She was feverish then?"

"Excuse me?"

"You said she was feverish. Did you see her with a fever? Did the doctor?"

Frau Buhler smiled thinly, as if trying to mask annoyance.

“No, I didn’t see her whilst she was sick, no one did, and the doctor didn’t arrive until dinner. I simply meant that she would most likely have been feverish, with the influenza. When Heinrich caught it back in May, he was terrible with fever; groaning and babbling for days, sweating the sheets sodden.” She stopped and closed her eyes, as if mastering a pain. “I’m sorry, it’s just the idea of Johanna like that, alone…”

Von Trelow forced down hot, bitter bile with the last mouthful of his breakfast. The rest of the unspeakable coffee he left on the table.

“But in Johanna’s case she was fine at breakfast and dead by dinner,” he observed with forced calm. “I’ve seen men with influenza too, and you’re right, it usually takes several days before they recover, or they don’t.”

Her lips were now a tight purple line. “So, what do you think that means?” she asked pointedly.

He pushed back the chair and stood. “Probably only that it was a very bad case,” he said. “It’s fortunate that no one else seems to have caught it.”

“Very,” she agreed.

Seconds ticked past with neither of them speaking. There was a weight there, he could feel it, something he didn’t understand, information missing.

“Excuse me,” he said at last. “I shall go and see Paul.”

“Good,” she said as he rose and left the table with a bow, “that’s probably best.”

Alaric’s mind whirled with troubling questions as he crossed the hall. Frau Buhler had always been a beacon of reason. She neither indulged speculation, nor tolerated narrow thinking. So why try to explain away what he’d found? Von Trelow reached the foot of the colossal wooden staircase as Herr Gephart descended, one hand firm upon the carved banister, to steady his weight. Von Trelow knew he owed the man an apology. Honour—and good taste—demanded it. He put aside his doubts, halted, and offered a polite bow.

Gephart, at sight of him, hesitated and stopped, regarding him with wary eyes.

"Von Trelow," he said curtly. His brusqueness was deserved, though it still stung, and Alaric accepted it as his due.

"Herr Gephart, I'm glad to find you. May we speak?"

The older man's eyes narrowed uncertainly and von Trelow read hauteur—with more than a trace of nerves—in his face. He was looking for a reason to refuse. There was no choice but to be explicit and throw himself on the other man's mercy.

"I wish the opportunity to apologise."

Relief, and faint curiosity, appeared in Gephart's eyes. He nodded gravely.

"Of course."

In a house of a certain stature, certain rooms are held in common and open to both sexes: the drawing room, dining room and library. But the billiard room, like the study, belonged to the men.

It was usually only occupied after dinner, once the ladies had retired to the drawing room. So early in the day, it stood reliably empty—and it was there that Alaric led Herr Gephart.

The room was dark and smelt fragrantly of expensive cigars, its long, heavy curtains still closed from the night before. He flicked on the electric lights. The space was dominated by the billiard table that ran the central length of the room, whilst at the far end a pair of card tables, each with two chairs, nestled beneath the windows. A finely carved chess set rested atop the drink's cabinet to the right of the door, and a pair of duelling sabres, which Alaric was certain had never seen their intended use, were crossed above the fireplace. He stood back to allow Gephart to enter and the businessman, assuming an unconcerned air, began to peruse the selection of gloomy hunting scenes hung upon the walls.

"Herr Gephart," he began once the door was closed. "Please allow me to apologise to you, and through you to your wife, for my boorish and uncouth behaviour last night. It was neither consistent with my character nor appropriate to an officer and gentleman, and I can present only my recent tragedy as an exculpatory defence."

He paused and waited to allow Herr Gephart to magnanimously forgive him or to churlishly, although perhaps understandably, refuse. Instead, the man looked him with evident confusion and said nothing. It gradually occurred to von Trelow that, rich though he might be, the businessman may not fully understand what had been said. He could imagine no other reason for his increasingly awkward delay.

He was considering how to say it again, more simply, without obviously insulting the man's education, when Herr Gephart finally cleared his throat extravagantly and raised his several chins.

"Of course, Herr von Trelow und Ehlinger. It is of no matter at all; no harm was done. Completely understandable given what has happened. Think nothing of it." He even assayed a light and clearly forced laugh that jarred uncomfortably.

Von Trelow's attention awakened, clearing the fog of grief. The fat industrialist was shaking; sweat beaded his brow, and his eyes, in constant motion, refused to meet von Trelow's gaze. Von Trelow was familiar with fear, even fear of him. But this? The man was terrified, and it was entirely unclear why. Von Trelow's behaviour the night before had been extraordinary, certainly disturbing, but could it truly account for such ill-managed fear? Was Gephart that faint of heart?

Abruptly the businessman stuck out his chest, threatening to burst the buttons on his bow-fronted coat, and gave a nod that was all posture and bravado. He was a man mimicking the confidence and pride he was imagining he should be feeling at having someone such as Alaric von Trelow as his supplicant. It was strangely unreal and then, with a final tense swallow and cough, he made to go.

"Thank you, sir, you are a gentleman." He offered a crisp bow, but he watched the businessman leave the room with a frown of confusion upon his face.

Chapter 7

Paul was upstairs in the nursery, as Frau Buhler had promised. He sat at a low child-sized table, concentrating intently on a large sheet of architect's paper while the housemaid, Trude, looked on encouragingly. He didn't respond when his father greeted him—his focus fixed upon his colouring.

Von Trelow felt a pang of disappointment but had no idea how to proceed. They barely knew each other. He leaned closer to see what the boy was doing. Someone had sketched simple outlines of fruit and vegetables in small groups down one side of the page, and Paul was busily colouring them in with wax crayons. Beside each group, he had carefully and accurately written the number of each. The numbers were rather unsteady and the colouring a little haphazard, but von Trelow was still impressed.

"That's very good," he told his son.

The boy flinched but continued scribbling red crayon onto a group of four apples. Von Trelow wasn't sure what to say. He glanced at the maid, but she had withdrawn to one side and was staring at her shoes. He'd get no help there.

"Do you know who I am?" he asked uncertainly.

There was the vaguest impression of a nod, but nothing more. His own father would have been barking about standing up, looking a man in the eye, and showing respect. It wasn't who he wanted to be.

"I'm your father. Do you remember me?" he asked, but again, there was no reply. "Do you like drawing?"

Not even a flinch this time, the boy just kept his fair head down. He hadn't been like this the last time he'd seen him, but then that had been almost a year ago and the boy, little more than a babe, had been content to chuckle at a teddy bear being danced in front of him.

Von Trelow glanced around the nursery for inspiration and spotted a group of carved wooden soldiers painted in dark green parade uniforms. He picked up a pair. "These are rather fine," he said lightly. "This one is an Uhlan," he waved one of the soldiers, "and this one is a Guardsman, like me."

Paul didn't even look up.

Seeing that he was making no progress, von Trelow placed them back in their place on the nursery floor. He tried to think of something else to say.

"Are you well?" he asked his son. When no reply came, he turned in desperation to the maid. "Is he well?"

She seemed rather surprised to be included in the conversation but nodded, before remembering to bob.

"Yes, sir, quite well."

At least someone would speak to him.

"And do you look after him often?" he asked. "My wife wrote that Frau Rentz had left."

The nursery nurse's departure had prompted several distressed letters.

"Not usually, sir, but at the moment..."

He understood. With the boy's mother gone, someone had to care for him. She was taking her turn.

"Yes, of course. Thank you, Trude."

She glanced up in surprise to hear him use her name.

"It's no trouble, sir, really. He's a good boy."

"I'm glad to hear it. There seem to be fewer servants than on my last visit."

"Yes, sir," she said, her voice unsteady but gathering pace. "Gretel moved to Brandenburg for munitions work, so did Frau Rentz, sir. And Dora married her young man on his last leave and went to Frankfurt where he's from. Then Krista and Bruno, they took jobs at the cement works in town."

He wasn't sure he'd ever heard her say so much. On his previous visits, she'd seemed a little shy, a little reticent. Now, she spoke more freely, even wistfully, as if these were marvellous adventures on which her former colleagues and friends had departed.

"Is it only you in the house and Herr Klosel outside? I remember Retzen with perhaps a dozen staff in and around the house. Johanna said there were twice that before the war."

She shook her head.

"No, Cook—that is, Frau Jahnik—is still here too, but she's married to that kitchen." He caught her blush at her own boldness in saying so.

"You must be worked off your feet."

"It's hard work," she admitted with a shrug. "But I like it here… most of the time." Now was perhaps not one of those times.

"Why did the others leave for the factory and the cement works?"

Trude seemed faintly amused.

"For the ration, sir. They're both classed as heavy labour—the ration's much better, and so is the pay."

He'd expected as much. Perhaps her newfound talkativeness was to fill in for those no longer there.

He glanced at Paul, still absorbed in his colouring, and nodded toward the door. The maid followed without complaint. Von Trelow stopped in the doorway—where the boy could see them, but beyond hearing.

“May I ask you a question?” he said quietly.

She looked uncertain, glanced at Paul, then nodded. “Of course, sir.”

“Is he always this quiet?”

She seemed embarrassed. Had he asked something a father wasn’t expected to?

“Not always, sir.” An awkward silence eloquently completed her answer.

“Only since his mother passed?”

“Yes, sir.”

“Of course.”

What was he expected to do? He felt adrift—his thoughts: shattered wreckage upon a cold, dark sea.

He grasped at something that he could understand. “Was it you who found my wife?”

Trude clutched at her apron and chewed her lip. Her voice fell with her gaze.

“Yes, sir.”

“That’s all right,” he said gently. “It must have been a terrible shock.”

She nodded again but kept her eyes downcast.

“I wonder, would you tell me how she was when you found her, please?”

He saw her brow furrow beneath her fair fringe, like she was girding herself against a pain.

"When she was… dead, sir?"

He thought she was right to pause—it did hurt to hear it; and probably hurt her to say it.

"Yes. Please."

She took a few breaths to collect her thoughts, and when she spoke, it came at a rush.

"It was terrible, sir. She didn't answer when I knocked, so I opened the door, and it was dark. I called her again, but she didn't reply, so I switched on the electric light and there she was."

The memory tangled her voice—tight, breathless. She sniffed and brushed a trembling hand across welling eyes.

Paul glanced up from the table with a little frown of concern and at once Trude turned her back to shield him from seeing her cry.

"It's all right," Alaric reassured her again, even as he fought with the chaos of his own emotions. "Please, go on."

She sniffed again before she did.

"She was in bed, but the bedclothes were thrown about, and her arms were all outstretched, like she was Jesus on the cross." It wasn't an image he enjoyed but he stayed quiet and let her carry on. "And she was the most terrible colour, sir. I'm sorry, but you wanted to know…" She paused as if to let him change his mind.

"That's right, I want to know," he assured her, though his heart felt like lead.

"She was blue, sir, the most dreadful dark blue. Her pretty face was all blue, and there was blood."

Von Trelow jolted. He lost all breath. The vivid image—horribly, terribly familiar. Questions whirled into his spinning mind. He stilled it, ordered them, and spoke.

"Blood where?" he demanded.

She winced at the sharpness in his voice, but he pressed on. His veins filled with ice, pounding building in his head with a steam hammer beat.

"On the sheet. It was on the sheet," she explained nervously, her voice beginning to fail.

His insistence had nearly driven her back into silence. He fought to calm the storm of his emotions.

"Do you recall where the blood had come from?" he persisted evenly, though his fists ached and shook.

She thought for a moment, then glanced up at him, surprised by the remembrance.

"Her nose and mouth," she said, "and her eyes. There was dried blood around them all, it was horrible." She shuddered hard, but there was still something more von Trelow needed to know.

"Her hands, Trude? What about her hands?"

She looked at him blankly and shook her head.

"Her hands, sir? I don't know what you mean."

He felt a knot of frustration but pressed on.

"You said that her arms were thrown wide, like a cross?"

"Yes, that's right."

He tried to smile encouragingly, but it didn't seem to help.

"Good. Well, what were her hands like?" The hammering in his head still building. "Think, Trude, it's very important. Were they curled up?"

"Curled up, sir?"

"Like an eagle's claws."

She frowned again, struggling to recall—then flinched, horror sweeping her face.

"They were, sir, they were curled up!" She looked at him, perhaps expecting some explanation, but his face was now a mask.

The pounding ceased. His heart froze.

When he spoke, his voice came calm, clear, and cold.

"If you please, would you tell me everything that happened earlier in the day?"

She frowned. "Everything, sir?"

"Yes. please."

Her expression betrayed her bewilderment, but he didn't explain. Eventually she simply obeyed.

"I got up at half past five, sir, as usual, and helped Cook with preparing breakfast. Herr and Frau Buhler like to eat early, so it needs to be served at half past six."

He nodded; it had always been so.

"Who was at breakfast?" he asked.

"Everyone, sir, except Frau Gephart. She had a headache and came down at about eight o'clock."

"Who is everyone, please? Who was here?" he persisted.

She took a moment to consider.

"Herr and Frau Buhler of course, Herr Gephart, Herr Friedrich, and Frau von Trelow und Ehlinger, that is, your wife." She seemed embarrassed to have mentioned her.

"That's very good, Trude. But not Frau Gephart and not Paul?"

"No, sir. Frau von Trelow und Ehlinger would usually let him sleep or play in the nursery until eight o'clock, and then either she or Frau Buhler would give him breakfast."

"In the nursery?"

"Yes, sir."

"And who gave him breakfast on Tuesday?"

She considered for a moment.

"Frau Buhler," she decided.

"You're certain?"

"Yes, sir. Frau Buhler said that she would do it because she had planned to walk with Frau Gephart, but she wasn't up yet."

Von Trelow nodded.

"And Joha… my wife, what did she do?"

"I'm not certain, sir. She said she was tired. I think she went to rest."

He frowned thoughtfully.

"Tired? Why?"

Trude shrugged.

"The family had stayed up late because Herr Friedrich was coming home. He arrived on the half past midnight train."

"I'm sorry, what train?" he asked curiously "Isn't the last train the one that arrives at nine o'clock?" It had been the one he'd arrived on.

She nodded.

"Oh yes, sir, usually. But Herr Friedrich got the night express to stop, because he is an officer of the OHL."

"I see," said Alaric.

Friedrich had used his position in army headquarters to halt a train off schedule. Was it ego? Impatience?

“And the Gepharts—when did they arrive?”

Again, she took a moment. “Friday, sir. They arrived in the afternoon on Friday.”

A weeklong visit. Gephart, another man of business. Were they combining professional discussions with a social call, or was it something more?

“Very well. What about after breakfast?”

She glanced back into the nursery at Paul, but he was still studiedly colouring, occasionally stopping to hold the page up to the light to enjoy the brightness.

“After breakfast I usually clear away the dining room, but Frau Gephart hadn’t eaten. So, I covered the dishes, then went up to make the beds and clean out the grates in the rooms.”

He nodded encouragement.

“I saw Frau Gephart leave her room at about eight o’clock, so I did her room then.”

“Did you see anyone else?” he asked.

“Not upstairs, sir. A little later I happened to look out one of the windows and saw Frau Buhler and Frau Gephart going for their walk. That must have been a little after half past eight. I believe the gentlemen were already in the library.”

“All three of them?”

“Yes, sir, and Herr Braun.”

The mention of that name came as an unexpected surprise.

“Braun? The same Herr Braun who is here now?”

“Yes, sir. He arrived after breakfast, although I didn’t see him myself. Herr Klosel collected him from the train station.”

What was Braun doing there on the Tuesday, then back again two days later? He itched to ask her about his comings and goings, but stopped himself, knowing that with patience he would hear it all.

"And they were all in the library together?"

"Yes, sir."

"All morning?"

"All day, sir. They didn't even come out to lunch. Frau Buhler had Cook make them up sandwiches and took them in herself when she got back from her walk." The maid seemed rather shocked at the idea, and von Trelow agreed. At his own home, at Tangdau, his patrician father might well subsist on sandwiches and meals snatched from the pantry, but the Buhlers were of the haute bourgeoisie; appearances mattered.

"But you were upstairs?" he asked.

"For most of the morning, yes, sir. I did come back down to clear the dining room once Frau Gephart had breakfasted. Then I went to watch over Master Paul." She glanced in the boy's direction.

"Why?" he asked gently.

"Frau von Trelow asked me to, sir."

"When was this?"

She creased her brow in the effort of remembrance. "Eleven o'clock, sir. She was coming upstairs. She asked me to bring a cup of tea to her room, and to look after Paul."

"Because her mother was out walking with Frau Gephart?" surmised von Trelow.

"Yes, sir."

"And you're certain of the time?"

She nodded adamantly. "Yes, sir. The clock in the hall had just struck."

That seemed proof enough, Frau Buhler was pedantically proud of the clock's accuracy.

"And you fetched her the tea?"

"Of course, sir."

"Did you make it yourself or did Cook?"

She had to pause again to recall.

"I did, sir."

"You're sure?" he pressed her.

She shifted uncomfortably.

"Are you certain?"

She gave a firm nod. "Yes, sir. I made the tea and carried it up to her."

"And no one else touched it? You didn't leave it anywhere?"

She seemed shocked at the idea and flushed brightly. "Leave it anywhere? Of course not, sir. I'd never..."

He raised a calming hand.

"Of course. I just need to be sure what happened. Please, continue. You took the tea to her room. What was she doing?"

"She was writing in her diary, sir. The blue one."

"Did you know where she kept her diary?" he asked. After all it wasn't impossible that its hiding place was a secret only to him.

"No, sir, she kept it hidden. I only saw it a few times when she was writing in it."

He nodded.

"And how was she? Was she angry, upset, tired, sick, excited?"

Again, the maid took her time to replay it in her memory before she replied.

“She seemed excited—writing quickly, talking to herself.”

He nearly smiled. She always muttered to the page when something had seized her imagination. What had captured her interest?

“Did she say anything?”

“Nothing, sir. I just put down the cup, said, “Your tea, Frauline…” she paused, embarrassed, “Sorry, sir. We often called her ‘Frauline’, rather than Frau Trelow und Ehlinger.”

For a moment he was caught between frustration and amusement.

“Of course, it’s a very long name and you’ve known her since before she was married. It must be far easier.”

She nodded, allowing him a thin grateful smile.

“Yes, sir, much easier.”

“And, having given her the tea, you went to the nursery?”

“Yes, sir. Since Frau Rentz left, Frau Buhler and Frau von Trelow have mostly taken it in turns.”

“But you sometimes assist,” he filled in.

She looked abashed but presently nodded.

“Sometimes. Where I’m needed, sir.”

“You’re a good person, Trude.”

She blushed. “Thank you, sir.”

“And the others, where were they?” he asked.

“I’m not sure when they returned, but Frau Buhler and Frau Gephart were back by lunch. Frau Buhler looked after Paul in the afternoon. I don't know about Frau Gephart, sir, she may have gone to her room, or she often reads in the parlour. The gentlemen were in the library until a little after four o'clock."

"What does she read?" he asked.

She looked surprised by the question. "Frau Gephart? Uh, romance novels, sir. Not very good ones." Another blush, this time at her own boldness.

Von Trelow merely nodded his understanding.

"I see. And the others, you're certain that they were in the library until four?"

"I saw them leave myself."

"Good, that's good. And how did they seem when they came out?" She shrugged, as if unsure.

"I don't know, sir. Serious, I think. But not angry or upset."

"And they didn't say anything? They weren't speaking to each other?" he asked curiously.

"Nothing, sir, nothing at all."

"Very well. And anything else before…"

She understood and saved him the pain. "Only that Herr Braun left for the station just after dark. I reminded Herr Klosel to be careful on the road. It can be difficult at night."

"And everyone else, other than my wife and Paul, were at dinner?"

"Yes, sir."

"And when my wife didn't appear?" He left the question hanging.

"Frau Buhler said that the food would get cold and asked me to go up to see if she would be joining them." She winced at the memory of what happened next.

He didn't leave her to dwell upon it.

"I see. Thank you, Trude. You've been most helpful." He read relief in her suddenly relaxing shoulders. A final thought struck him. "One last thing if I may?"

"Of course, sir." The tension returned.

"When you made the beds and cleared the grates yesterday morning. Did you clean my wife's room too?"

She shuddered at the mention of it but nodded.

"After the undertaker came, sir, to take Frauline Johanna away. Frau Buhler told me to take the sheets and burn them. I cleaned the grate, stripped the bed, and then gave the bedding to Herr Klosel to burn." She had screwed up her face at the memory—but had told him what he needed to know.

"The undertaker, do you know which one?" He had no idea if there was more than one in the town, but it wasn't impossible.

She shook her head. "No, sir, I don't. I didn't see them."

He nodded; it had been worth asking. "Thank you, Trude."

He glanced past her to where Paul had stopped colouring, watching them with uncertain eyes. He caught his father's glance and looked nervously away.

"Please look after Paul. I have to go out for a while."

"Of course, sir," she said agreeably.

He was already stalking away.

Purpose carried him down the hall. He had been bereft—adrift without Jana. But now, he had animus. A cause.

He could see the cobalt blue of her skin, the dried blood speckling her lips.

Someone had murdered his wife. He would find them—by analysis, by discipline.

And before his leave was done, he would kill them.

Chapter 8

A chill wind swept across the open, flat country, cutting through even the heavy wool of an army greatcoat. It promised a hard winter. The trees stood already bare; fields lay stripped. The only things moving were a few circling crows and gently drifting smoke, rising from the town and from a distant steamer winding downriver towards the Elbe. Von Trelow quickened his pace, a crisp military rhythm pumping blood into his limbs. Ten minutes brought him to the edge of town; two more to the house of the doctor.

The address was a solid, red-brick, white-shuttered gentleman's townhouse, indistinguishable from its neighbours save for a brass plaque fixed beside the door. Von Trelow ignored a polished baroque doorknocker and rapped the wood with his knuckles.

Footsteps shuffled faintly. A key turned. The heavy door swung slowly inwards to reveal a small, pale woman of indeterminate age—anywhere from fifty to eighty. She peered at von Trelow from behind thick, round spectacles, her gaze finding his midriff and slowly rising until she finally reached his face.

"Good morning, ma'am," said von Trelow, dipping his head.

Her eyes, magnified to saucers, gave the impression of a startled owl.

"Who?" she asked, perfectly completing the portrait.

"My name is von Trelow und Ehlinger. I'd like to speak with the doctor."

She blinked, sifting his words like grains of sand.

"Please come in," she said at last in a high, reedy voice. "He is with a patient at present. However, he should be free soon." She stepped unsteadily aside to allow him to enter the narrow, chequerboard-tiled hallway. "If you will wait in the parlour, I shall inform him you are here once he is free." She pointed to the left-hand door.

Von Trelow followed her instructions into a rather cluttered parlour, where a worn horsehair-stuffed sofa and matching armchairs huddled amidst cabinets and side tables crowded with Dresden china figurines and assorted cut glass. He lowered himself cautiously into an armchair, careful not to disturb the fragile ornaments.

A few newspapers and magazines lay upon the table for waiting patients, all at least a month out of date. He turned instead to a decent little oil painting of a ship in a storm. There had been a time that he'd dreamt of joining the Navy, an idea his father had blamed upon his English mother, though he couldn't recall her ever mentioning it. The dream had vanished during his first North Sea crossing, lost to a heroic bout of seasickness that had returned every time since. Still, he liked the look of the sea; its romance still appealed.

A door clicked and creaked somewhere down the hall. Voices murmured, footsteps passed. The front door opened and closed. A moment later, a shadow crossed the window. Someone returned along the hall, pausing outside the parlour. He heard a hushed exchange—then the door swung open.

He judged Doctor Meissner to be a little older than himself, perhaps thirty, with a lean, sallow face and dark, expressive eyes. His sandy brown hair lay unruly across his head, and the hand he extended was long and delicate—unlike the heavy, imprecise thing that von Trelow wrapped around it. They shook.

"Doctor, thank you for seeing me."

The doctor sketched a brief smile. It must be difficult, thought von Trelow, to strike the right balance between genteel politeness and sober reserve when speaking to the bereaved. It had been a good attempt.

"I am sorry for your loss, Herr von Trelow und Ehlinger," he said, withdrawing his hand.

"Please, call me von Trelow—or, if you prefer, Alaric. And thank you, for your thoughts, and for what you tried to do to help Johanna."

The doctor nodded, relaxing a little—just as von Trelow had intended.

"Alaric then. And please—call me Eduard. I only wish I'd done more. I arrived too late—far too late." The doctor stepped back and gestured down the hall. "Please, come through to my consulting room."

Von Trelow followed him into what had once served as the dining room of a respectable middle-class home, now converted into a doctor's office. An examination couch lay against one wall, whilst a large wooden desk occupied most of the space. One chair was set before it, and another to the side. The doctor gestured von Trelow to the patient's chair, then shut the door and took his accustomed place.

Glass-fronted cabinets lined the walls, their jars and bottles neatly labelled in a fine gothic hand. A skeleton hung from a stand. Framed anatomical prints filled the remaining space, with the doctor's university diploma in pride of place.

"How may I be of service?" asked the doctor. "Are you unwell?"

Von Trelow shook his head.

"No, I'm quite well, thank you. I wish to ask about Johanna."

Meissner's expression tightened. His brow creased in professional sympathy.

"Of course. A dreadful thing to have occurred, especially for one so young—but unfortunately common in the current circumstances. A lack of nutrition, thanks to the naval blockade, has weakened the population's resilience to disease. Increased cases of influenza are just one of the maladies taking their toll."

Von Trelow nodded, though his fingers dug into his knees. He forced them to relax.

"I understand, but you have eaten at the Buhlers' house. You know that a lack of nutrition was not a concern."

The doctor shifted awkwardly in his seat. "Well, I wouldn't wish to comment on any domestic arrangements..."

Von Trelow interrupted him. "But, Doctor, you said nutrition as a possible factor. Did Johanna seem malnourished to you?"

"No," admitted Meissner, "but you have to understand that I had not seen her in a professional capacity for some months."

Von Trelow nodded. "Of course. But a doctor remains a doctor, even when not in his professional capacity—does he not?"

The doctor frowned and moved in his seat again. "I don't quite understand..."

"Well, allow me to clarify. You saw her often: at church on Sundays and for dinners. You are a frequent guest at the Buhler house, I believe. Is that not correct?"

The doctor's face was fixed in a frown, troubled and even belligerent.

"Yes," he admitted.

"So, you must have seen her what, six or seven times a month?" suggested von Trelow.

The doctor shrugged. "Perhaps, yes."

"And in that time, did you at any point see anything that might have indicated a lack of nutrition?"

"No, I did not," he finally admitted. "In fact, she looked to be putting on a little weight; she seemed in fine health."

Von Trelow nodded, rose, and began to pace—two steps across, two back—all the room would allow.

"You were at the house on Wednesday night, at dinner. You were there when Johanna was discovered. Is that correct?" asked von Trelow.

"Yes, it is," replied the doctor, voice cooling, "and you clearly have a point to make. Please make it. I have patients to attend."

"My point, Doctor," said von Trelow sharply, "is that you ruled my wife's death as caused by influenza."

"That's what her symptoms were consistent with," insisted Meissner.

Von Trelow snorted. "Really? I've seen dozens of men die of influenza this past year. None of them whilst turning blue; cyanotic, isn't that what you doctors call it? With blood around the eyes, nose, and mouth. That was how my wife was found. The state of her bed suggested violent spasms and her hands had bent into claws. Rictus, that's the word—yes? Are those symptoms of influenza?"

Doctor Meissner, irritated and defiant, stood up and faced the larger man.

"Yes, they can be. These are all possible symptoms of severe influenza."

"Perhaps, each of those symptoms may appear in some cases, but all together? I've never seen it. I've also never seen them die in a matter of a few hours, in a house with no other cases." The doctor tried to speak, but this time von Trelow didn't let him. "But what I have seen, Doctor, is men die in a few hours or less in just that manner; their faces blue, their mouths and noses, even their eyes and ears, full of blood, after thrashing about in an agonised fit and their hands clamping into claws, but it wasn't influenza. It was phosgene, doctor. Poison gas."

The doctor stared at him in disbelief.

"Are you suggesting...?" he allowed the question to fade, apparently unable to complete it.

"I am suggesting that she was poisoned, Dr Meissner. Murdered."

The doctor glared, then stepped around him and yanked open the door.

"You are overwrought, sir. I would prescribe a sedative—though I suspect you would think I was trying to poison you too. So, instead I suggest you go and rest. I am entirely content with my diagnosis. Your wife died of severe influenza. That is my opinion and that is what the death certificate states. Good day, sir." He gestured stiffly to the open door.

Von Trelow glowered, pausing on the threshold.

"You're very young to still be in a practice like this, Doctor. Mostly there are only old men left behind. All the medical men your age have been called up to serve in the military."

Doctor Meissner's lip curled into an annoyed snarl. "I have weak lungs, from childhood bronchitis. I was medically exempt."

"Really?" said von Trelow, and left.

Von Trelow hunched in the corner of the telephone booth, one arm across his chest so the door would close. The booth stank of old cigarettes and unwashed bodies. It was the price of privacy. Three attempts, four operators—but he'd finally made the connection.

"Louis?" he asked the Bakelite mouthpiece. A dull crackling, then a stretched, tinny voice.

"Alaric, mon frere—how is it you're not dead yet?"

Despite everything, von Trelow smiled. That was Louis—he made you smile. Louis Randolf Beck was an Alsatian, born to a proud German winemaker and a mercurial French mother who walked out when he was five. Louis, von Trelow, and Erich Freisinger had trained, lived, and marched off to war together. Louis had taken a piece of shrapnel to the knee outside Riga the year before, and Erich had died on the Somme. Only Alaric escaped unscathed; yet Louis insisted he was the lucky one.

"How are you, Louis? How's the leg?"

"It hurts in the cold and the cane is now a fixture—but at least I'm no longer of use to His Majesty's Army. For that, I offer thanks to the Russian artillery. And the ladies like it; it adds character," said his friend. He could imagine the grin.

"As if you needed the help, you half-French reprobate."

"My inconstancy is not my errant mother's fault, mon ami… Well, perhaps it is. Women are a delightful mystery: a man cannot do without one for long, nor endure one for long. My mother felt the same way about my father. So, perhaps you're right. Now—to what do I owe this pleasure, mon colonel?"

"I need your help, Louis," said von Trelow, lowering his voice. "It's important."

"What do you need?" replied his friend, his voice sharpened to a razor's edge. No question of why. Closer than a brother.

"Jana's dead," said von Trelow. "I need a doctor I can trust—in Retzen. Today."

He waited through the silence—only static on the line.

"Christ, Alaric, I'm sorry." He was too, von Trelow could tell. "What was it?"

Von Trelow sighed and lowered his voice still further.

“The local medico says it was influenza. But she was blue, Louis, blood on her lips and clawed hands.”

He heard Louis swear hard, away from the mouthpiece.

“Phosgene? Are you certain?”

Was he? He felt sure, but being able to prove it was another matter.

“Not yet. That’s why I’m calling.”

“I understand,” said his friend. “And any doctor not a hundred years old is in a field hospital somewhere?”

“Something like that,” admitted von Trelow. “What about Lise?”

He let the idea float along the line.

“Lise Freisinger?” asked Louis, uncertainly.

“Of course. She should have finished her residency by now and have her licence. Can you find her?” If anyone could find Erich’s sister it would be Louis, of that he remained certain.

Louis took his time to consider.

“Yes, I think so. But give me a day and perhaps I can find someone who doesn’t wish you dead.”

“I can’t wait, Louis. My leave ends on Tuesday. Can you find her?” demanded von Trelow urgently.

“Yes, but it may take a little time. Can I call you at this number?”

“Yes, I’ll wait,” replied von Trelow.

“Very well. I’ll see what I can do.”

“Thank you, Louis.” He really meant it, and Louis would know it.

“Always...” said his friend,

"…the same," replied von Trelow. It was the First Foot Guards regimental motto, it meant everything.

"Alaric, if you need help…" added Louis. He didn't say with what, he didn't need to.

"I'll call," promised von Trelow.

"Good." And he was gone.

Von Trelow replaced the earpiece, wrestled free of the booth, and bought a paper from the post mistress. Then he took a place at the end of the counter and leant upon it to read.

Von Trelow read the *Berliner Tageblatt* from headline to sports, then flicked through a copy of *Ulk*. At last, the telephone rang. The postmistress dropped from her perch behind the caged counter, but von Trelow was already there.

"It's for me," he said, tossing paper and magazine into a wastepaper basket. He wedged himself back into the booth and lifted the receiver. The operator's clipped voice announced a call from Berlin. He thanked her and waited for the connection.

"Alaric?" came the static-shrouded voice.

"Louis, any news?"

"I found her. You were right—she's qualified and working at a hospital."

"In Berlin?" asked von Trelow, pulse quickening. Dresden or Cologne wouldn't help him.

"Yes," said Louis. "Krankenhaus Moabit. It took some persuasion, but she'll come once her shift ends tonight."

Von Trelow let himself breathe—just a little easier. He'd been certain of Louis. If anyone could persuade her, it was him.

"Thank you, Louis. I owe you."

A short laugh, scrambled by the wires. "No, you don't, and you know it."

"Thanks anyway." He waited for Louis to ring off—was about to do so himself.

"Alaric, are you sure this is wise? She did say she'd kill you."

"I can take care of myself, Louis." A full-throated laugh followed—and, as always, von Trelow smiled too.

"I know you can, you great ox. But she wasn't thrilled to hear from me. What makes you think she'll help you? She may come only to yell at you again, or to really shoot you this time—not merely threaten it."

She might. He didn't know. He hadn't even been sure she'd agree to come.

"I don't have much choice. Unless you know of another doctor who's available and trustworthy?"

"She's available, but how do you know that you can trust her?"

Von Trelow shrugged—not easy jammed into a booth—then remembered that Louis couldn't see him.

"I don't, but I hope she'll do it because Erich would want her to."

Another static-warped laugh down the line.

"You'd better hope so. You're not as charming as I am."

Von Trelow laughed too.

"No one is, Louis. I'll be fine. Auf wiedersehen."

"Auf wiedersehen, you oaf." And Louis was gone, leaving him with a smile.

Same old Louis. He'd check the timetable, though she'd likely arrive on the same train he'd taken. Louis wasn't wrong, though—the thought of seeing her again twisted his stomach into a tortured knot. The last time, her grief for Erich had turned entirely on him. Had it faded at all? He'd know soon enough.

Chapter 9

The Retzen police house amounted to little more than a modest dwelling, distinguished from its neighbours only by the Prussian eagle above the door and a curt sign reading *Landgendarmerie*. Funded by the state, the upstairs housed the local sergeant, whilst the lower floor offered a lifeless reception: a dust-veiled counter facing a single, hard wooden bench. Behind it lay a cramped office and, tucked at the rear, a cell barely large enough for two drunks, or a more serious felon awaiting transfer to Brandenburg.

Von Trelow laid a gloved hand on the scarred counter, rang the bell, and let his gaze wander across the clutter of warning notices—new regulations, censorship edicts, government mandates, and the penalties for involvement in the black market. He wondered if the policeman ever dined at Herr Buhler's table. Did he turn a blind eye, or did they serve up special 'ration dinners' whenever he visited?

He turned at the scuff of boots on tile as a green-uniformed gendarme senior sergeant limped through the door behind the counter.

"How may I help you, sir?"

The sergeant's voice was flat, distant—devoid of warmth or concern. His collar bore the insignia of a Vice-Wachtmeister, and the square set of his shoulders implied former army service. His dark moustache had been sculpted into precise waxed curves, whilst his right leg dragged stiffly—whether from an old wound like

Louis's, or the work of a field surgeon's saw, von Trelow couldn't tell.

"Oberstleutnant von Trelow und Ehlinger. I understand you attended the Buhler house two nights ago, following the death of my wife."

The sergeant offered no trace of sympathy. He simply nodded.

"Yes, sir. That's correct."

"I wondered if I might ask you about the manner of her death?" said von Trelow.

"What about it?"

"I have reason to believe that it may not have been as simple as a case of influenza. I wished to speak to you about the investigation."

The waxed ends of the policeman's moustache stirred as he weighed his response.

"Sir, there is no investigation."

"May I ask why not?" von Trelow demanded.

The sergeant remained impassive.

"Because there are no grounds for suspicion of anything other than a natural death."

Von Trelow felt a surge of anger and mastered it.

"Hardly natural. She was twenty-three years old and in excellent health," he insisted, voice taut.

"That may be, sir," the sergeant replied, unmoved. "But the doctor was clear. Death by natural causes. Influenza."

"I understand what he said," replied von Trelow, steadying himself. "But the symptoms she showed were consistent with phosgene poisoning, not influenza. She died in hours—not days."

He hesitated. “Have you at least requested a post-mortem examination?”

If the Vice-Wachtmeister felt anything, it appeared to be boredom.

“No, sir. Unless the death was in some way suspicious, a post-mortem is not required.”

Von Trelow leaned both hands on the counter between them.

“Suspicious? She wrote to me. She said she was afraid—something wasn’t right at the Buhler house. Now she is dead, showing all the symptoms of phosgene poisoning. Yet everyone insists it was influenza, even though no one else in the house is ill. Is that not suspicious?”

The policeman shifted his weight, easing the pressure on his bad leg.

“Not really, no. Not when the doctor is says it was influenza. Women worry—that’s not unusual. And poison? Where would anyone even get something like that? This is Brandenburg, not Belgium, sir.” The emphasis was unmistakable: *You’re not in Belgium now. You’re not at the Front. You hold no authority here.*

Von Trelow drew a long breath and mastered his frustration. He would get nothing there, except, perhaps, arrested.

“Very well. I’m sorry to have wasted your time.”

He turned to leave.

“No trouble, sir,” the sergeant said flatly, “Careful how you go.”

The pink, steaming ham hocks lay on a thick bed of pease pudding and sauerkraut. Chilled white wine from the Mosel filled the crystal glasses. The Buhler family and their guests sat ready in their places, silverware in their hands—about to eat—when von Trelow entered the room.

“My apologies for being late. I went for a walk and lost track of the time.”

He moved to his usual seat at the table and sat as Klosel—elevated, it seemed, from chauffeur and handyman to footman for the day—swiftly laid a place and went to discover if the cook had prepared an extra ham hock.

“Glad to see you out and about, getting some air,” said Herr Buhler. “Fresh air is good for the health—clears the lungs and improves the circulation. A good thing, especially in the circumstances.”

Klosel returned with another plate of *eisbein* and placed it before von Trelow.

“Thank you, Klosel.”

The place across from him, where Jana used to sit, gaped like a socket without an eye. He flinched and looked away. His gaze fell to the steaming food. He could barely stand to touch it; his stomach recoiled. But years in the army had taught him to eat when he could, so he dutifully began slicing pieces of ham and forced himself to chew as he quietly observed the others at the table.

“Tolerable weather,” said Gephart, slicing a sizeable lump of meat from the bone and forking it into his mouth.

The comment had been to the table, but Herr Buhler responded, setting down his knife and fork, and nodding thoughtfully, as if the matter required careful consideration.

“Certainly, less rain than usual for the time of year,” he said at last. He then resumed eating, eyeing the food with something close to dismay.

“Lovely ham,” said Louisa Gephart brightly. Her eyes widened and flicked to von Trelow, before dropping back to her plate.

Frau Buhler pretended not to notice.

“Thank you, dear. It’s from one of the local farms. Good people.” She sipped her wine. With conversation stalled, the women resumed eating—careful, precise, as if under judgement.

At the head of the table, Herr Buhler picked at his meal, nibbling, whilst Gephart tore bright chunks of meat and devoured them with enthusiasm. Friedrich, by contrast, seemed off his food, whilst Braun ate with methodical focus—as if he hadn’t eaten properly for months, which, if he’d been living on the ration as they all should have been, was likely true. Von Trelow ate mechanically, giving little notice to the food on his plate, his attention reserved for the other diners.

“Is this Cook’s sauerkraut?” asked Friedrich. No one answered. “It tastes rather sweeter than usual.” He looked to both his parents for reply and, not finding one, he returned to the wine. The glass was at his lips when he abruptly started, spilling the contents down his tunic and drawing every eye at the table. Both elder Buhlers glared at their son. Herr Gephart, only momentarily distracted, quickly returned to his *eisbein*. Frau Gephart, seated opposite the now blushing young officer, let out a light peal of laughter—joyous and woefully out of place. She stifled it at once, looking away with a muttered apology, and joined Friedrich in flush-cheeked embarrassment.

Braun, who also seemed to be unaccountably embarrassed by the little incident, looked about the table and met Herr Buhler’s distracted eye. He appeared to feel the need to say something.

“Business is good, I hope, Herr Buhler?”

Buhler looked at him rather blankly. Across the table, Frau Buhler scowled—as fiercely as if the question had been an insult.

“I suppose that depends upon the news from Berlin,” said Herr Gephart, answering for the other businessman. His small eyes peered down the table at Braun with something like disdain.

Braun looked away. It was now his turn to flush red—more with anger than embarrassment.

Von Trelow said nothing, simply observing.

An awkward silence settled over the table as plates were cleared and replaced with thick slices of apple tart and whipped cream. Von Trelow's stomach rebelled. Military training or not, it was too much. There was a limit to how far he could flaunt the rationing restrictions without beginning to feel rather sick.

Friedrich, too, had declined the dessert. "I think I'll get some air," he said to no one in particular.

"Good idea. Very healthy—good for the lungs and the circulation," said Herr Buhler, returning to his theme. He seemed about to go on, but another stifled giggle from Frau Gephart and a sharp, irritated glare from Frau Buhler stopped him short. He subsided into silence, waving Friedrich away as the young man stepped out onto the terrace. A moment later, von Trelow followed.

Friedrich held an open silver cigarette case in his hand. He took one for himself and offered the case to von Trelow.

"Thank you—I don't," von Trelow reminded him.

Friedrich rolled his eyes.

"Of course, sorry. I always forget. Something about the smell?" He snapped the silver case closed, slipped it back into his breast pocket and lit the cigarette, drawing in the smoke and coughing roughly. "Damned cough."

"It's not the smell so much," explained von Trelow, moving upwind. "It's that it deadens your sense of smell. That can make all the difference in no-man's land."

Friedrich hawked and spat into the flower bed, quickly glancing back towards the house to be sure his mother hadn't seen.

"I would have thought not being able to smell would be rather an advantage out there?" He smiled wryly.

Von Trelow simply shook his head.

"No. The smell is terrible, but you get to know it. The death and cordite, they're everywhere, eventually you can ignore them. But the smell of bleach or mown grass, that can mean gas hanging in a depression. If you don't notice, especially if you're crawling, and you're always crawling, you'll be dead before you can get out again. The smells of a trench; food, shit, and sometimes soap, can tell you how far you are from the enemy on even the darkest night." Friedrich nodded, apparently impressed despite himself. "But tobacco is the best, cigarette or pipe smoke," insisted von Trelow.

"Why so?" asked Friedrich, taking another drag, and stifling a cough.

"It carries. You can smell it a hundred metres away. Sentries and scouts know how to shield a flame and the glow of a cigarette, or they don't last long, but the smell of the smoke, you can't hide that. If you smoke yourself, it becomes almost impossible to spot it. But with practice, and a little observation of the wind, you can tell what direction they're in, how far away they are, and you can even get to know something about who they are."

Friedrich laughed at his brother-in-law. "Don't be absurd."

Von Trelow shrugged, unoffended, he'd been sceptical too until he'd picked up the talent.

"British tobacco doesn't smell like French tobacco, and neither smell like American. Pipe tobacco, which engineers and gunners often favour, is different to the smell of cigarettes. You can even get to tell the quality, whether it's cheap soldiers' tobacco, like English '*Players*' or '*Woodbines*', or French '*Gauloises*' or '*De Troupe*', or if it's a rich custom blend, that only an officer could afford."

Friedrich stared at him, drew in the smoke, coughed again, and shook his head in mild disbelief.

"You're a very strange man, Alaric."

Von Trelow merely smiled.

"I prefer 'meticulous'. In any case, it's helped keep me alive."

The suggestion of mortality smothered the conversation.

"How are you, Friedrich?" asked von Trelow eventually. "You look tired."

He did too. Shadows hung beneath his eyes, his skin pallid, like a man who'd missed the sun.

The younger man nodded and sighed deeply.

"I feel it, Alaric. I can't believe it—Johanna, I mean."

"I know," replied von Trelow, not knowing what else to say.

"I feel so damned helpless."

"Yes."

"I suppose it's all part of God's plan..." said Friedrich weakly.

Von Trelow felt his rage surge, his fingers twitch. He'd always quite liked Friedrich, although their army duties meant he'd seen desperately little of him. He was cheerful and good-natured, if a little foolish and self-absorbed. But now von Trelow had to check the urge to hit him or grab him and shake him like a ragdoll for his stupidity, his blindness, and his faith. Instead, shocked by the unexpected ferocity of his fury, he said nothing. He concentrated on simply breathing, watching as Friedrich finished his cigarette, dropped the butt into the flowerbed, and led the way back through the front door. Von Trelow followed, his mind whirling, barely under control.

The dining party were emerging into the hall as they entered, and Herr Buhler, who seemed to have eaten little but drunk well, crossed to meet them and, to Alaric's surprise and discomfort, suddenly took him by the arms. It was so unexpected, so out of character, that Alaric flinched as if burned and almost yanked away. If Herr Buhler noticed he showed no sign.

"It is a terrible thing that has happened, my boy, truly terrible. No one feels it more than I, but we must think of the living. It's what Johanna would have wanted," he insisted earnestly.

Von Trelow froze. His fragile self-control trembled. Fingers cracked. Raw emotion flared, too fast, too hot. He fought to contain it. He almost managed it.

He heard his words over the pounding in his head.

"Herr Buhler," he said, drawing himself up to his full impressive height. "I shall contend with anyone as to how much they feel Johanna's loss, even with you. And on the contrary, I believe that what she would have wanted is for me to find out who killed her."

There was a frozen silence for some seconds, then a startled squawk of nervous laughter from Frau Gephart. Then the hall erupted—voices scolding, pleading, berating him for suggesting such a thing. Only Herr Braun stayed apart, keeping his distance, before quickly slipping away towards the stairs.

Alaric stood, a prisoner of his righteous anger as they protested around him, until Frau Buhler brought them all to silence with a shout belying her size.

"Alaric, what in the name of God are you talking about?" she insisted, quickly suppressing her husband and son's explosions of agreement.

Von Trelow waited for quiet, realising as he did so that he'd crossed the Rubicon.

"It is perfectly simple. No matter what the doctor says, Johanna didn't die the way influenza kills. It was too fast. Too violent."

The voices rose again, a babble of objections tumbling over one another. Von Trelow raised a commanding hand and his voice.

"If I might finish!" They fell silent at once. "Her death was too sudden and too brutal," he insisted. "Her symptoms were nothing like influenza. But they correspond, in every regard, with something I have seen too many times: phosgene poisoning." For a moment there was stunned silence. "Someone killed Johanna, and I intend to discover who and why."

The cacophony of voices now began to rise once more, and again Frau Buhler silenced it.

"Alaric, this is a preposterous suggestion. There is no one who would wish to harm Johanna, least of all anyone who was in this house. And the idea of poison gas, it is too much. Do you imagine that someone crept about the house releasing gas under her door?" Her voice cracked—sharp and incredulous.

"Nothing so clumsy," he insisted. "Phosgene dissolves in water; the battlefields are steeped in poisonous pools. A little, slipped into a drink or food—it would be all too easy."

"This is absurd!" shouted Herr Buhler, his face ruddy with wine and outrage.

"It really isn't," replied von Trelow stiffly.

Frau Buhler took her husband's arm firmly in her hand, clutching at it until her knuckles were white.

"Heinrich, please take me away. I cannot listen to this madness."

Herr Buhler took a moment to realise what was being asked of him. He gave her hand a vague pat before turning to go.

"Quite right, my dear. He's clearly unhinged by it all: the war, poor Johanna." As they retreated Frau Buhler ushered the startled and sympathetic Gepharts ahead of her.

"You could prove me wrong very easily, Herr Buhler, Frau Buhler. Demand a post-mortem. You are important people in this town, respected, the police will listen to you." There was a noticeable shudder from them both, but they did not stop. "Don't you want to know the truth?" demanded von Trelow to their retreating backs.

Herr Buhler stopped, despite his wife attempting to coax him onwards, and half turned against her strident pulling.

"I will not subject my Johanna to a butcher's blade, sir, and if you loved her, truly loved her, nor would you!" He allowed himself to succumb to his wife's forceful entreaties, vanishing behind a slammed door.

Von Trelow found himself left with Friedrich, who seemed too shocked to speak or even to leave. The young man simply stared at him as though he were truly mad.

"Well?" said von Trelow, taut as a spring.

"You can't mean it," Friedrich finally managed.

"I do."

"It's not possible," he insisted. "You're upset, we all are, but Mother's right, no one would hurt Johanna."

"But they did, Friedrich. The manner of her death, it's as plain as day."

Friedrich began to pace about the hall in anxious frustration.

"But I was there," he pleaded. "I saw her, it wasn't some poison gas, it was just a terrible illness, you have to believe me."

Von Trelow flexed his broad shoulders as if for a fight and settled to the 'at ease' stance.

"You saw her, Friedrich? Her body? Well, what did she look like? Was her face cyanotic?" Friedrich looked confused. "That's blue." He paused a moment as Friedrich looked at him but seemed unable to speak. "Was there blood on the sheets and around her nose and mouth?"

"I'm not... I'm not sure," Friedrich finally stuttered.

Von Trelow nodded and carried on.

"Had she thrown back the covers like she'd been kicking or thrashing about? And were her hands locked, like this?" He made tight claws with his fingers and forcefully presented them to Friedrich.

The other man shook his head in confusion and clutched his blonde head in one hand. "I don't remember, perhaps, I'm not certain," he admitted shakily.

"In which case how can you be sure it isn't poison?" challenged Alaric.

"Because it can't be!" howled Friedrich, throwing his hands up in exasperation. "You're wrong."

Where burning rage had ruled before, now something cold had taken hold of von Trelow and his next words came automatically, without conscious will or thought.

"How many phosgene poisonings have you seen at general headquarters, Friedrich?"

Friedrich took a moment to understand the question, then brindled defensively.

"What does that mean?"

"Not many, I'd wager."

"I do my duty," Friedrich insisted.

"How many corpses have you seen up close?" persisted von Trelow, staring at him with icy calm.

"I don't..." began Friedrich, but his voice faltered.

"Do you know how many I've seen, Friedrich?"

The other man shook his head, unable to look him in the eye.

"No, nor do I. It must be thousands, perhaps tens of thousands: Germans, Belgians, French, English, Russians, Americans. I see them in my sleep, whenever I close my eyes. The men I've killed, the comrades I've seen killed."

Friedrich looked like he wanted to say something, or to run, but von Trelow was as much an observer as he. There was something inside him that raged to be heard, and Friedrich was its witness, whether he wished to be or not.

"I've seen every kind of death, Friedrich. I know the look of a man who's been shot and died on the spot, or one who's been wounded and bled his life out in the mud. I know how they look when they've been stabbed, or torn apart by shrapnel, or bludgeoned to death, or strangled, or died in flames. I know the faces of the ones who refused to burn and chose to jump from planes or balloons. I know how they look when they're shattered by explosives, or suffocated under the earth, or drowned in mud. I know the look of the ones who starved, who froze, or who simply died of fright. And I know those dead by gas too, by chlorine, mustard gas, and phosgene, and of dysentery, typhus, typhoid, cholera, TB and, yes, influenza as well. I know them all, Friedrich, like the faces of old friends, very close friends."

Friedrich stood rooted to the spot, his face as pale and waxy as if he were a corpse himself, and without another word von Trelow straightened his cuffs, turned on his heel, and stalked away.

Chapter 10

Behind the house stood a line of brick-built stables and outbuildings, forgotten and forlorn. Once they had been filled with riding horses, carriage horses, a pony for the children, and a multitude of busy servants tending to the needs of the family and the estate. Now they were deserted, horses and servants both gone to war, so it was here that von Trelow gravitated in his cold rage.

He found himself there without recalling the journey, standing in the block-paved stable yard facing a great pile of sawn logs ready to be split for the winter. In desperate need of some physical channel for his anger he stripped off his Waffenrock and shirt and hung them on a convenient hook, pulled the axe from a log-end chopping block and set to it.

He worked with mechanical precision: place, lift, swing, and bend to place again. It was hard, tiring and purging. Slowly the dissonant howling in his head—not quite the screams of dead men, nor the whine and shriek of shells, nor his own wailing at Jana's loss, but something of all three—began to fade.

"I brought you a cup of tea, sir," said a voice breaking through his rhythm. He let the last swing drop and split its log cleanly in two and found Klosel carrying cup and saucer. "Cook made it in the English way, sir." He didn't entirely disguise his disdain.

"Thank you, Klosel. Most kind. I should thank Cook as well, for remembering." He stepped to the old stone horse trough full of recent rainwater and plunged his head in. It was cold, crisp, and shocking, making him gasp. He straightened up and rubbed the drips from his face and from his short-cropped scalp, then walked to where the chauffeur was still waiting and took the cup and saucer from his outstretched hand. “Thank you.”

“It seemed only equitable, sir, since you were doing one of my jobs for me.” He nodded to the still substantial pile of logs. It hadn’t occurred to Alaric who would have to chop the wood, but it clearly wasn’t going to be Herr Buhler, so Klosel it had to be. He glanced at the thin shoulders and the age-stooped back; it hardly seemed fair.

“It’s good to work up a sweat,” he assured him as he sipped the tea. “I’ll see if I can do the rest before I leave. It’s good exercise for me.”

Klosel managed a self-conscious, grateful smile and began to turn back to the house but stopped.

“Did you mean what you said, sir?” he asked suddenly. Von Trelow wasn’t sure what he’d meant.

“About the wood? Of course.”

“No, sir.” The chauffeur was clearly uncomfortable and glanced towards the back of the house to see if they were being overheard, but there was no one else to be seen. “About Frauline Johanna being killed.”

“You heard that then?”

The old man shrugged.

“You have a powerful voice, sir, it carries well.”

Von Trelow sipped a little more of the tea before he replied.

“I meant every word of it, Klosel. Can you help me?”

The chauffeur looked suddenly very old and very sad, but he nodded.

“I will if I can, sir. I loved her too. We all did, in our own way.”

Von Trelow reached out a large hand and laid it on the old man’s bony shoulder and squeezed it gratefully.

“Thank you, Klosel. I know you did.” Klosel, for his part, seemed awkward and abashed by such contact, but smiled sadly, nonetheless.

“She is at least with God, sir.”

Half an hour earlier, the suggestion would undoubtedly have fired Alaric’s anger, but now he was left with only a melancholy purpose—and in any case, it was meant with nothing but kindness and he understood that.

“Let us hope so.”

“There can be no doubt, sir, she was a good woman.”

On that they could agree.

Half an hour later in the sacrosanct depths of the kitchen, where the Buhlers and their guests would never condescend to be seen, von Trelow sat at the broad kitchen table and finished another cup of tea, feeling considerably wiser. Frau Jahnik, the cook, had easily been taken into their confidence. She too had served the family since Johanna was a child:

“I could not have loved the dear girl more if she were one of my own!”

Her own tears were heartfelt and freely flowing. They ran down sagging red cheeks which in better times had been full and plump. Between her tears she did most of the talking—“Listen to me carrying on, sir,”—with Klosel filling in the gaps.

It seemed that this was the Gepharts’ third visit in a month:

"He eats enough for three and she barely has a bite, so proud of her figure she is. And the fuss if any of the laundry comes back anything other than spotless!"

"From her?"

"From him!"

It certainly struck von Trelow as rather overstaying their welcome if they were simple houseguests. Both Friedrich and, more recently, Herr Braun had been repeated visitors too, and there had been others, names he didn't recognise, businesspeople and men whose profession and reasons for being there had never been explained. Braun was certainly one of these. Neither of the servants quite knew who Braun was. He spoke little and cautiously, like a man used to minding his words, but he was undoubtedly erudite and clever:

"He's always watching, from behind those glasses. Up to no good, mark my words."

Friedrich's presence was a puzzle too; an OHL staff officer during the most devastating Allied offensive of the war, the army exhausted, the workers threatening revolution, and Friedrich had time for leave, not once but repeatedly?

"Coming and going at all hours. Exhausted he was when he got back this time, chilled to the bone. He took one of my special hot toddies right off to bed. It's inhuman what that army asks of you young men." If only she knew what it was truly like, thought von Trelow, but he wouldn't disillusion her.

He was now certain Johanna had been right. There was something odd going on at Retzen, and there was no doubt in his mind that it all tied back to her death. He finished the tea, warmly thanked them both and received both their blessings in return. Then he headed for the stairs and his room, to clean up after his exertions at the log pile, his mind ticking as methodically as the clock counting down the hours of his leave.

It was in the gloom of the upstairs corridor that von Trelow spotted Braun emerging mole-like from his door. At first sight of Alaric, he shrank back, as if he was about to return to the safety of his room, then he lowered his head and instead moved quickly, mumbling something that might have been a greeting, or could have been a prayer.

"Good afternoon, Herr Braun," said Alaric, stopping to speak with him. Braun nodded but kept walking, keeping his eyes downcast so that only his wild and impressive eyebrows could be seen. "I wondered if you had a moment?"

The round-faced man waved vaguely and shook his head without hesitation or breaking his stride.

"Excuse me, perhaps later," he muttered and, giving no further explanation, briskly made for the head of the stairs.

Alaric, his curiosity sharpened to a razor-edge, watched him out of sight, then approached the recently vacated room and tried the door. It was locked. He gripped the doorknob and pressed his shoulder to the wood, testing it. Its weight resisted him. He let go and glanced toward the stairs, where Braun had disappeared.

"Very well, keep your secrets for now," he said quietly, then headed to his own room further along the corridor.

The much-lauded grandfather clock was sounding three o'clock when he descended the stairs, washed, and refreshed. As he looked down into the hall, he saw Friedrich watching him, evidently having just left the library. The younger man was shuffling anxiously, tension apparent in face and limb.

"I was looking for you," said Friedrich as von Trelow reached the foot of the stairs. That came as rather a surprise, Alaric had thought that he'd avoid him all day, if not for the rest of their stay.

"I was chopping wood," he explained.

The look on Friedrich's face eloquently conveyed that he had absolutely no idea why someone would do that, but didn't wish to say so and risk annoying him again.

"Oh," he said finally. "I wanted to apologise."

Another surprise.

"What for? I seem to recall that I was the one upsetting everyone. Surely if anyone is expected to apologise it would be me," replied von Trelow.

Friedrich looked uncomfortable and something else, ashamed.

"You're not a man to jump to conclusions and I… we should have listened. It's just, we're all so shaken by what happened to Johanna. But the idea of it having been more than just a random act of God…"

Von Trelow winced at the phrase, but Friedrich didn't seem to notice.

"We reacted poorly, so I'm sorry. I'm sure father and mother will be too, eventually." They both smiled at that, knowing that an apology from either elder Buhler would be a long time coming.

"I apologise too," von Trelow admitted. "My nerves are close to shot, Friedrich. I need rest, and there's been none to be had, and now with what's happened to Jana, I just don't have anything left."

Friedrich nodded.

"But I am convinced that her death wasn't simple influenza."

"Do you really think it was phosgene?" asked his brother-in-law desperately. He didn't want to believe, but he was trying—Alaric gave him credit for that.

"I'm afraid I do, or something very like it."

Friedrich sighed and rubbed his fingers through his short blonde hair.

"But why? Why on earth would anyone want to hurt Johanna? It just doesn't make sense."

Von Trelow shrugged his broad shoulders expressively.

"I have no idea, but she wrote to me a few weeks ago that she was concerned about something. She just didn't say what. Then her diary was tampered with. She wrote in it on the day she died, and someone tore those last pages out and burned them. I found the ashes in the grate."

Friedrich was wide eyed, shocked, and appalled.

"My God, someone really might have killed her." He was silent for a moment, as if taking it in. "What are you going to do?"

Alaric smiled, calmly and confidently, this much at least he was certain of.

"What I'm trained to do: gather intelligence, analyse it, and draw a conclusion. In this case, who killed her and why."

Friedrich nodded approvingly.

"Good. What will you do then?"

"What do you think I'll do, Friedrich?" said von Trelow icily.

Friedrich's complexion went a little pale, but he didn't protest, and he didn't disagree.

"If there's anything I can do, Alaric." Von Trelow nodded, but he persisted. "I mean it, anything. She was my sister, my little sister." For a moment he almost looked like he was going to dissolve into tears.

Von Trelow saved him with a question.

"Why are you here, Friedrich? Why have you been here so much recently?" Friedrich's eyes glanced up in surprise.

"Here?" he said.

Von Trelow nodded.

“Yes. We have the Allied armies attacking up and down the Front, and our own allies are failing and collapsing around us. Are you really so surplus to the needs of the OHL that they can let you go at a time like this?”

Friedrich could have become upset at the implied slight, but this time he didn’t, he only laughed quietly.

“They probably could; I don’t think my planning abilities are essential to the General Staff,” he admitted. “But if you must know, I’m here negotiating on their behalf.” He seemed rather proud of that.

“Negotiating what?” asked von Trelow.

“Concrete,” said a gruff voice behind him. They both turned and found Herr Buhler standing in the doorway of his study. “Not that Friedrich is supposed to be discussing it, however, I suppose it’s hardly a great secret.”

“That the largest cement company in Germany is making concrete for the army? Probably not,” admitted von Trelow.

Herr Buhler sighed,

“On which subject, we have requisition orders and delivery schedules to review, Friedrich.” He gestured back into the study and his son dutifully went inside. Herr Buhler looked to von Trelow before he followed. “We both said some regrettable things earlier. I’d drunk too much with lunch; Johanna’s death…”

“Of course,” said von Trelow. “I apologise for my manner and if I offended by the matter of my suggestion. I’ve been at the Front for far too long.”

The businessman nodded. “It’s bad?” he asked, his eyes dark with worry.

Von Trelow wondered what to say, to convey what he knew, what he lived, to someone who had never seen it.

“Each time I go out, I lose a little more of myself, and the best of us are already dead.”

Herr Buhler stood silent, unable to find words. “We are all very proud of you, Alaric,” he said finally, his voice thick. “Johanna loved you very dearly. Let us put today behind us, eh?”

Von Trelow nodded too, if only to calm the waters.

“I agree, sir.”

“Good, then if you’ll excuse me, Friedrich and I have some work to do.” He turned to go.

“Just one more thing, sir. I’ve been introduced to Herr Braun, but I have no idea who he is.”

Herr Buhler paused, as if carefully considering his answer.

“He’s a lawyer. He brought papers from Berlin relating to the contracts.”

“The army contracts?” asked von Trelow.

“That’s right,” said Herr Buhler. “Now, you’ll have to excuse me.”

“Of course,” replied Alaric and watched the dark wooden door close on them both.

He stopped for several minutes, remaining where he was, just thinking, allowing information to flow through the machine of his mind. Eventually his body began to wander aimlessly whilst his brain ticked over all that he’d heard and what he knew.

In due course von Trelow found himself in the drawing room, gazing blankly out across the front terrace, over the drive and the ornamental lawn beyond. Movement drew his eye to the left. Someone was walking briskly down the drive towards the road to town. It was Braun, taking short quick steps, and glancing over his shoulder, not once but twice.

Von Trelow was out in the hall in moments, plucking his greatcoat from the hook where he’d left it that morning. His pistol belt hung beneath, and he fastened it about his waist out of habit. There was no one in the hall as he let himself out of the front door and so, unseen, he set a strong pace towards the town in the wake of Otto Braun.

Chapter 11

The flat, featureless country was easy to observe. From his vantage point striding along the long curving road, von Trelow could see over the hedge and catch sight of Braun's hat as he passed farm gates and gaps. He was gaining on him, his long legs and Guardsman's stride easily outpacing Braun's gambolling gait.

The moment he'd seen him leaving the grounds of the house the barbed hook of suspicion, that the man was trying to flee, had lodged in his mind. He hadn't taken a bag. Of course, he could have stuffed the pockets of his coat or simply abandoned his belongings at the house. Wherever he was going, he was in a hurry. This was no stroll; it was too quick and purposeful. The man was almost running down the road that led straight to the train station on the far side of the town.

The gnawing idea that this was the man's destination was now fixed in von Trelow's mind, bringing with it an attendant suspicion. If he was running, why? Von Trelow tried to tell himself that it might be something else, nothing to do with Jana, but his rage would not listen. It was building, like a boiler gaining pressure—the needle on the dial climbing steadily higher, only barely held in check.

The two sides of his mind grappled with what he'd seen. Braun had fled the room when the question of murder had been raised. Was he that squeamish, or was it guilt? If he went to the train station, he would have to stop him. He needed to know. He quelled the violent images that swirled into his mind. He'd only ask him questions, but those questions would need to be direct—he wouldn't have much time, they could be interrupted at any moment. He didn't need to hurt the man, but he would have to abandon any subtlety and rely on simple fear. He wished he'd brought a knife; knives scared people better than almost anything else, but a pistol was a good alternative.

The dusty bulk of the cement works loomed into view on the right. The dirty grey puffs of a shunting engine showing where a train of trucks, that had brought raw materials along the spur from the mainline, was preparing to leave. As he rounded the bend, he saw Braun trotting ahead, then the train slowly cut across the road between them in a cloud of hissing steam, clanking and wheezing as it hauled its wagons back towards the junction east of the town. He marched quickly to where the line crossed the road. The sluggish engine and its consorts rumbling past with frustrating apathy. Von Trelow crouched and peered between the passing bogeys but could see nothing. He paced impatiently, but the train kept its stubborn, steady meter until eventually the last of the wagons finally passed and rattled off down the line. Braun was nowhere to be seen.

Von Trelow hastened forwards, but four years of war had taught him to recognise a potential ambush. His fingers flicked open the button on his holster. The reassuring weight of the Luger slipped easily into this hand, and he thrust it into his pocket, as if he were simply keeping his hands warm against the autumn wind. His eyes scanned the hedge line with practiced acuity, looking for the slightest glints or unexplained shadows as he moved lightly on the balls of his feet. Yet no one leapt from cover, no shot was fired, no trap sprung, and he found himself surprised, almost disappointed.

He reached the entrance to the cement works unaccosted and stopped. There was no sign of Braun further down the road. The town wasn't far beyond, but the man would have had to have run like the devil. No, he couldn't imagine it. Which left the works. It was the only explanation left.

There was no watchman on the gate, although a small, pitch-roofed sentry box, styled rather like a Bavarian cottage, had been built for the purpose. He supposed it was impossible to spare a man to guard cement and sand when Germany needed every able man at the Front or in a factory.

He walked around the barrier and into the wide, cobbled yard, past a large steam excavator busily scooping up great mouthfuls of limestone gravel from a huge heap left by the offloading of the train. It chugged as it rotated, its engine belching smoke into the cold air, and disgorged its load into an iron storage bin the size of a dreadnought. Elsewhere a gang of men were busily shovelling gravel onto a conveyer belt that carried it clanking up and through the wall of the impressive main building. Still there was no sign of Braun.

A man in dusty overalls, a shapeless navy-blue cap upon his head, was crossing the yard and having no other options von Trelow stopped him.

"Excuse me, I was supposed to be with Herr Braun, but I was delayed. Do you know where he's gone?"

The man appeared nonplussed, although apparently impressed by the uniform.

"It's about the army contract," von Trelow said experimentally. It didn't seem to help.

"No idea, sir, sorry. I don't know the man."

"He's about forty-five, moustache and round glasses, wearing a brown coat and a black Homburg hat."

The man looked him over, then, evidently deciding that he was not an enemy saboteur, nodded.

"He's just gone into the office building, over there." He pointed back the way he'd come, where a red brick block three storeys tall stood aside from the bustle of the main works.

“Thank you,” said von Trelow and followed his directions across the cobbles, surreptitiously slipping the Luger out of his pocket and back into its holster.

Fifty metres from the building, by merest chance, Alaric caught sight of Braun’s profile and hat through one of the ground floor windows. The man had just entered a room from somewhere beyond. Von Trelow stepped quickly out of the line of sight and approached the building with long swift strides. He was at the red brick wall in moments and slipped along it towards where he’d seen Braun. He stopped before he reached the window and leant back against the building in the manner of someone waiting for a friend.

He could hear voices from inside, but though he strained to catch their words, they were an incomprehensible muddle of muffled murmurs that rose and fell beneath the shunting of machinery and the chuffing of engines. At points they seemed quite animated, the speakers, or at least one who didn’t sound like Braun, surging angrily, but soon subsiding. Try as he might, it was quite impossible to hear anything clearly enough to make sense of it.

He was still none the wiser when, after a quarter of an hour, the harsh squeak of chairs being scraped across a hard floor heralded movement in the room. Von Trelow took his chance: A snatched glance through the window.

Braun, hat in hand, his back to the window, moving around the table towards the door. Beyond him, a man wearing a workman’s leather jacket over a thick pullover and worn dusty trousers of heavy dark corduroy. He wore a narrow brimmed black bowler on his head with short salt and pepper hair showing beneath it. He was facing the door as he opened it, but he didn’t look happy. Something in the way he moved, spoke of frustration and annoyance. Braun followed him out.

It would take perhaps thirty seconds for them to exit the building. He needed to be hidden by then. Von Trelow moved swiftly past the window, along the front of the block and around the corner. The shadows there were deep, perfect to wait and watch.

The door to the building opened and the two men emerged. Braun made a show of offering his hand to his companion, who evidenced every sign of continuing frustration. The other man refused it. More words were said, and if von Trelow were any judge, Braun was having to work hard to placate him. The worker moved through expressions of surly annoyance, to gesticulating agitation, and finally sullen compliance. When he finally took the proffered hand, it was obviously only grudgingly, shaking his head and slouching away towards the works, his every step speaking of dissatisfaction.

Braun stood and watched him go, then, after a moment of reflection, turned and walked cautiously but quickly in the opposite direction, across the uneven cobbles towards the gate.

Von Trelow, observed from cover as he tallied the questions the little drama had raised. He went to follow. The sharp scrape of hobnails on cobblestones—Someone at his back—Damn! He'd been a fool.

A quick glance over his shoulder. Three men, all dressed in dust-covered work clothes and caps, brows creased by curious, hostile frowns. Idiot! He'd made the mistake of a raw recruit. He felt a flush of fury, as the anger he'd built up on the walk to the plant, that had begun to fade whilst he was waiting, roared back into his breast. The trio eyed him with open suspicion.

"What's this? An army spy?" said one, thrusting out a chin he hadn't shaved in days. His words at no point dislodged the hand-rolled cigarette stuck to his lip. It was an impressive, if entirely wrong, guess, given how close to the truth it was. This man might fight but preferred to talk.

Von Trelow glanced back to the yard, Braun was already halfway across, his odd, rapid gait almost skipping.

"He's here to snoop on the union," said the second worker, drawing von Trelow's attention back. He was an older, heavy, man with the wheezing rasp of a life spent amongst the dust and fumes. No immediate threat there.

The third man had said nothing but had knocked off the tip of his cigarette and stowed it in the band of his hat. He now began to move to von Trelow's left, circling him, his left hand disappearing deep into his jacket pocket. It was probably not because he was cold. Here was the danger.

A final flick of the eyes found Braun almost at the gate. Von Trelow damned his own foolishness again and the time this absurd, unnecessary distraction was wasting.

"He's a strike breaker, some kind of spy," said the first man, now stepping closer to jab an accusing finger. "Is that what you are, Herr Officer?"

No point in talking, it would take too long to try. The accusative finger was still raised. The man was far too close. Grab it, yank it sharply down. A snap and a howl of pain, cut off by a fast right cross to the jaw, cracking the man's yellow teeth shut. He let go as the worker stumbled back, his weak legs folding beneath him, taking him to the cobbles.

The scuff of boots on the cobblestones at his back. The familiar flash of cold fear, quickly overcome. Turn fast to meet the quiet man sliding in, the gleam of a blade in his hand. A slap to the wrist moving the knife aside. A hard kick to the knee winning a cry of fierce agony. Then grab the sleeve of the knife hand, and the back of the man's head in the palm of his hand, and swing. Face struck brick with a satisfying crunch, and the figure in his grasp collapsed. The knife fell clattering from nerveless fingers.

The third man had barely had time to gasp and deal with the resultant wheeze. Von Trelow faced him, his right hand hovering threateningly over his holster.

"Get out of here," he snarled.

The rattling, heaving workman nodded breathlessly, paused, made a decision, then grabbed at his dazed but conscious comrade, pulled him with difficulty to his stumbling, unstable feet, and dragged him away. The third man was entirely unconscious and would need to be carried, probably to the doctor to have his nose set.

Von Trelow looked across the yard. Braun was already out of sight. He headed after him, briskly marching to the gate and out onto the road. Looking towards the town, there was no one to be seen. He felt a lurch of concern. Where was he? A glance the other way, back towards the house. There, Braun's hat jogging along behind the hedge.

Relieved, von Trelow followed for about fifty metres, crossing back over the railway tracks, then he stepped through a farm gate and began to run with long steady strides across the empty fields towards the distant monstrous architectural amalgam. The shorter distance of his direct route, cutting off the road's gentle curve, combined with his swifter pace, ensured that by the time Braun began to make his way up the driveway, von Trelow was already waiting, striding across the lawn as if returning from a vigorous stroll.

Braun saw his approach and glanced about for some avenue of escape, but there really was no way to go without simply turning tail and running. Instead, he made directly for the front door with a new burst of speed.

"Out for a walk too?" asked von Trelow in his heartiest voice.

Braun nodded reluctantly and offered a vague, "That's right."

Von Trelow came up alongside him as he approached the steps of the Corinthian pillared portico, inserted his arm under the other man's and, before he could flinch away or cry out, grasped his wrist and bent it sharply back.

Braun yelped.

"Keep your voice down, there's a good man, and come with me or I'll break your arm." He turned to walk them both around the end of the house.

Braun fearfully tried to pull away, back towards the front door, but the pain in his wrist was too much and he instantly succumbed.

"Y-you're mad!" he yelped, although he was clearly trying to be as quiet as he could.

Von Trelow continued to march to the corner and around it towards the back.

"If I am, you'd be very well advised to do exactly as I say, wouldn't you?" he suggested.

Having rapidly considered his point, Braun shut up and allowed himself to be led.

Once at the rear of the stables, under the line of dark pines that stood shading their back wall, von Trelow released him. Braun staggered away, massaging his bent wrist, and staring at him with unconcealed terror from behind his spectacles.

"I have some questions for you, Herr Braun. Answer them and you shall leave here entirely unharmed. Refuse, or lie to me, and I cannot make the same promise. Is that clear?" He loomed over the other man, who had backed into the stable wall, his left wrist still cradled protectively to his chest.

"Yes, it's clear," he conceded shakily.

"Good. Let us start with who you are please," began von Trelow.

"Braun, Otto Braun. I… I'm working with Herr Buhler. I brought him some papers to review and sign. Then I'm to return them to Berlin for filing."

"What papers?" asked von Trelow.

Braun shook his head.

"I don't know, I was just told to bring them. They were given to me."

"By whom?"

"Herr Schmitt... uh, he's my employer." Braun was looking all about, desperate for some way to escape. He hadn't given up hope, that meant his words couldn't be trusted. There was no infallible way to tell if someone was lying, instinct could tell a lot, but a good liar could fool anyone. If Braun was a lawyer, as Herr Buhler had said, it was a professional skill, and so one had to assume that he was at least better at it than the average. Von Trelow tried a different tack.

"You went to the cement works today. Who did you meet?"

Braun looked even more shocked than when he'd grabbed him.

"You followed me?" he said, outraged.

"Answer me, or I promise you'll wish you had," threatened von Trelow in a level voice that left no room for doubt.

Fear was etched across Braun's face, but he was still not entirely cowed. Von Trelow was impressed.

"I can't tell you. I went on behalf of Herr Buhler. You'll have to ask him." He saw the reaction in von Trelow's face and quickly tried to mollify him. "I swear it was only a business matter to do with the running of the works." Von Trelow glowered menacingly. "I swear by God and Germany, it was nothing more than that!"

That, von Trelow finally believed. He wasn't sure why, but there was an earnestness in Braun's voice that was hard to ignore.

He was about to press further, to ask about his previous visits, but Braun spoke first.

"You want to know about your wife, yes?" he asked quaveringly.

Von Trelow nodded, cautious and still within arm's reach.

"Listen to me, I beg you—I don't know anything about her death, I swear it. I only met her once. She seemed charming. But when I was leaving here on Wednesday evening, the chauffeur swung the car around the circle before the house."

Von Trelow nodded. He would have to have done that if he'd collected someone from the front door.

"And?" he asked meaningfully.

Braun was pale and breathless, shock still holding him, but he went on.

"As the lights passed over the end of the front terrace—where it curves around the far end of the house—I saw two people there." He stopped speaking, as if something was preventing him from saying more. His lips were clamped shut and his arms, right hand still protectively gripping the left, were crossed across his chest.

"Who did you see?" insisted von Trelow, he took a half step closer, almost pressed against the other man.

Braun whined, an odd sound, half appeal, half complaint.

"I'll tell you if you swear not to hurt me," he said desperately.

"I swear I'll hurt you if you don't," snarled von Trelow. But something in Braun's eyes caught his attention, magnified by the lenses of his glasses. He had something to say, something he wanted to confide, but was truly scared. Von Trelow nodded curtly. "All right, tell me and I swear I won't hurt you."

"Whatever it is?"

Von Trelow's mind was spinning now, a machine racing for an answer.

"Whatever it is," he agreed.

Braun's fractured breathing steadied, if only slightly.

"It was two people in an embrace, a man and a woman and I couldn't see the man because he was behind her. I only had the impression of him and his arms around her back, but..." He had to take a breath before he could bring himself to complete what he'd begun. "I believe the woman was your wife." Braun flinched, despite the promise he'd extracted, waiting for the punishing blow.

Von Trelow's mind was filled with noise, the steam whistle cry of a boiler under pressure, his pounding heartbeat an engine's frantic rhythm.

"I only saw them for a moment, then they ducked out of sight," Braun continued to chatter fearfully, but von Trelow was barely listening. The machine of his disciplined mind was howling, shaking, ready to burst. Then a voice cut through the screeching.

"Forgive the interruption, sir. Frau Buhler has asked me to inform you that the pastor is here to discuss the funeral arrangements." It was Klosel, standing at the corner of the stables, his eyes blankly taking in the scene without any sign of emotion.

Braun took his chance and stumbled past the motionless von Trelow, half running back towards the house. Klosel waited until he was gone.

The howling in von Trelow's mind had started to ebb, but in its place were whirling questions. Questions he couldn't bear to ask, questions he'd never considered having to ask. He felt sick even to think of them, but you heard it all the time. Soldiers, officers and men, were constantly receiving such letters from home. Wives and sweethearts left alone for months or even years, succumbing to other men, wanting divorces, or simply admitting their guilt, perhaps worst of all the dilemma of a guilty wife wanting forgiveness, but bearing another man's child. He'd seen it all, but never, not for a moment, had he imagined it of Jana. Did that make him a fool?

"Sir, Frau Buhler and the pastor," Klosel reminded him.

Dazed by his own imaginings von Trelow turned and walked slowly back towards the chauffeur.

"Thank you, Klosel. I'll go now." His voice was flat—dulled by uncertainty.

"I'm sorry for disturbing you, sir," said Klosel as he passed, "I was concerned."

Von Trelow stopped and nodded, without looking him in the eye.

“That’s all right, Klosel,” he said flatly. “It was all under control.”

Chapter 12

Von Trelow went through the motions of the meeting with the pastor in the manner of an automaton. He met the man, greeted him, sat, and drank tea, and offered perfunctory responses whenever his opinion was sought, but by the end of the interview had no recollection of what had been said or agreed, or even of the man's name. He barely noticed when Frau Buhler stood to show the pastor out, whilst he remained, his gaze fixed upon a knot in the parquet. She did not return, and he was left to the turmoil of his own thoughts and suspicions.

If Braun was being truthful—and von Trelow believed that he was—then was he right? Was it Jana he had seen?

Perhaps he was mistaken. In the darkness, with only a passing glimpse, might he have confused her with Frau Buhler—older yes, but the resemblance undeniable. Or perhaps Frau Gephart: taller, certainly, but still youthful and slim. Trude, too, was a possibility if the glance had been brief enough.

Only Frau Jahnick he discounted—there were limits to what even the poorest light could disguise. Undoubtedly Braun's eyesight was poor; the ubiquitous spectacles spoke to that. So, could anything he said be relied upon?

And yet, von Trelow could not rid his mind of the fear.

If it had been Jana, then who had she been with? The idea circled him, snarling. Her brother... her father... Innocent, perhaps—offering comfort. But then why would neither man have mentioned it?

If not family, then who?

Herr Gephart? Unthinkable, despite his taste for younger women.

The doctor—young, intelligent, there when he was not. Von Trelow recalled the anger in Meissner's eyes. And the fear…

The confines of the drawing room had become suddenly intolerably oppressive. Von Trelow stumbled to his feet and made his way down the hall to the library. There the single window was a glazed door. He crossed to it, turned the key, and stepped out onto the terrace that wrapped around the end of the house.

Finally, in the cool and the dark, he could breathe.

This was where Braun had seen someone—possibly Jana—in an embrace. Von Trelow walked to the corner and stood where they must have been, trying to reconstruct the angle. Here, in deep shadow, the light from the library door barely reached halfway across the terrace.

If they had been distracted—his stomach turned at the implication—they might not have heard the Mercedes, or imagined themselves safe, until the headlights swept across them.

Yes, it could have happened. Must have happened that way—unless Braun was wholly given to flights of fantasy. He did not seem the type.

It was too dark to see anything more, even if some trace remained. He turned back towards the open library door, his mind still reeling.

The air cracked. Stone splintered.

He hit the paving before he knew what he'd heard—hand snatching for the pistol hung with his coat in the hall.

No second shot shattered the night. Only the swishing crackle of flight through fallen leaves.

Back on his feet. His mind shifted gear—clear and focused now. He gave chase, keeping low, weaving erratically, making a hard target. It had been the soft bang of a pistol, not the hard snap of a rifle—whoever carried it, he was close.

They knew the ground, plunging eastwards, deeper into black woods unwashed by the slivered moon. Von Trelow followed the crackling footfalls through the leaves, raising his arms to shield his face against branches as well as shots.

None came.

His quarry was rushing headlong, confident of the ground—but their stride faltered and stumbled. Von Trelow could hear it, each step unsteady.

Abruptly, the prey slithered to a stop.

Von Trelow stopped too. He stepped flat against thc broad trunk of a tree, pressed his body to the bark and stilled his breath.

He waited for the shot… A return to flight…

Only the night.

High branches creaked. An owl called its melancholy cry. Near at hand, the small rustlings of tiny night timc creatures returning to their foraging beneath the leaf-fall.

His breath was even, his pulse steady. He'd played his game a hundred times.

The snap of a twig – loud as a rifle shot.

He was already running.

All stealth was abandoned; speed was his defence. He hurled himself after the noise, saw a shadowed movement between the trees.

Bodies collided and fell. A man cried out amongst the leaves. There was worn wool beneath von Trelow's hands and a short, coarse beard. He wrestled him onto his front, planted his knee in his back, despite his struggles.

A quick search with flickering hands. No gun, only a small knife worn smooth by use, coils of wire, and an old bread bag.

"Please, I'm sorry, I'm sorry. It was only a few rabbits. Please!" gabbled the man beneath him. "I won't come again, I'm sorry."

"Be silent," hissed von Trelow, close to his ear.

Instant obedience. Still, his frightened breathing drowned out the soft sounds of the wood.

He had caught an old poacher, and whoever had fired the shot was gone.

Von Trelow arrived at the train station at a quarter to nine. He waited alone in the shadows beyond the flickering gaslight. It was best to be cautious—especially if someone was trying to kill him.

The train arrived—predictably prompt. A firefly glow, swelling, until the engine's heaving breaths were heard, shredded by the scream of steel wheels along rattling rails. Then the blunt bulk of the train burst from the darkness, shrieking its passing, as its brakes screeched and set sparks dancing.

The train slowed to a halt amidst a gout of steam and clatter of doors. A woman with a baby. An old couple. A handful of working men with tool bags. A railway worker in his uniform. Finally—alone—a young woman of remarkable height, in a long grey coat and an austere broad-brimmed hat. She held a sturdy carpet bag in one hand, in the other a doctor's Gladstone. She scanned the platform both ways and, seeing no one she recognised, set her bags down to wait.

Von Trelow waited until the last of the other passengers had left the platform and the train had begun to haul itself noisily away. Then he stepped into the light.

She saw him without sign of recognition and let him come to her.

Lise Freisinger—now Doctor Freisinger—hadn't changed that he could see. Still uncommonly tall and willow-wand thin, with her ice pale blonde hair tightly tied up out of the way. Her eyes, hidden beneath the shadow of her hat, he remembered as bright blue and unwavering. As he drew closer, she picked up her doctor's bag. She left the larger one for him.

"Hello, Lise," he said as he bent to pick up the carpet bag.

With the words still on his lips, she hit him.

He'd barely grasped the grip, words yet in his mouth, when her gloved right hand slapped him hard across the cheek. The side of his face felt like fire and his head rang. If she hadn't practiced the whole manoeuvre, she had a formidable talent. She'd even had him lean down to make it easy for her.

He stifled the instinct to respond and stood up, rubbing his face appreciatively.

"As I was saying, thank you for coming. I know it can't have been easy."

He saw her take a deep breath and met her glare.

"He trusted you," she said accusingly.

"I know."

"You couldn't save him." It wasn't even a question this time.

"No. I tried. I truly tried."

He could almost feel Erich's weight across his shoulders and his throat raw from crying for a medic.

"I don't hate you because you couldn't save him, do you know that?"

He frowned in mild confusion. "No, then why?" he asked.

"Because you promised me you would. You lied to me and gave me hope and then you took it away." Her voice was fierce and unsteady. "Anyway, I swore the next time that I saw you I'd hit you as hard as I could. But I don't suppose you even felt it, did you?"

"It hurt, if that's what you wanted." He didn't just mean the pain either, although he'd had far less painful blows from far larger assailants.

"Good," she said and walked past him down the platform towards the gate.

He caught up in a few long strides and fell into step with her. He tried again.

"Thank you for coming, I do mean that."

"Other than to hit you in the face I'm not entirely sure why I did. I think it's what Erich would have wanted me to do, so perhaps that's it."

He smiled to himself. "That's what I said to Louis," he admitted.

She nodded. "And what did he say?"

"That you might shoot me."

She didn't laugh. "I couldn't get a gun," she said coolly. "Poison on the other hand is readily available."

Von Trelow's eyes fell on the gleaming black doctor's bag in her hand, and he wondered how much she was joking, if at all. "Then it's probably a good job that I brought the food."

She glanced at him finally. "I'm starving," she admitted. She wasn't exaggerating. Up close, he could see her clothes hanging loosely on her never-full figure and the shadows deep beneath her cheekbones.

"Do you want to eat now?" he asked, pointing out a bench on the platform. He'd half expected a politely outraged refusal, but she nodded keenly without protest and walked to the seat.

She ate the sandwich he'd brought for her as if it were the first thing she'd eaten in a week. He waited, watching quietly, then handed her his own. She didn't say no.

"There are a couple of apples too, and coffee. It's ersatz, but it's hot." Frau Jahnik had happily provided from the kitchens.

She finished the mouthful and swallowed hard. "My God that's good," she admitted as she unwrapped the second sandwich.

"How long is it since you've eaten properly?" asked von Trelow.

She was already eating it and shrugged. "It depends on what you mean by 'properly'," she said finally. "I've had food, but most of it has no right to the name. The ration keeps being cut, and even if you have the ration for something, it probably doesn't exist."

"But you're a doctor, surely you have money?"

She took another bite of sandwich and ate it ravenously before she replied. "You mean the black market?"

He nodded.

"I work at a hospital and volunteer at a clinic. One doesn't pay a lot, the other doesn't pay at all. If patients pay me, they don't eat," she said simply. "My hospital pay's usually enough."

"Hardly," he said meaningfully.

She stopped eating and scowled at him. "Well, what's the choice Herr Oberstleutnant Alaric von Trelow und Ehlinger? We don't all have country estates and preferential military rations. Most of Berlin is starving and the winter's not yet begun. I thought it was bad enough last year, this time it will be a catastrophe. It will be like the Turnip Winter all over again."

"Unless the war ends," he said quietly as she returned to eating.

She nodded vigorously. “Yes,” she finally managed. “If the war doesn’t end soon the only choice will be if we die of starvation, disease, or are killed by our neighbours.”

He let her finish and handed her an apple.

“May I have some coffee?” she asked, placing the apple in her lap.

He unscrewed the lid of the flask and poured her a cup.

“I saw protestors marching in Berlin when I was passing through,” he said. “With red banners.”

“You can’t be surprised,” she said, taking the cup from him. “Thank you. People are desperate. There are strikes somewhere or another all the time, until they send the police in to break them up.” She sipped the coffee and didn’t even flinch at the taste. “It’s just people wanting food, but the communists and socialists are the only ones who seem to want to help them and the government acts like they’re the enemy. It’s becoming frightening.”

He wanted to ask her if she was safe, to offer her help, but he was certain she’d throw it in his face. Instead, he quietly waited whilst she drank her coffee and ate her apple. He offered her the second one.

She took it and tucked it away.

“I’ll keep it for later,” she said without guilt. He’d find something to eat when he got back to the house, she probably knew that, or simply didn’t care. She stood, brushing crumbs from her coat and picking up her doctor’s bag from the bench.

“There’s an inn in the town, I’ve rented you a room,” he explained.

“Good.” She headed for the gate. “You can tell me about your wife on the way. I’m sorry, by the way. I don’t think I said.”

“No, but thank you.”

“A lot of people are dying, von Trelow, and not just at the Front.” They were on the street now, moving from pool of gaslight to pool of gaslight.

“I know,” he said calmly. “I see the reports. You can call me Alaric by the way.”

She strode quickly, easily keeping pace with him.

“I could, but I don’t want to. We’re not friends. You’re someone I’m trying not to hate too much, because I don’t want to waste the energy.”

He found that hurt more than he’d anticipated, but didn’t reply. He simply led the way to the inn, and on the way, he told her all that had happened, and all that he’d found.

*

The Maxim gun to von Trelow’s left was pumping out fire with methodical efficiency, slowly twisting from left to right, sowing bullets in a murderous arc. Other guns answered up and down the line, firing from strongpoints and bunkers to blanket the ground, but still they were coming.

A dull thump sent a mortar round on its way as screaming whistles heralded its British brethren’s reply.

A crashing explosion close at hand rained grey earth and pale chalk that pattered on von Trelow’s stahlhelm.

“Steady men,” he bellowed to be heard above the insane din. “Wait for the signal.”

He saw nervous men crouching, hugging their rifles and knees. “Remember, they have to come to us,” he told them.

“Keep your heads down!” he yelled at the brave and the new replacements who didn’t know any better, some still too young to shave every day. “Wait for the signal.”

Then the signal came, a red flare, rising and bursting high overhead. Then another and another, turning the trench into a carmine hell.

"Australia!" Battle-cries drifting over the parapet.

The whistle in his mouth, piercing and sharp over the dull thumps of mortars and chatter of the guns. The men mounting the firing step, raising rifles.

A boy's head snapped back, blood pouring before a shot could be fired.

Rifles cracking up and down the line, men falling, littering the duckboards. Voices yelling, words in German and English battling and merging.

He rounded the dogleg as something hit the boarding across the parados wall and thumped down onto the floor. He saw the pinecone shape and had time to desperately duck back before the grenade exploded.

Primal shrieks, a man with shredded stumps where legs had been.

Von Trelow stumbled into the trench over dead and dying. Another man fell, his face a lurid mass of red.

Another missile arcing over the parapet.

Von Trelow dropped to his knees in the slaughter, grabbed the grenade and threw it back. Another came, clattering down and landing on a corpse—he threw that one too. Another, and another.

On hands and knees, he scrambled, grabbing them from broken boards and shattered bodies, throwing them back where they'd come.

On and on. Never-ending. More and more, falling.

An explosion close at hand—the punch of the blast—no time to check for ripped flesh; he'd soon know.

Another grenade. Another. Another. Endless.

“Australia!”

Boots in the trench.

He scrambled at his belt, Luger in hand—

Erich.

Helmet gone. Blood on his face. But alive. Blue eyes bright like fever.

“They’re coming!”

And then they came.

Rising over the sandbags, soup-bowl helmets over khaki.

Von Trelow shot the first man. Another took his place. He fired again and again until the pistol clicked empty.

Then they were in the trench, dropping, scrambling, falling into the pit with him.

He grasped at a rifle, wrestling as the soldier tried to twist the bayonet onto him. He wrenched it from his hands, smashed his face with the butt. Over and over. Pummelling him into the German dead.

Another screaming face. Knock the bayonet aside. Plunge his own in. Shots singing past. Muzzles flashing. Blood flooding from behind rotten teeth.

Wrestling again as hands clawed at his rifle. A scramble to draw his knife and then a frenzy of stabbing as the Australian fell, dragging the rifle with him.

Corpses and blood. Knee deep. Still coming.

Grasping up an entrenching tool like an axe—laying about him, chopping down on arms, cleaving faces. His knife slashing and stabbing.

“Alaric!”

A voice above the screaming.

Erich.

Down amongst the fallen. His tunic bright with spreading scarlet.

Pushing through the press of khaki and grey.

An enemy figure looming above the fallen man, bayonet poised.

Eyes wide—white—as von Trelow’s shovel sheared through collarbone, deep into the chest. Falling away.

Dragging Erich up and onto his shoulders. Hot blood seeping across his neck.

“I’m sorry, Alaric.”

“Shut up, Erich… Medic!”

Stumbling for the communications trench.

“Medic!”

Grabbing a fallen bayonet, long and saw-backed, like a small sword.

Barging past the grey, stabbing and slashing at the khaki.

“Medic!”

“I’m sorry, Alaric. I’m sorry…”

“Shut up! Medic!”

*

He awoke in the too soft guest bed, sheets bunched tight in his hands and stared at nothing. He waited whilst his breathing steadied and the sheen of sweat dried in the cold of the room. Then he wrapped his coat about him and went to Jana's bed.

Chapter 13

Breakfast was a cold affair. Although they currently shared the same roof, it was clear that the rest of the household—Buhlers and Gepharts alike—no longer entirely trusted von Trelow's judgement. Or his temper. He could hardly blame them for that, particularly when he had his own dreadful suspicions of them in return. He exchanged stiff good mornings with them all, except Frau Gephart, who had again remained in her bed.

"Your beds are far too comfortable, Buhler," joked Herr Gephart between mouthfuls. "She never sleeps so late at home."

The Buhler's laughed politely, but she was not the only one missing.

"And where is Herr Braun this morning? I hope he's not unwell?" asked von Trelow.

No answer. No curiosity. Either they all knew where Braun was—or none of them thought his absence remarkable. Von Trelow did not feel the same.

"He went back to Berlin on the late train," explained Friedrich eventually. "He said he had people to meet."

"I see," said von Trelow.

"Alaric, there have been a number of letters I should let you have," said Frau Buhler abruptly, before he could ask more. "They are letters of commiseration and regret from certain ladies of the town. I was going to write to them, but I thought you may like to read them and send your own replies." She was clearly trying to distract him, to give him something to do, but he could see opportunity there too.

"Thank you, I'd like that very much," he replied. "I was going to see Paul at his breakfast. Perhaps after that?"

"Of course," she responded agreeably. "If you are going to the nursery, I shall leave them on the table in the hall."

"I shall be sure to collect them."

Von Trelow was true to his word. He went to the nursery after breakfast and found Paul about to have his own.

"Good morning, Paul." His son once again declined to look up, eyes fixed upon his plate. "How are you this morning?"

After a long pause had become truly awkward Trude nudged the boy.

"Answer your father, Paul, be a good boy."

He shrank into the seat, but a small voice did manage to say, "I'm well, thank you, sir."

Von Trelow went and crouched across the table from the child, trying to reach his level so as not to tower over him.

"I'm glad. What do you plan to do today?"

Paul answered with only a shrug.

"Well, what would you like to do?" Another long, uncomfortable silence.

"Paul," said Trude encouragingly, "you should answer your father, it's polite."

"I want Mutti," said the little boy softly.

Von Trelow felt his heart painfully contract.

“So do I, Paul,” he said truthfully, “but she’s gone.”

The child looked up, his eyes, so like Johanna’s, full of tears.

“You go away, then she can come back. I want my Mutti!” he wailed. He turned and clung to Trude’s legs, burying his sobbing face in her apron.

She wrapped him in her arms and held him as he wept.

Von Trelow stood, then stepped back. The maid’s eyes watched him—full of expectation.

He was entirely at a loss.

What did she expect? What was he supposed to do? He wasn’t the boy’s mother.

“I’m sorry, Paul,” he said at last. “I wish it were that simple.”

Then he turned and left him to his tears.

The iron-grey sky hung bloated with rain as von Trelow crouched beneath the dark trees at the end of the house, brushing gently at the fallen leaves. A boxy flashlight moved in his hand, side to side, its beam carefully angled as he sought a glimmer of reflected light.

He’d found the bullet easily enough—a flattened lump of useless metal buried in the concrete of the end wall. Still, he’d winkled it free with a knife and dropped it into an envelope taken from the side table in the hall.

His current search was speculative. If the shooter had used a revolver, there would be nothing to find. But he believed in being meticulous—and he needed something to occupy his mind. So, he was there.

Passing over the same ground a second time, a vision of his son’s tear-streaked face rose in his mind like a spectre.

He froze—a fist in his throat.

He was failing as a father—an agony he could not deny—but he had no idea how to bridge the gap.

Where else he'd been inadequate? Had he failed as a husband too?

He paused, eyes shut tight, until he could breathe again. The whirlpool of doubt, jealousy, and guilt slowly released its hold.

When he opened his eyes, he had regained some semblance of control.

He continued his search.

He'd worked backwards from the point of impact—past where he'd been when the shot was fired—into the trees. There was a place there, shaded by branches at the side of a large elm, where he'd have stood if he had done the shooting. He'd started there and been crouched, hunting the ground, for half an hour by his watch and still had nothing, but patience tinged with a dash of stubbornness was one of his virtues, and he persisted well past the point he'd given up any real hope.

Then there it was. A gleam of brass amongst the yellows and browns of the leaves. With a thrill of discovery, he reached down with his broad, gloved fingers and picked it up—a cartridge case, marked on the butt end: '7.65x17'. He dropped it into a second envelope and placed that too into his pocket with the envelope containing the bullet, and the letters from the ladies of the town.

The tracks from the night before proved easier to locate, now that it was light. Previous rain and fallen leaves had left plenty of places for a fleeing man to leave his mark. Von Trelow moved through the woods again, this time with cautious precision, scanning to either side whilst following the clearly visible trail.

He stopped as the tracks crossed a clearing. Rain had left broad patches of thick mud and both he and his assailant had run through them. His own larger prints were easy to discount, and of the others, several were badly distorted and blurred by slipping. One was clear; the worn boot-print of an average sized man. What was more, they confirmed something he'd suspected the previous night, the man had an uneven gait. A limp or some other imbalance?

Having committed the boot-print to memory, he carried on. It was clear that the man had moved quickly and surely, knowing his way, heading east through the woods before looping back towards the road to town.

He found the place where he had sheltered against the tree, and the place where he'd tackled the poacher. The old man's footprints were smaller, badly worn, and had approached from the south. From there von Trelow ranged out in increasing arcs until he eventually found what he was looking for.

The footprints of the man he'd been pursuing had stopped behind a sturdy elm tree, less than ten metres from where von Trelow had taken shelter himself. He'd felt his pursuer almost upon him and gone to ground. The footprints from the night before were still clear in the mud and showed just the balls of the feet. The gunman had been crouching, waiting, likely with his pistol levelled, an ambush waiting to spring. Von Trelow's instincts had saved him.

The man's trail then led away from the tree, moving in short, careful steps, whilst von Trelow had been wrestling with the poacher. He'd made off to the south-west, out across fields of wet earth, wheat stubble, and patchy grass, for another half kilometre before joining the road and vanishing. Whether the man had turned left towards town or right towards the house was impossible to say, but von Trelow had an appointment to make in the town, and so he turned to the left and made his way towards Retzen's smoking chimneys.

He found Lise waiting for him in the neat little coffee house on the Hochstraße. The place smelt of bitter roast, floor wax, and fried ham, and the empty plates before her suggested she'd eaten a substantial late breakfast. She was sipping black coffee watched by the elderly proprietress. He crossed to the table, ordered a coffee for himself—certain it would be terrible—and sat down.

"Good morning, Lise."

"I still hate you," she stated conversationally.

"I hadn't assumed otherwise." He placed his cap and gloves on the chair next to him, but left his coat buttoned up against the chill of the unheated room. She had done the same.

"Then why do you insist on calling me Lise?"

He shrugged. "It's what I've always called you, since before the war. It's difficult to think of you any other way."

"Try," she insisted coldly.

He could see her eyes this morning. They were still the same startling blue he remembered, and they were glaring disdain.

"Then I shall do so, Frauline Doctor Freisinger."

She scowled and pursed her lips as if struck by a sudden pain.

"Somehow, when you say it, it's actually worse. I suppose Lise will have to do," she admitted through gritted teeth. She returned to her coffee as the owner brought his.

He took a sip and grimaced in disgust. That at least seemed to amuse her.

"I didn't tell you last night, in case it worried you, but someone tried to shoot me yesterday evening," he said quietly, trying to avoid the woman at the counter from overhearing.

Lise raised a single curious eyebrow.

"Well, it wasn't me, I told you, I couldn't get a gun. Anyway, you know when I arrived."

He scowled and sighed. "I know, I just mean that we need to be careful. Whoever is behind this, they're not afraid to kill over it."

"I thought we knew that already?" she said coolly. The reminder stung and he let it show. She didn't apologise.

"You're right of course. But this is a little more overt."

"I suppose so. Anyway, I'm going to go and talk to this Doctor Meissner, I'll see if he will speak to me." She sipped at her coffee, seemingly quite content with it, whilst von Trelow left his on the table.

"I think you're wasting your time. He's either so arrogant he can't conceive that he's wrong or he's involved somehow and will deny it all the way to the executioner's block."

"Arrogant doctors are almost as common as arrogant army officers," she sniped. "But it's the correct thing to do; she was his patient; he wrote the death certificate. I'll at least try to do things the right way. Anyway," she added, "you never know, he might like me. I'm likeable."

Von Trelow laughed at that, a short scornful bark.

She met his eyes and smiled back. "When I choose to be. In any case there may be some point of connection, other physicians we both know. You said he was in his late twenties? He's in practice and has been for some time, so he can't be too young; he wouldn't have completed his residency."

"You have," pointed out von Trelow.

"And I worked twice as hard and did twice the job of any of the men, to manage it," she replied acidly. He didn't doubt it.

"I'd say he's close to thirty," judged von Trelow.

"Three or so years older than me. We could have overlapped. Do you know where he studied? Was it Freiburg? I don't remember his name but it's not impossible that he was there too."

Alaric could recall the diploma in pride of place on the doctor's wall, but for the life of him he couldn't bring to mind the name of the university.

"I don't know," he admitted. If anything, her look of disdain grew deeper and he almost apologised. He caught himself in time and shook himself out of it. "Very well, go if you wish. But if he does refuse to help, what then?"

She finished the last of her coffee and placed the cup down.

"Then I shall enquire at the funeral homes. According to my landlady there are only two in the town." It was one more than von Trelow had assumed in a town of that size.

"And why would they tell you?" he asked. He found that he had absent-mindedly picked up his coffee cup, thought better of it and replaced it on the table.

She was smiling again. "I told you, I'm likeable. In any case funeral directors are typically very courteous to physicians. We're often their best source of new business."

He scowled at her black humour, but didn't disagree with her plan, they were certainly more likely to speak to her than to him.

"And if they won't let you see her?" he asked, already knowing the answer.

"Then I presume you're capable of breaking in once it's dark?" she whispered theatrically.

He sighed. "I'm an intelligence officer, not a burglar. I don't know how to pick a lock any more than you do."

Lise smiled sweetly, collected her hat from the chair beside her, and fixed it upon her head.

"Well then, you have all afternoon to learn, don't you?" she said. "I'll see you at the inn at a half past one and you can buy me lunch."

He glanced at the plates from her recent breakfast.

"If you keep eating like this, you'll get fat," he taunted her, as unlikely as that seemed.

She flashed him a brilliant and very false smile. “It is my life’s ambition. By the way, I told the nice woman that you’d be paying.” She left him there under the proprietress’ watchful eye and went on her way.

Two streets over von Trelow found a small, neat shop with attractive leadlight windows showing a distorted view of hunting coats, fishing rods and rubber gumboots. It was a family business under the name of Kallenbach, founded in 1872, according to the sign above the frontage. He stepped inside, jangling a bell as he opened the door and ducked the low lintel.

“Good morning, sir,” said a short, shadowed figure emerging from the back of the shop. He was a small man, sixty or older, with a bald pate and white tufts of hair floating cloudlike above each ear. He was dressed in a trim and traditional green hunting jacket, buttoned to the neck and he smiled welcomingly. “How might I be of service to you today?”

He reminded von Trelow of the illustration of a gnome in a book of fairy tales his mother had read to him and his siblings when they were children. He warmed to the man immediately.

He glanced about the shop. Many of the shelves were empty, or near to it, but that was only to be expected. What was there was of a good quality, be it for fishing, hunting, boating, or just walking in the country. Between the two men was a long glass counter, inside which was a shelf of green baize displaying handguns, knives, fishing lures and the like. Shotguns were on a rack on the wall behind, no rifles of course, not with the war on.

Von Trelow reached into the deep pocket of his greatcoat, removed the big pistol he'd taken from the American major, and laid it on the counter.

“I wondered if you had any ammunition for this?” he asked.

The old shopkeeper removed a pair of wire-framed spectacles from his breast pocket and hooked them over his ears, then peered at the large automatic.

"Colt 1911, .45 inch." he said appraisingly. "May I?"

Von Trelow nodded and gestured to the pistol. "Of course."

The little man smiled gratefully, picked it up and expertly checked it to see if it was loaded. It wasn't. He removed the magazine, worked the slide, replaced the magazine, cocked it and dry fired it with a loud clack. He admired it from every angle and then replaced it exactly where he'd found it.

"Thank you," he said warmly. "An unusual weapon, at least in Germany."

"I took it from its original owner in France."

The little man chuckled.

"I dare say. Well, it's a treat to have seen it, but I'm afraid I can't help you. It's a very unusual round and there's just demand, and no way to get it of course."

"Of course," agreed von Trelow. "It was an idle thought. I suppose everyone buys 7.63 Mauser and 9mm Luger?"

The shopkeeper shrugged.

"A lot do, but some people still have old weapons from before the war, revolvers and the like. In times like these people want to ensure they have spare ammunition."

Alaric nodded understandingly and pocketed the Colt.

"But pistol rounds?" he asked.

"We have some 9mm Bergman-Bayard, although we haven't sold any in years, some 6.35mm for pocket pistols, ladies' guns and the like, and of course, 7.65 Browning."

Von Trelow carefully contained any reaction. He was simply someone else interested in handguns, passing the time of day.

"Browning? Is there much call for that?"

The old man seemed distracted. "Hmmm? What, oh yes, some. I wonder, would you consider selling the Colt? I'll give you a fair price."

Alaric pretended to consider the offer. "I don't know, I hadn't thought about it." He paused, as if thinking. "So, who needs Browning ammunition?"

"Around here, the police mainly. A lot of them carry Mauser 1914s. Like this one." He leant over the counter and pointed to a compact but rather elegant pistol a little larger than von Trelow's palm. Alaric looked at it appreciatively.

"May I see?" he asked.

The shopkeeper cheerfully obliged.

"What about the Colt?" he asked as he unlocked the case.

Von Trelow feigned hesitation but had never intended to sell it.

"Thank you, but I think I'll keep it. Perhaps I'll find some ammunition eventually. It's a big gun and it fits me well." He showed his large right hand to make his point, winning another small chuckle from the old man, who placed the small Mauser onto the glass countertop. Von Trelow picked it up and examined it, admiring the quality and certain rather interesting innovations.

"So, the police use these?" he asked.

"Hmmm?" mused the little shopkeeper. "Yes, or the Dreyse 1907. They're rather larger but chamber the same round."

"I see," said von Trelow, dry firing the little automatic with a click. "How interesting."

Chapter 14

Lise was in a secluded box-like booth at the rear of the inn. The dark wood was nearly black, the open side shielded by carved panels inset with frosted glass. Matching windows behind allowed in light but preserved privacy—only someone seated directly opposite the entrance could be seen from the room. Lise was not. She was deep in the corner, waiting.

"I'm surprised you haven't eaten already and left me with the bill," said von Trelow, slipping into the narrow booth.

"I only just got here, or I might have done."

The landlady took their order with weary efficiency, von Trelow ordering tea with milk in the English manner, earning the usual look of bewilderment.

"He really does like it like that," explained Lise, as if excusing the behaviour of a particularly eccentric relative. She waited for the landlady to leave.

"I wonder how much of the bread and sausage will be sawdust."

Von Trelow shrugged, "Out here in the country, it may not be too bad."

"It is in the city," she said simply. "You don't see many dogs or cats these days, even rats are growing scarce." Her smile sharpened. “Though I imagine it’s different at divisional headquarters.”

“You’re a vicious little savage, aren’t you?” he snapped.

Her eyes narrowed, her smile rigid. “Tell me I’m wrong.”

“You’re wrong. If I get good food, I’ve probably taken it from an enemy trench.”

“Hail the conquering hero,” she replied sourly. “Do you want me to polish your medal for you?”

This time he bit his tongue.

“No, I want you to tell me about the doctor.”

A sour look crossed her face, like he’d deprived her of her favourite sport.

“I think you’re right; he’s hiding something. He couldn’t get me out of there fast enough.”

The landlady returned with their meagre meal—thin soup, a slim red sausage, a dash of sauerkraut, and the ubiquitous k-brot. Its arrival temporarily distracted Lise from her taunting, and she fell upon it ravenously.

“He was the same with me,” said Alaric, steeling himself. “I think I may know why.”

She raised a questioning eyebrow.

“Well?” she asked over a gulp of ersatz-coffee.

He didn’t want to say it—but discipline compelled him.

“He and Johanna may have been having an affair.”

Lise’s other eyebrow had joined its twin, framing her surprise.

She swallowed a mouthful. “I presume you had no idea?”

He shook his head, not trusting his voice.

"How did you find out?"

"I didn't. I mean, I'm not sure. But I spent half the morning thanking the matron ladies of the town for their condolences. They were quite forthcoming. He's carried a torch for her since she was fourteen. He'd been away at university..."

"Halle," she interjected.

"What?"

"He studied at Halle-Wittenberg; it was on his diploma."

He sighed. "I know it was on his diploma, I just couldn't remember which university he'd attended."

"Halle-Wittenberg," she insisted with the infuriating, stubborn precision he remembered from when she was a girl.

"I know, you said. Does it matter? Are doctors from Halle-Wittenberg particularly known for having affairs with married women or poisoning their patients?"

She shrugged and smiled sweetly. "It wouldn't surprise me, but not that I've particularly heard."

He closed his eyes for a moment and swallowed his frustration. "In which case..."

"Carry on," she allowed, returning to her food.

"Meissner courted her the summer before the war. I met her the following spring, when I was on leave." He paused. "We married that November."

Lise nodded, still chewing, waiting.

"Paul was born the following August." Why had he said that? Reassuring himself... nine months between.

He found Lise's eyes upon him—open, mocking—as she slowly chewed the k-brot.

He silently hoped she'd choke.

"In any case, he's apparently been attending the house a lot this past year." He felt a little sick and pushed away the remaining food.

"Are you eating that?" Without waiting for his reply, she pulled his plate and bowl across the table.

He watched her attack the remaining food with grim efficiency.

"What?" she demanded, catching his stare.

"Nothing. Just wondering if you were bothering to chew."

She glowered but said nothing—too busy eating.

"Anyway, I went through her diary," he continued. "It's all in code. Most of it I can read, but some sections are in a far more complex numerical cipher. Possibly a Playfair, or even a double Playfair."

He found Lise glaring at him again—she clearly cared nothing for codes.

"Those sections could be about an affair, I can't tell."

She had now finished the sausage and bread and paused over the remaining soup.

"It's a possible motive," she admitted. "If she'd threatened to tell you or was pressing him to make a commitment. He might have panicked. A scandal like that could ruin his career. Or perhaps he finds you intimidating, I understand some people do."

He smiled acidly.

"As the attending physician, he could write what he wanted on the death certificate," she said. "Who's going to question it?"

"I know." It was precisely where his own analysis had brought him. "I need to go and see him, to ask him straight out. It's the only way."

She finally stopped eating and put down the spoon.

"And if he denies it? Even worse, what if he admits it?"

He didn't answer.

She leant forward, glancing out into the bar to make sure no one was close enough to overhear. She lowered her voice anyway.

"If you kill him, what good will it do? She's still dead, and you'll be hanged—or shot—or whatever they do to soldiers. If she was unfaithful, then she's not worth your life."

"What?"

She refused to yield the floor. "If she was innocent, that's different. But you will not get yourself killed over an unfaithful wife."

"I thought you wanted me dead," he said quietly.

She still glared. "Only if I do it. And on balance, I think I'd rather have you alive and suffering."

"Well, that seems reasonable," he said bitterly. "So, what do you suggest? Because I can't see how to find out what's going on without getting him to talk. He lives above his consulting rooms, and even if we could search them, what's there to find? He'd have to be a fool to leave a phosgene canister, or whatever he used, lying around."

She finished the last of the bread and sat back, warming her hands on the coffee cup.

"Very well. We talk to him. Together." She held up a hand before he could protest. "Otherwise, I'm on the next train back to Berlin."

They locked eyes across the table, testing their resolve. She meant it, and he needed her.

"All right," he growled.

Her smile, for once, was genuine.

"Good. I've also found out where they took your wife's body. It took all my considerable charm; they're a distrustful lot around here. I had to pretend I wanted to send flowers."

He nodded before realising the incongruity of what she'd said.

"Flowers, in October? Anyway, who grows flowers when they could be growing food?"

Her look of utter disdain had returned.

"Tissue paper flowers, Herr Intelligence Officer. No one's had real flowers at a funeral for years."

The rain that had been threatening all morning had finally arrived, hammering down on streets and houses, splattering off the cobbles, sending turbulent streams rushing along the gutters at the side of the road. Alaric paused in the doorway, chided himself for not having brought an umbrella, and pointed Lise towards the alley at the side of the inn, where the overhanging eaves of the buildings provided some degree of shelter.

"Down here," he called over the drumming rain, turning up the collar of his coat and courteously placing her on the inside, closer to the wall. It merely earned him another scowl.

"How did I survive without you?" she shouted over the noise.

"Without me paying for all your meals? You almost didn't."

She was preparing a reply when he became aware of figures in the alleyway ahead. Four men, hair plastered down by rain, jackets soaked from the shoulders to the waist, spread across their path, blocking the way. Heavy boots and sturdy clothes—working men toughened by hard labour—workers from the cement plant.

He glanced behind. Two more had entered the alley, faces set and grim. He thought of the Luger at his belt, but the holster was buttoned down—they'd be on him before he could draw. His eyes passed over their weapons; sturdy clubs, a knotted rope, half a broom-handle as a baton. This was to be a message then, not a murder. He'd reply in kind.

One of the men stepped towards him, pointing with his club.

"You need to stop—"

Von Trelow didn't wait to hear what he was supposed to cease doing. Never allow an enemy the first move. He moved fast—too fast for a man of his size—seized the club with one hand and punched the man in the mouth as hard as he could.

The man's grip went slack, and he fell backwards with a grunt.

There was a moment where surprise favoured von Trelow—but only a moment. He drove the length of wood into the belly of the closest of the other men, then swung it into the side of his head with a sharp crack. The man dropped.

Then they were on him.

He met the swing of another club with his own—the sharp smack echoing off the walls. A knotted rope struck his ribs, painful—nothing more. He repaid it—a hard blow across the wielder's arms. The man howled.

The remaining club-bearer swung again. Von Trelow leant back, feeling the wind of its passing spatter his face with rain. He struck at the exposed belly.

His opponent hopped back just in time.

Von Trelow pressed forward. The men behind would be on him at any second.

He dropped his own cudgel and caught the next swing across his forearms, grasping the wood. The attacker tried to wrench it free—exactly as von Trelow had expected. He drove his elbow into the man's face, then a knee into his unprotected groin, folding him and leaving him in the gutter.

Fire blazed across von Trelow's back. The men behind had finally arrived—he saw the scene like a map on a planning table: two men ahead, injured but still mobile, two to the rear, one with a club. He was the threat.

He spun and grasped the startled thug by his lapels, driving him backwards across the rain-slick cobbles and into the wall. The man's eyes rolled up, dazed. Von Trelow slammed him again to be certain, drilled a stiff punch into his midriff, and kicked him hard as he fell.

Two conscious but still down, nursing injuries, one more behind—

No one there.

A glance found him, still half a dozen steps up the alley—Lise struggling to hold him back. On her knees, her long skirts tangled about her feet as she clung to his leg, teeth bared, screaming obscenities not taught in medical school.

Von Trelow saw it all, as the back of a fist cuffed her hard in the face.

Lise Freisinger slid to the ground, blood streaming from her nose, still grimly hanging on.

Something broke free. He bellowed in rage—flew across the cobbles—meticulous, ordered thoughts drowned in a howling maelstrom of wrath.

The thug had time to see him coming. No time to act. The chain in his hand impotent at his side.

The huge Guards officer—face twisted in unleashed anger—bore down on him. With a bestial roar, von Trelow unleashed a deluge of pummelling blows.

Von Trelow had learned to box, years before—this was none of that. Furious, savage, relentless—the man crumpled before the onslaught, curling up against the pounding storm.

Von Trelow dimly registered a dull blow across his shoulders. He barely noticed.

He continued to hit.

Another blow struck his back.

He kept hitting.

Something skated past his skull, sparking stars.

He rose and spun, snarling, and took a hard blow in the face.

It stopped him cold. He tasted blood.

The man with the knotted rope waited wide-eyed for him to fall.

Von Trelow's hand snapped around the worker's throat like a snake's strike. His heavy fist flew back and smashed into the startled face—back and again and again—a brutal piston as he bore the man backwards to the wall—nose crumpling, lips splitting, blood flowing. And the thing inside him roared...

The sharp crack of a gunshot echoed in the alleyway, cutting through his rage like a blade. He froze, fingers tight about the man's throat, breathing hard. He began to make out the shape of the world.

He saw the shiny spiked helmet and dark green raincape of a Prussian Landgendarme, an archaic uniform of a former age. The Vice-Wachtmeister had his Dreyse pistol raised toward the sky. Now he lowered it and levelled it at von Trelow.

"Let him go," he ordered.

For a few defiant seconds von Trelow's rage refused to yield. His fingers tightened their grip. His instincts measured the steps to the man with the gun. Finally, breathlessly, his thoughts began to clear. Discipline returned.

He released the man, to slide insensible into the wet.

"Get out of here, all of you," roared the policeman at the battered and bloodied men.

"What?" yelled von Trelow.

The thugs needed no further urging. Those still able to stand gathered those not and pulled and dragged them, stumbling and slip-sliding from the alleyway.

Lise, one hand to her bloodied nose, shoulder pressed to the wall, stooped to recover her hat from the gutter. As one of them passed, she lashed him with it—viciously—doing him no great harm and it no great good. She gave what remained a sour look, then pulled it down upon her head.

"You're letting them go?" demanded von Trelow, still at pistol's point.

The sergeant stepped forwards, his right leg dragging, and nodded.

"I am," he said simply.

"Do you really need the gun?" asked Lise testily.

The Vice-Wachtmeister's eyes flickered to her for only a split-second, but von Trelow in that moment had already closed the long step between them and torn the gun from his hand.

The startled sergeant stumbled backwards on his bad leg, suddenly staring down the barrel of his own pistol.

"Now," snarled von Trelow, licking blood from his split lip, "you're going to tell me what's going on, and who killed my wife." The safety flicked off with deliberate precision.

The sergeant, his rain-soaked face pale but still, watched the pistol and spoke slowly and clearly, hands motionless and on show.

"You have the gun, so I'll play along, but I have no idea what you're talking about." He barely flinched as Alaric raised his aim to eye level.

"So, it's a coincidence that a man with a limp tried to kill me last night with a pistol, the same calibre as this?" he demanded.

The policeman considered for a moment, then nodded, slowly and apparently calmly.

"I suppose it must be, because it wasn't me. I wouldn't have missed."

Something in the man's voice sparked a moment's doubt in von Trelow's mind.

"You were a sharpshooter… sniper?" he asked.

"Town champion," said the policeman bitterly. "Before the war. The army wouldn't take me—my leg." He shifted his awkward stance.

"What happened?" asked von Trelow.

The policeman scowled, his pride clearly grazed, but he answered anyway.

"It was crushed by a wagon when I was ten. But I assure you, Herr von Trelow und Ehlinger, if I were trying to shoot you, you'd be dead."

Von Trelow lowered the pistol slightly—as far as the man's chest. Years of interrogations had taught him to read men—everything about this one spoke of the truth.

"I took you for a soldier."

"I took you for a bumbling, entitled Junker; it seems we were both wrong."

Von Trelow couldn't help a half-smile. The barrel of the pistol dipped lower until it faced the cobbles.

"Then if you're nothing to do with this, why wouldn't you investigate my wife's death? Were you paid? Did you receive orders?"

The sergeant shook rain from his eyes.

"I'm not investigating your wife's death because there was no murder. The doctor certified the cause of death as influenza—no case to answer. And her father is the most important man in the town; I'm not poking about in his family business without cause or evidence.

I have two shell-shocked men and myself to do the work of a dozen. Thieves, agitators, Bolsheviks, deserters. And the plant workers have just been paid, so tonight they'll get drunk, and blood will flow." He met von Trelow's eyes. "So, tell me, Herr Oberst—just exactly what do you expect me to do?"

"Help," snapped von Trelow.

The sergeant's laugh held no humour. "Help? Your wife ate cake in the coffee house whilst my family lived on k-brot and cabbage soup. She lived like a princess while we all starved." His voice hardened. "Why the hell should I help you?"

"I didn't know," said von Trelow quietly.

"Would it have mattered if you had?"

"I hope so."

They stayed facing each other for some moments before von Trelow asked another question, but when he did all the anger was gone.

"If you're not involved, why did you let those men go?"

The sergeant almost smiled. "Because I have one gun and a single cell fit for two men. If I need them, I know where to find them—union thugs from the cement works. But arresting won't get you answers. They won't turn on their boss."

He left von Trelow to draw the obvious conclusion.

"The union boss at the plant?" he said, and the sergeant nodded. "Who is he?"

“If I tell you that, I’m a target and so is my family, but if you’re forced to ask for yourself, they’ll know that you didn’t get it from me. So, I’m afraid you must do your own leg work, Herr Oberstleutnant.”

Alaric nodded, flicked on the safety catch and handed back the pistol.

The sergeant took it, regarded it for a moment and replaced it in the holster beneath his rain cape. When he looked up von Trelow already had his hands out before him, palms upwards.

“What are you doing?” asked the policeman.

“Surrendering to your custody.”

The Vice-Wachtmeister looked at him like he was mad, then laughed.

“You really are an idiot, aren’t you? You’re a bereaved war hero with the Blue Max, whose father-in-law owns most of the town. You’d be out before I finished the paperwork. You couldn’t get arrested here if you shot someone on the Hochstraße.” He turned and began to walk away.

“I might yet test that theory,” said von Trelow to his back.

“Please don’t,” said the police sergeant meaningfully. “You should probably both see a doctor, you know,” he added as an afterthought.

“Thank you,” Lise called after him. “We will.”

Chapter 15

The owlish old lady was visibly shocked to find a battered and bloodied officer and lady standing on the doorstep. She showed them quickly into the cluttered parlour before going to fetch the doctor. It struck von Trelow that if they'd contrived a ruse to get the doctor to see them, they really couldn't have come up with a better one. His lip was split, and the side of his face was swelling nicely. Beneath his coat, tunic, and shirt he could feel the breadth of his shoulders and back beginning to bruise and stiffen. His ribs ached horribly, and his knuckles looked like they'd been worked on with a steel rasp.

Lise looked little better. Her nose was bloody, although probably not broken by her own estimation, however she would undoubtedly have a stunning black eye by the morning. It was her clothes that had borne the brunt of the attack. Her hat looked like it had been sat on, then thrashed, before being drowned, her coat was mud-streaked, soaking wet, and marked with patches of black soot or oil, and the hem of her dress was savagely torn. She picked at it in irritation.

"It's the only one I have with me. And it's my best," she complained bitterly.

"I'll buy you a new one," said von Trelow.

"I don't have the ration."

"Then I'll get you something from the house," he promised. "You're taller than Johanna, but..."

Her bloodied face darkened, and she began to tell him what he could do with the ill-fitting clothes of his dead wife. She was saved from further indelicacy by the opening of the parlour door.

They both stood, von Trelow wincing rather more at the movement than he'd hoped to.

"Oh, it's you," said Dr Meissner coldly, although it was unclear whether it was directed at one of them or both.

"We've had an accident," said von Trelow. "The lady is hurt."

"The lady is a doctor herself," Meissner pointed out tersely. "I don't see why you need me."

"I don't have my medical bag, and... and I think I may be a little concussed," said Lise, capping her performance by swaying terrifyingly close to a glass-fronted cabinet of delicate objets d'art, before slumping to the sofa with a somewhat theatrical groan. If Dr Meissner was suspicious, he didn't show it. He only hesitated a moment, before the demands of professional duty took command.

"Bring her into the consulting room," he snapped at von Trelow, before turning and walking out without a backward look. Von Trelow moved stiffly to where Lise was sprawled on the couch, bent, with considerable discomfort, and went to scoop her up.

"Don't you dare," she hissed, snapping her eyes open. She stood with far more ease than he could manage and grabbed onto his arm. "This is fine," she insisted, and nodded toward the door.

He didn't argue and led her to the next room.

Meissner was gathering iodine, cotton swabs and gauze from a cabinet into an enamelled kidney dish when they came in.

"Help her to the couch," he instructed. "Then sit down yourself, before you fall."

Von Trelow did as he was bid, leaving her perched as he walked stiffly to the patient's chair and awkwardly lowered himself into it.

"What happened?" asked the doctor with professional detachment. He pulled a lighter from his inside pocket, sparked it and slowly waved it back and forth before Lise's eyes, instructing her to follow the flame.

"We were attacked," admitted von Trelow. "Men from the works." He watched the doctor's face for some reaction, but there was nothing.

"These protests are getting out of hand," Meissner opined. "They're getting bolder and more dangerous. It starts with broken windows and ends in broken bones."

"They're starving," snapped Lise. "Ouch!" she flinched as he pressed at her nose to assess the damage.

"Hardly," replied Meissner. "The plant workers' ration is almost three times the standard."

"If there's anything to buy," she retorted.

"Which there is, it may be plain and repetitive, but it's filling and nutritious. I've made sure. There are people in need here, but it's not the plant workers."

She regarded him with vicious contempt, and von Trelow enjoyed for once not being the immediate subject of her disdain.

The argument died into uncomfortable silence and Meissner finished his examination.

"No concussion, no break, maybe a little shock. You'll heal perfectly well, Dr Freisinger. Rest and an aspirin for the pain." He turned toward the desk and found himself staring down the gaping barrel of the Colt.

The doctor froze, the kidney dish falling to the floor with a metallic crash.

“Come and sit down please, Doctor,” said von Trelow, waving him towards the other chair.

Meissner did as he was told—pale as a ghost and visibly shaking, eyes frozen on the big American pistol.

“Now, Doctor, you’re going to answer my questions immediately and honestly, or I will shoot you, and my friend here will swear that it was a terrible accident whilst I was removing the gun from my pocket with my poor injured hand.”

Meissner glanced disbelievingly at Lise, who shrugged her complicity.

“But you’re a doctor!” he stuttered.

“I won’t be doing harm,” she said with chilling calm. “He will.”

Meissner looked between them, apparently unsure as to who to be more scared off. He settled on the man with the gun.

“You won’t get away with it.” There was still the thinnest shred of the defiance he’d shown the day before.

Von Trelow sighed complacently. “My dear Doctor Meissner, as the local Vice-Wachtmeister has only just pointed out to me, I’m a war hero who’s recently lost his wife and whose father-in-law effectively owns the town. I couldn’t get arrested here if I tried.” He paused long enough for the reality to sink in. It was obvious when it did, Meissner slumped in the chair as if he’d been deflated.

“What is it you want?” he asked dully.

Asking the question was hard, like climbing the parapet. At least his gun hand remained steady.

“Were you having an affair with my wife?”

The doctor’s head jerked up—eyes wide.

“With Johanna? No!” His indignant answer was like a splash of cold water in von Trelow’s face.

"Think carefully, Doctor, I'm not bluffing." He jerked the pistol to make his point.

Meissner looked suitably scared but didn't change his story.

"I swear, it's not true. Anyone's who's said so is lying."

"But you were in love with her?"

"What? Well... once maybe, when we were much younger. But she met you." There was only the trace of resentment in his voice—a tale from long ago.

The weight on von Trelow's heart could hardly be said to have lifted, with his wife still lying dead, but it now at least seemed something he could bear.

"But you were at the Buhler's house on Tuesday night?" persisted Alaric.

"Yes, I've already told you that I was."

"So, who were you with on the terrace?"

The doctor looked at him in total bewilderment.

"No one!"

Lise raised her hand like a child in class and waved it at them.

"Wait. You said you weren't having an affair with Johanna." Meissner looked sick, his paleness almost grey. "So, who are you having an affair with?"

The trapped doctor looked at the unyielding door, at her, and finally at the floor.

"Doctor?" pressed von Trelow, reminding him persuasively of the gun still pointed squarely at him.

"Marla Buhler," the doctor murmured.

It took a few seconds for von Trelow's mind to encompass this new information.

"Frau Buhler?" Meissner merely nodded, eyes remaining firmly downcast. "For how long?"

The other man shrugged vaguely. "Almost three years."

Neither von Trelow nor Lise said anything, and after almost a minute Meissner surrendered to the need to fill the silence.

"I went to see her, after you'd swooped in and dazzled Johanna. I don't know why, I just wanted to talk to someone... It just happened."

"And kept happening," sniped Lise as she hopped down from the examination couch and went to peruse the contents of his cabinets.

He didn't bother to reply.

"So, was it her you were with on the terrace last Tuesday?" persisted von Trelow.

"What? No, I told you, I was never on the terrace." He paused for a moment, breathing heavily. "When was this?"

"A little after dusk, as Herr Braun left for the train station," said Alaric.

Meissner nodded, a frown creasing his brow.

"What is it?" von Trelow pressed him.

"I did arrive at the house as the car was leaving, I'd walked across the fields. I didn't know it was this Braun person in the car, I don't think we've met, but while I was in the hall taking off my hat and coat, Frau Gephart came in from the library. She was practically running, and she looked rather shocked. I asked her if she were all right and she said she was, but she didn't look it. I believe the library has a door that opens onto the terrace. Perhaps it was her. Anyway, that's the truth."

Von Trelow considered this piece of information carefully and began to make connections. Behind him Lise was removing bottles from the shelves, peering at the labels with professional interest and returning them again.

"And Johanna. You didn't see her at all until the maid called for help?" he finally asked.

Meissner shook his head firmly.

"No, I told you before, I wish I had, but even if I'd seen her straight away it wouldn't have helped."

"Why is that?" asked von Trelow.

"Because she was already dead long before I arrived," replied the doctor.

Alaric nodded, having expected as much.

"How long before?" he asked.

The doctor shrugged. "It's impossible to say for sure, it's not an exact science."

Von Trelow looked to Lise for confirmation.

She glanced over from the cabinets and nodded. "He's right."

Von Trelow sighed in frustration. "But if you had to guess?"

The doctor looked for a moment as if he were going to refuse, then his eyes fell again upon the Colt, and he sensibly changed his mind.

"At least four hours before," he said.

"How can you be sure?" asked Alaric, but Lise answered for him,

"Because rigor mortis takes at least four hours to set in. She was in a state of rigor?"

Meissner nodded. "Yes."

"What time were you called to see her?" asked Lise over her shoulder as she fished in the back of an interesting shelf.

"About seven o'clock. Frau Buhler sent the maid to see if Johanna was joining us for dinner. Two minutes later we heard her scream."

"And you noticed nothing out of the ordinary, no strange smells? No glass or cup or signs of food?"

Meissner sighed. "You mean like the smell of cut grass?"

Von Trelow almost leaped up. His bruised ribs prevented him.

"Exactly!" He stifled a groan.

Despite the levelled pistol, Doctor Meissner still looked at him with tired pity in his eyes.

"No, nothing. I'm certain. I do read the medical journals, Herr von Trelow, I know what phosgene smells like. I did not smell anything like it, nor see anything unusual that she may have consumed. The only crockery there was a teacup, which the maid said she'd brought to her in the morning, long before a poison like phosgene would need to have been administered. I tell you; this was nothing but a tragic case of severe influenza." He swallowed hard, realising that this was not what the armed man wanted to hear, but there was no sign of von Trelow's anger.

"Damn," Alaric exclaimed softly.

"So, do you believe me?" asked the doctor nervously.

Von Trelow looked at him as though he'd forgotten that he was there for a moment.

"Hmmm? Oh, yes. I believe what you say about your relations with Johanna and her mother, and what you saw."

"And the cause of death?" asked Meissner curiously.

"I believe that you believe it, Herr Doctor. But you've never seen someone who died from phosgene poisoning. Someone wants you, and everyone else, to think it was influenza, but I don't believe it for a moment."

A further thought occurred to him.

“By the way, Doctor, how have you avoided military service? You obviously don’t have bronchial lungs, not if you can walk across the fields to the Buhler house on a damp autumn evening.”

The doctor’s cheeks flushed. He paused before answering, as if considering a lie. He thought better of it.

“Marla... Frau Buhler, paid for a medical exemption,” he muttered.

Lise turned from the cabinets to scowl her continuing contempt, von Trelow simply nodded.

“I thought it would be something of the sort.” His bland acceptance seemed to sting more than Lise’s disdain.

Meissner seemed for a moment to recover a modicum of his old defiance, stiffening in his chair.

“Is that all? I’ve told you everything I know.”

Von Trelow raised a calming hand.

“One last question, Doctor. Did Frau Buhler, or anyone else, suggest you should rule the death as caused by influenza?”

The doctor bristled.

“You may consider me a coward, Herr von Trelow, even immoral, but I am a professional. I did not and would never allow anyone to colour my medical judgement. I did my job that night to the best of my ability, as I do every day.” It was a little of the old confidence and pride, and to von Trelow’s ears it rang frustratingly true.

Chapter 16

Von Trelow returned to the house via the gun shop, arriving a little before dusk. Lise he'd left at the inn with instructions to wait there until he collected her at eleven. From the hallway of the house, he could see Frau Gephart reading alone in the parlour. He entered and closed the door behind him.

"Good afternoon, Frau Gephart." She looked up with a welcoming smile, her elegant, aristocratic features beautiful in the soft yellow light.

"Good afternoon, Herr von Trelow." She noticed the bruises as he approached. "Good heavens, are you hurt?"

He waved her concern away, although his ribs protested with every move.

"It's not as bad as it looks," he lied. "I slipped on some wet cobbles and fell rather hard."

She seemed genuinely sympathetic. He regretted what he had to ask her. "Do you mind?" he asked, indicating a nearby chair.

She shook her head obligingly and he sat down as naturally as he could manage.

"I think your fall was rather worse than you're admitting," she said kindly.

He nodded. "Perhaps a little. You're very observant."

She smiled at the small compliment.

"I am too, it's part of my job—my training," he explained. "Unfortunately, it means I notice things I'm not supposed to notice."

The slightest furrow appeared between her elegant brows.

"Like your being on the terrace with a certain someone on Wednesday night. Like your sleeping late each morning."

She was quite pale now and her red lips were a perfect O. He said nothing more, leaving her to fill the silence when she worked up the courage.

"What? What do you know?" she asked quietly, flicking a fearful glance to the closed door.

"It's all right, we're alone," he assured her, "and I have no intention of revealing your secret to anyone or embarrassing you in any way."

She didn't relax, she either didn't believe him or was expecting some other price to be demanded for his silence.

"What do you want?" she asked, her voice betraying a quaver of fear.

"Only the truth. I promise, on my honour as an officer, that whatever you tell me shall go no further, but I need to know what is going on and who you were with."

She looked at him closely, measuring her trust. This close he could see that her eyes were hazel more than green, her hair had streaks of auburn amongst the strawberry blonde and her features bore the faintest lines, betraying that age was beginning to catch up with her beauty. She made her decision.

"I'm not what I seem, Herr von Trelow," she began cautiously. "I come from a small town near Breslau. My father was the postmaster."

Von Trelow let his surprise show. Her looks and her manners had suggested origins in an impoverished Junker house, much like his own.

"I met Udo in Berlin before the war and pretended to be more than I was. By the time he discovered the truth…" she shrugged. "He didn't mind so much."

"I understand."

"We were married nine years ago." She left the statement hanging.

"He wants a son; an heir," he surmised.

She nodded with a sheen of tears sparkling in her eyes.

"I was pregnant twice…" Her words carried defiance.

"I understand." Two miscarriages must have crushed them both. And her husband increasingly old, fat, and impatient, and she wholly dependent upon him for everything she now had.

"He's tried all sorts of things; herbs, potions, cold baths…" Her words dried on her lips, but von Trelow understood. Nothing had worked—she'd become desperate.

She'd fallen silent, unwilling to cross the line. Von Trelow did it for her.

"Then you met someone? Friedrich?" he surmised.

She flashed a look of wide-eyed panic. It slowly subsided. She nodded.

"He was young and handsome, and he flirted with me very prettily, but that wasn't why I did it." She was pleading, needing him to believe her; actually, he did.

"Of course. You needed to give your husband an heir."

"I didn't have a choice." She was crying now and from inside his tunic he presented her with a neatly folded handkerchief. "Thank you." She dabbed at her eyes. "I overheard Udo with friends after dinner—they were drunk. He said that if I couldn't provide him an heir, he'd have to find himself a wife who could… And they laughed!" She shuddered, tears flowing freely.

She took a little while to recover. Hiccoughing softly as she steadied her breaths.

"And when did it happen?" asked von Trelow finally.

"When we came here last month."

He'd guessed as much. "And does your husband know?"

She looked at him in panic and he tried to reassure her.

"That you're pregnant, not that he's not the father."

She sighed heavily and relaxed a little.

"No, I haven't told him yet. Not until he and I… If he even suspected the truth… he'd throw me out. He can be ruthless, truly." There was a catch of fear in her voice. Was it fear of disgrace and destitution as an aging beauty, or something more?

"He'd divorce you?" he asked.

She nodded firmly.

"At the very least." She seemed to have regained her composure and held out the handkerchief to return it to him. "Thank you."

He returned it to his pocket.

"Does Friedrich know?" he asked.

She shook her head.

"No, he's a sweet boy but naïve in so many ways. I think he's in love with me and… I think he might do something foolish."

That sounded right to von Trelow's judgement.

"Like demand that you leave your husband and marry him?" he suggested. He could easily imagine it.

"Yes."

"Except the Buhlers would never allow it, and when it came right down to it, Friedrich would never go against them."

She shook her head, just a little sadly.

"He could never survive without money, and I don't want to." She was right again, and von Trelow found himself coming to rather admire her.

"You must end it with him, you do know that? I assume that you haven't." There had been enough small signs looking at it in retrospect, midday yawns from Friedrich, fleeting moments, and glances between them.

"No, and I know, you're right."

"Even Friedrich can count to nine. This is your last chance to be able to convince him that it's not his."

She nodded; her sad smile now set in resolve.

"I will, tonight. We leave tomorrow anyway. I'll tell him that it was all a mistake. I'll be a little cruel so that he hates me just a little, then perhaps when he hears he won't want to think about it too hard."

Yes, he was beginning to admire her a great deal.

"That's good," he agreed. "Are you sure your husband will believe it's his?" he asked.

She smiled with quiet confidence.

"Yes, he's already eager to try out his newest concoction. I'll pay the midwife well to say the baby came early."

Von Trelow stood stiffly and bowed, taking her hand and kissing it lightly.

"Good luck to you, Frau Gephart. Please consider me a friend, if you should need one."

She blushed as she took back her hand and held it in her other palm.

"Thank you, Herr von Trelow, I would consider that a great honour."

"Before I go, may I ask one more thing?"

She nodded agreeably. "Of course, anything."

"In your time here, did you see anything that might explain what happened to my wife? Any reason anyone might have had for wanting her silenced?"

She couldn't hide her shock.

"I know," he said, "but I remain convinced that there is more to this that simply sickness. Please."

She sat still for some moments, her brow once again creased, this time in thought. Finally, she looked up.

"Perhaps. She seemed worried. She and I had been quite friendly on our previous visits, but this time she almost seemed to be avoiding me. Then on the day she died, I passed her as she was coming in from the garden. She was upset, in a hurry, she nearly knocked me down. When I asked her if she was all right, she just said she had to write her journal. I didn't even know she kept a journal."

"What time was this?" asked Alaric thoughtfully.

"Just about eleven o'clock, Frau Buhler and I had come back from our walk a short while before."

Slowly in his mind cogs were clicking into place. "If I might, did you notice what was she wearing on her feet?" he asked.

"Her feet? House shoes."

“You’re certain? Can you be sure with her skirts covering them?”

But Frau Gephart was adamant. “Oh yes, because she hiked up her skirts as she ran up the stairs.”

A piece of the mechanism clicked home. “Thank you, Frau Gephart, you have been most helpful and enlightening.”

She smiled. She was really very beautiful when she smiled. “Please, call me Louisa.”

He nodded, “Then I am Alaric. Good day, Louisa.”

“Good day, Alaric.”

He walked to the door, but before he opened it, one more question came into his mind.

“What is it that your husband’s company does?”

She looked up from where she’d returned to her book, a little surprised. “His family owns the Baden Chemical and Gas Company, they make dyes, inks, and other chemicals. Why?”

He smiled and waved it away. “I realised I didn’t know.”

Alaric wasn’t looking for Friedrich, in fact, he would rather have avoided him at that moment, but Friedrich found him and seemed to want to talk. He’d been drinking, brandy by the smell of it, and it had made him cheerfully gregarious.

Seeing that he wasn’t about to lose him, and given that the rain had for now stopped, von Trelow took him out through the front door onto the front terrace in the twilight.

“What happened to you?” Friedrich asked upon seeing his bruises.

“Someone tried to hit me, but fortunately I blocked it with my face,” said von Trelow dryly.

“My God, who?”

Alaric shrugged. “Oh, some union types, I think. I expect they have something against the army.”

Friedrich scowled. “That sort have something against order and decency altogether. They should be shot like rats.”

The comparison amused von Trelow. “Shooting rats is harder than it looks—they’re fast and very unpredictable. Trust me, I’ve tried.”

Friedrich wrinkled his nose in distaste but didn’t comment.

“Has there been a lot of trouble with the unions?” asked von Trelow.

“Some... yes. Quite a lot actually: Strikes, pickets, machines damaged.”

“Sabotage?”

Friedrich shrugged. They’d walked the length of the terrace and turned to walk back.

“They don’t smash anything beyond repair, that would be risking their necks in wartime, but they remove parts or loosen bolts so that they shake apart and the line has to be shut down until it’s fixed. There have been bricks thrown at windows, foremen beaten up, and someone left nails out in the yard when father drove down in the car.”

Von Trelow could imagine Herr Buhler’s reaction to a set of burst tyres on his precious Mercedes.

“I don’t suppose that your father was very amused.”

“Not at all, from what I hear,” agreed Friedrich.

“So, what is it they want? I heard that they get a decent ration here.”

Friedrich nodded, warming to his subject.

"They do; that's the damnable thing of it. There are some who still yell about bread and hunger, but it's just slogans. There may not be a lot, but they get their share."

Perhaps not as much as Herr Buhler though, thought Alaric, detecting the smell of something meaty and delicious rising from the grates over the sunken kitchen windows.

"Mostly they talk about workers' rights, increased pay, works councils and representation—Marxist stuff," spat Friedrich, leaving no doubt as to his feelings.

They reached the other end of the terrace, where it turned about the end of the house, Alaric led them round it to where someone had taken a shot at him just the night before.

"There must be some kind of ringleader though, some boss?" he asked with studied disinterest.

"Oh, I don't think so," replied Friedrich vaguely. "You don't get a leader with... germs and so forth." He looked at Alaric as if expecting him to grasp his meaning. "Bacterium!" he said triumphantly. "That's what they are you know, bacterium multiplying and infecting the body of the State."

The voice was Friedrich's, but the words were someone else's. He wondered whose.

"I see. That must be difficult," von Trelow commented without commitment. He had reached the door into the library, and it now occupied his interest. The white chip in the concrete where the bullet had struck was a hand span away from the doorframe. More cogs, more ticking.

"Oh, it is difficult," pronounced Friedrich warmly, "but there will have to be a reckoning. I tell you, Alaric, when the war is over, we'll have to deal with their type, and when the army is back, we will."

Something in his tone, the utter certainty of it, made von Trelow turn, his ribs and back still a mass of painful flesh.

"What do you mean?" he asked.

Friedrich smiled broadly, a boy who had a secret and wanted it known that he had it but wouldn't tell.

"Nothing, it's nothing," he said, his smile becoming a grin. "Just talking, hypotheticals and all." Friedrich was a bad liar; he always had been. He was lucky Herr Gephart seemed to be even less perceptive.

Von Trelow nodded and started back towards the front of the house.

"So, did you want me for anything?" he asked. Friedrich shook his head casually,

"No, I just wanted to see how you are." And to crow about having a secret. There had always been something a little insecure about Friedrich, a little spoiled, and having a secret that the family war hero didn't know about seemed to be enthralling him.

"Oh, I'm fine... as fine as I'm likely to be for now," said von Trelow rather dourly. "I think I'll go and take a bath, soak these bruises. I'll see you at dinner." With that he left Friedrich at the door.

Chapter 17

Hot water and bath salts had eased von Trelow's aches enough that he moved almost normally as he walked back towards the town in the cool October darkness.

He'd spent the evening at dinner and at cards, playing *Doppelkopf* with Herr and Frau Buhler and Herr Gephart, whilst Friedrich and Louisa played *Quartett* at another table. He'd played solidly, and occasionally well, although not well enough to compete with Herr Gephart. The corpulent businessman had played with ruthless focus, consistently taking reservations, and playing solo hands as many times as the rest of the table combined. By the time von Trelow made his excuses to retire he had been very glad that they'd been playing for points and not money—if Gephart's business ever failed, he clearly had an alternative career as a card sharp already prepared.

No one had seen von Trelow leave the house, and he'd seen no one upon his way. With the arrival of night, the rain had come again, leaving the streets deserted, but it was a light persistent drizzle now, not the driving sheets of earlier in the day. In any case he'd taken precautions, a waxed, hooded rain cape both kept him dry and hid the instantly recognisable uniform beneath. He reached the inn whilst the church clock was still chiming the hour to find Lise waiting outside, clutching her doctor's bag, and having done what she could to restore the sartorial acceptability of her clothes. She was sheltering beneath the eaves, and he scowled irritably to see her there.

“I told you to stay inside,” he chided her.

“And since you’re neither my father nor the Kaiser, I ignored you,” she replied.

He bit his tongue and tried a measured argument.

“I was simply concerned for your safety, that you might be attacked again.”

Now she laughed, but it didn’t seem to be at him for a change.

“I think they were attacking you. In any case, take a look for yourself.” She nodded towards the inn. There was certainly a lot of noise coming from beyond the heavy wooden door.

He stepped up and did as he she suggested.

It wasn’t a free for all brawl, not yet, but it might well end up there by the end of the night. The bar was full of drunken, rowdy, arguing workers, shouting and shoving at each other with more than a few Bolshevik slogans adding to the potent mix. He let the door close.

“I see what you mean,” he admitted.

She flashed him a self-satisfied smile.

“I have something for you,” he said somewhat grudgingly, he wasn’t sure he wanted to give it to her, now that it came to it.

“Not one of your wife’s dresses?” She wrinkled her nose in distaste.

“No,” he retorted, “you made your feelings on that subject quite clear.” He revealed his hand from beneath the rain cape and showed her a compact little pistol with shiny wooden grips.

“It’s a gun,” she said unnecessarily.

"It's a Mauser 1914 pistol—7.65mm," he corrected her. "Small enough to carry in a pocket or a purse, but it will stop a man; kill him if you shoot him in the right place."

She left it there on his hand, gleaming dully in the light from the frosted windows of the inn, and looked him in the eye.

"How do you know I won't use it on you?" she asked seriously.

He shrugged. "You said you preferred me alive and suffering, perhaps I take you at your word."

"I also said, that was unless I was the one to kill you."

"Then perhaps, I don't believe you." He saw her eyes flare defiantly. "Or maybe I just don't care that much if you do."

She stared at him until the fire in her eyes gradually dimmed and she crossly looked away, reached out and took the pistol.

"It's heavier than it looks."

"As I said, compact." He offered her the remainder of a box of cartridges which she placed in the doctor's bag, the pistol she slipped into the pocket of her coat.

"Why?" she asked him.

He shrugged, not entirely sure himself.

"Because you almost got hurt earlier, because you said Berlin was getting more and more dangerous, and because you're Erich's sister..."

She dropped her eyes and stared at the wet cobbles.

"Thank you, I suppose."

"You're welcome. Do you know how to shoot?" he asked.

"Point the end that goes bang at the bad man and pull the trigger?"

He sighed, the affront of an expert before a complete novice.

"Squeeze, don't pull; like you're milking a cow or a goat."

"And for those of us who didn't grow up on a farm estate?"

He just glared at her.

"All right, I get the idea."

"Good. And don't raise your arm to aim, not unless you're taught. Just keep it tight to your side and turn your whole body to face them." He showed her how, pointing his finger like a child playing at cowboys.

She rolled her eyes, as if it were all too foolish for words, but she did it anyway.

"Like this?"

"Like that," he said with a firm nod. From beneath his cape, he brought out an umbrella which he presented to her with a casually decorous bow, then he walked out into the rain.

She glowered at his back, but opened it anyway, then scampered to catch up with his long strides.

"I still hate you."

"I know."

The house on Havel Weg sat back across a courtyard, whilst the mortuary fronted the street. It had once been the stables, converted when the undertaker had bought the property. Suitably sombre black doors were set in spotless white walls and gave an appropriate impression of severity and weight.

No lights were showing in either the mortuary or the house and the soft drumming of the rain promised to muffle any but the most indiscreet sounds. There were two doors onto the road that ran down to the river, the smaller public door was built of thick hardwood set with polished brass fittings and would have taken a battering ram to force. Von Trelow had brought a small crowbar, borrowed from Klosel, but had no confidence in its faculty here. The second door, or rather doors, had been for the horses and now allowed access for the hearse.

Von Trelow moved along the wall, Lise close behind, until he reached the double doors used by the hearse. They bore the same glossy paint as the other door, but there the similarity ended. He tested them, finding them far lighter and with plenty of slack movement at their centre where they met. He peered down the crack with the aid of his flashlight and then examined the hinges to either side.

Lise watched, bored. “Are you actually going to do anything or are you just waiting until they rot?” she whispered irritably.

He offered her a withering glance, then pulled out his trench knife and worked at the hinges of the leftmost door. A minute or so later, with the hinges scraped clean of the worst of their rust, he flexed his aching shoulders, firmly grasped the cross brace and lifted. He heard pops and creaks of protesting muscle, then an answering groan above the patter of the rain, and a metallic snap.

The door lifted off its hinges.

Von Trelow, grunting under the weight, lowered it quickly but quietly to the cobbles. It was still linked to its fellow by the locks, but now the joined combination could be moved and opened as one. He took a breath, grasped hold once more and lifted it back a pace to leave a gap, then waved Lise inside.

“You’re just a shaved bear, aren’t you?” she hissed as she folded the umbrella and slipped into the building.

He didn’t bother to reply, he simply followed, then quietly hauled the door back into place, flush with the wall. He turned and in the utter blackness bumped into her.

“Be careful,” she whispered, her voice catching with nerves.

He ignored the urge to taunt her for her fear and pulled the flashlight from his pocket.

The torchlight flared off a great black shape that loomed from the darkness. He heard Lise gasp a stifled cry and dipped the light to stop its harsh reflection. It was only the hearse, polished and ready, it's glass and brass gleaming, lacking only a horse to pull it.

"Come on," he said quietly and moved cautiously past the great spoked wheels in search of a door. He found three, one that clearly led out into the courtyard at the rear of the building, the others internal, one to each side. A quick glance confirmed that the rooms to the right were meant for the grieving public, sombrely decorated and with suitable biblical prints upon the walls. Through the left door though, all was austere. Clean paint and tiled floors spoke of a workspace, and he followed the chill corridor past a door marked '*Office*' to a pair of double doors signed '*Mortuary*'. He had already grasped the door handle when Lise stopped him, laying a steady hand on his wrist.

"Don't," she said firmly.

He paused, glancing at her in the patchy glare of the flashlight.

"What is it?"

She sighed, apparently reluctant to say whatever she had to say.

"What?" he persisted.

"You shouldn't go in there." Her tone was determined, even when whispered. "That's your wife in there. No one who loved someone should have to see that."

"But you…" he began, but she spoke over him.

"I will not argue this. Go and keep watch, this is going to take some time."

There were several seconds of indecision whilst von Trelow wrestled with his conscience and his dread, then he succumbed.

"Very well."

She relaxed, clearly relieved.

"But there's one thing I have to ask you to do."

"What?" she asked suspiciously.

"Will you cut me a lock of her hair? I never had one, she thought it was bad luck, but that doesn't matter now…" His voice cracked, petering out to nothing.

She nodded, making no comment, then disappeared through the foreboding doors.

To sleep—on patrol or on watch—would get you killed. It was a lesson learned early. Alaric had learned it well. He kept his mind sharp as he waited, listening to the tiny insignificant sounds of the building and making sense of them: the rain on the windows, the wind across the rooftiles, the creaking of the building, the scrabbling of rats. He recalled the faces of brother officers, their fates, their families. When he'd honoured the dead, he allowed himself to think of Jana—not as she was now, beyond those cold stone walls, but how she had been.

Nine days before marriage, twenty since—not quite a month together all told. He recalled each day, as he had so many times on so many nights, each look, laugh, touch and kiss. He remembered all the things that they had done together, and how much they'd never done: never ridden together, never walked in the woods on his father's estate with the bluebells were thick upon the ground, they'd never skated, never danced at a ball, not a real ball like they'd had before the war. There was so much they'd lost.

He tried to hold on to what they'd had. He remembered a year previously, his fifth leave since they'd married almost two years before. He'd arrived at the house whilst Paul was asleep, and they'd excused themselves from dinner and from her parents, with unseemly haste. That had earned disapproving looks from her mother, not that Jana had cared. She'd run up the stairs trailing the scent of rose otto and was pulling off her dress before he'd made it through the bedroom door. The corsetry had slowed her down, particularly since they'd tried to remove it while wrapped in each other's arms, kissing ardently.

"Be careful!" she'd chided him as he tugged at her underclothes. They were her best, bought for her wedding and worn only when he was home. He'd managed to tear them the last time he'd seen her, and she still hadn't forgiven him. He'd kissed her hard and left her to manage them herself as he removed his own clothing. She'd been undressed faster than he'd ever witnessed, before sliding into bed, blushing that he'd seen her, despite her own enthusiasm. As for him, even a brief glimpse of her pale, smooth flesh had been enough to stun him. He'd stood in his underwear, staring, struck dumb. Jana had peered at him over the edge of the covers as she plucked out hairpins and tossed them towards the dressing table, then grinned coyly as she shook her hair loose.

"Are you going to just stand there all night?" she'd challenged him and wriggled down into the bed enticingly. He hadn't needed to be asked twice. He was naked, in her bed, and in her arms in moments.

They hadn't got up until lunchtime the next day.

When they were apart, her mind, through her letters, captivated him, but when they were together her body held him in thrall. He had loved her so very much, her smile, her laughter, her cleverness, and her eager desire. He had planned everything around her, a future, a life, now spent and gone.

His mind was still filled with her when, with a start, he heard the dog. The rain had stopped, drifting away to nothing in the morning cold. There was barking, deep and insistent, and not far off. It continued for several minutes, steady and persistent like the animal was prepared to put in time as well as effort. Then he heard the creak of a distant door and a muffled curse. The dog, excited and purposeful, ran across the courtyard on skittering paws, and up to the mortuary back door. Von Trelow heard the insistent snuffling, the scrabbling with its claws, and then the barking recommenced.

He'd grown up with dogs, he knew the signs, this one had smelt something wrong and was not to be put off. He climbed quietly to his feet and was about to go to warn Lise, although she must have heard it for herself, when the distant door of the house creaked again. An angry voice was drowned out by the dog's persistent barking, but it was drawing closer, clearer.

"You stupid dog, what is the matter with you? There's nothing there. Come away." The undertaker, irritable at being roused in the early hours, more so to be dragged out of his house by an agitated animal, tried to pull the dog away. There was a growl, deep and uncompromising, and then a snap. The man yelped, but not too hard. "Bruno, you're being a fool!" he insisted, but the dog kept scrabbling and barking with persistent confidence.

"God in heaven, very well!" the undertaker snapped finally. There was the jangling of keys, the click of a catch and then the door opened a crack. It was thrust wide by the impatient canine. It burst in, rapidly quartering the floor, nose to the ground. It circled the hearse, wove betwixt its wheels, snuffled at the doors, front, back and both sides. It ignored the door to the mourning rooms and instead paced the ground between the front door and the mortuary corridor. It settled upon the latter.

By now the undertaker had followed the dog inside, unhappy to be left alone in the cold and dark. He switched on the reassurance of the light. The dull orange electric bulb flickered into life setting strange shadows dancing, making the man's nervous breaths come short and shallow. He peered into the corners but evidently saw nothing unexpected. His stubborn shepherd dog was by now pawing at the door to the workrooms. The undertaker went to it, breathlessly laid a hand upon the handle, and threw it wide. The dog leapt through, past him, into the tiled corridor and ran its length, passing the office where a burglar might reasonably have been expected to have headed, instead skidding upon the slick floor and immediately recommencing his scrabbling at the doors to the morgue. His master followed, swift and irritable, although seemingly a little relieved now that the cause seemed evident.

"Stupid dog, you know you're not allowed the bother the clients. Your greedy nose is going to get you into serious trouble one of these days. That's not food, Bruno. No, Bruno, no!"

The dog yelped and whined as he was taken by the collar and dragged forcibly away, back down the corridor and out into the coach-house, where the door to the corridor was firmly closed.

"Go on," snapped the undertaker at the reluctant creature. "Go!"

Whining and yapping in pitiful pleading, the dog was hauled out of the building, held whilst the outer door was secured, and thence led back to the house.

Von Trelow waited several minutes as the barking and cursing receded and the door to the house creaked and closed. Then he waited a while more, before he cautiously raised the hinged hearse floor, rising from the hidden compartment for the newly dead. He unhitched the rear door and slid out of the glass-sided coach then replaced everything as he'd found it, before going to the mortuary. He tapped lightly on the doors.

"Lise," he hissed into the gap.

There was a light tread, and the door was softly pulled a sliver ajar.

"What?" asked Lise without any sign of concern.

"Are you all right?" he asked, suddenly feeling rather ridiculous.

She gave him a look that made him feel doubly so.

"Of course I am, why wouldn't I be?"

"The undertaker... his dog..." He was feeling more and more foolish by the second. "Where did you hide?"

Her look was once again irritable disdain.

"I didn't, I have work to do, keeping watch is your job." With that she closed the door.

She finally emerged, sombre and silent, quietly closing the door to the corridor and crossing to where he sat hunched, huddled beneath his cloak. He didn't bother to speak, he simply climbed to his feet, flexed his fingers, then set his hands upon the coach-house door and lifted it clear of the frame. She slipped out past him. He followed, then heaved the heavy door back onto its hinges and them into place. It was hardly easy, even his powerful muscles complained under the strain, but it was not complicated, and within moments it was done.

It was almost half past two by the glowing orange numbers of his watch, the streets were glistening damp in the light of the gas lamps, but there was no one about and they made their way quietly back to the inn. Neither spoke until they were well away from the mortuary, neither knew why, it simply didn't feel right.

"Here." Lise finally broke the silence as they passed the red-brick church at the head of the Hochstraße, holding out something in her hand.

He took it, a thick golden double loop of a curl tied by a thread. He stopped and stared at it, lying in the palm of his hand, then pulled it back beneath his cape and tucked it safely away.

"Thank you."

She nodded but said no more about it.

"I'll catch the early train back to Berlin."

"What did you find?" he asked keenly.

She glanced at him as he walked at her side.

"Are you sure you want to know? The cause of death isn't clear yet." There was something in her voice, a nervousness he disliked.

"You must have some idea."

“The symptoms were as described,” she admitted, “at least so far as I could tell. Immediate cause of death was asphyxiation due to fluid on the lungs, but what caused it I can’t determine here. I need to perform some tests.”

“What tests?” demanded von Trelow.

She glared at him.

“Tell me.”

"If the cause was phosgene poisoning there should be evidence of burns to the tissues of the nose or throat, but I need a microscope to examine the samples I’ve taken. If it’s influenza there should be evidence of Pfeiffer’s bacillus, for which I need to grow cultures.”

He had no idea what ‘cultures’ were but trusted that she did.

“How long will that take?”

She shrugged vaguely.

“At least three days, perhaps five or six.”

Von Trelow scowled. “The funeral is set for Tuesday afternoon. I leave Tuesday evening to return to the division. I need to know, Lise. I must.”

She simply shook her head.

“I’ll do what I can, von Trelow, but it can’t be rushed. It takes as long as it takes.”

He bit down on his frustration. Nothing he could do would change things. There was no choice but to wait. He nodded his acceptance and caught her furtive eye.

She started to walk away.

“What is it?” he asked, following her.

“Nothing,” she insisted with a shake of her head. It was a poor lie.

“Lise, what is it?” he asked again, grasping her shoulder to stop her flight.

She spun on him.

“You don’t want to know, von Trelow,” she snapped forcefully.

He weighed his answer for several beats.

“Tell me,” he said. “Just tell me.”

Her eyes fell shut, sighing regret. “Von Trelow…”

“Tell me!”

It still took some seconds before she replied.

“She was pregnant, perhaps three months,” she said softly.

He almost forgot to breathe: Berlin, July, the Adlon Hotel, their last night.

“Thank you,” he said dully, as drumbeats pounded in his head. He blinked at the cobbles and then looked up at her, “For everything.” He looked about himself, as if surprised to find where he was. They were only a few dozen metres from the inn. “I’ll leave you here. I look forward to hearing from you once you’ve done your tests.” His voice was wooden, threatening to break.

She nodded, but didn’t reply, she just watched him walk away.

Chapter 18

He lay beneath ridged concrete in the bunker's cool dampness. Strange—there was always someone about, sleepers snoring or shifting on a bed, making the iron frame squeak, or someone simply moving past the door. But there was nothing, not even the pattering of rats. He was entirely alone.

It wasn't quiet though, nor still. The ground, and the bunker within it, shook with the irregular drumbeat of shells: The frantic *allegro* of mortars and the steady, menacing *lento* of the heavy artillery. Yet it wasn't they which kept him awake, the rhythm of the guns had become as familiar as a lullaby. There was a presence, familiar, longed-for, yet entirely out of place.

He looked to his left, on a bunk barely wide enough to contain his frame, yet somehow there was space for her. She was dead, and yet not dead. Her blue eyes pale and glazed, unmoving, unblinking. She simply lay at his side and stared at the ceiling. Her skin no longer pale and rosy, but waxy and blue, and cold. He could feel her alongside him in the bed, her flesh drawing the warmth from him.

A shell exploding above shook the room, showering them with dust and making the lights flicker, the dancing shadows seemingly giving her life.

"Hold me," she begged without her dark lips moving. "Hold me, please." And of course, he did, despite the chill of her touch and the stench of decay. He held her as she kissed him, and the shells rained.

With a thunderous crack the roof rent open and fell. Cold, cloying earth tumbled. A choking, smothering cascade, covering them both. Trapped in that awful, devoted embrace. Buried together, the dead and the living bound as one.

*

Von Trelow woke hard to find himself in Jana's bed. Their bed. His mind cleared, sifting memory from imagining. He hadn't bothered to go to the guest room; there hadn't seemed to be any point. He'd known he'd end up here.

It was still dark, still early. He'd barely slept at all; the dreams plagued him. But where being in her bed, in her place, had previously calmed him and kept the nightmares at bay, now she was in them.

For the remainder of the night, he barely closed his eyes. He counted the quarter hours until he heard the servants wake on the floor above. Then he went and sat at the dressing table, staring at his dim reflection in the mirror, letting her small precious possessions lie in his hands. He opened the wardrobe and let the familiar gowns flow through his fingers, recalling in meticulous detail when she'd worn each one, what they'd said, how he'd felt. He gathered them to his face and breathed the soft scent of rose otto and her, feeling his throat catch and his eyes fill with tears until he could bear it no longer.

He went to the bed, sat down, and simply stared at the lock of her hair, letting its golden strands caress his fingers. Then he drew the broken silver pocket watch from his tunic and unclipped the back. He removed the seized and useless mechanism and the painted watch-face and dropped both into the wastepaper basket. In their place he carefully coiled the beautiful lock of her hair, safe under glass. He clipped the case closed and opened the watch. There was her photograph, there was her hair. He stared at them both and, finally and silently, he wept.

A little after seven o'clock he descended for breakfast, aching, stiff, and horribly tired. Frau Buhler had already eaten and departed the table. Frau Gephart was still abed. Of Friedrich there was no sign, and von Trelow assumed he was sleeping off his disappointment, assuming Louisa had kept her word.

The breakfast table belonged to Herr Buhler and Herr Gephart, speaking of politics and chewing over the morning papers. Von Trelow dully said his good mornings, made himself a plate and sat in his usual place. For once he didn't notice the taste of the coffee.

"God in heaven, what happened to you?" asked Herr Buhler, noticing him properly. "You look terrible."

Von Trelow touched the swollen bruise that occupied the side of his face and had made shaving such a trial.

"This? I had an encounter with some of the fellows from the trade union. They expressed their opinions on the army and the war. It was a frank and open discussion."

That brought an angry snort from Herr Gephart.

"You see, Buhler, it needs to be stopped. It's a cancer."

Their attention slipped away from him. Herr Buhler looked a little uncomfortable but dutifully nodded.

"I dare say. They tried to burn the milling building at the works last night. I had a note this morning. They poured petrol under a door and set light to it."

"Much damage?" asked Gephart whilst chewing.

Herr Buhler shook his head.

“No, the night warden found it and doused it before it could take hold. But they’re relentless.”

“Barbarians, the lot of them,” continued Gephart on his theme. “Vandals out to destroy civilisation, that’s all they are. They need stamping out.”

“Who exactly are they though?” asked von Trelow, forcing his sluggish mind to engage. He received two blank stares in response. “I mean forgive me; I’ve been at the Front. These acts, even trying to give me a beating, just seem like the behaviour of disgruntled workers.” He adopted a blank expression of studied ignorance.

“It is rather more than that,” said Buhler, finishing the last of his toast. He seemed to search for words to explain without insulting his son-in-law’s intelligence.

Herr Gephart had more to say and evidently less scruples over saying it.

“They’re not workers—they’re communists, revolutionaries—out to destroy the state and murder anyone who doesn’t bow to their savagery. You can see what they’re doing in Russia. It’s no good saying that it can’t happen here because it can. They’re in every factory and plant across Germany, and they’re ruthless. We need to act, and act decisively, or it will all be too late.” Now von Trelow knew whose words Friedrich had been repeating.

“One step at a time, Gephart,” said Buhler placatingly.

Alaric wondered what he meant, but Herr Gephart seemed to understand him and grunted amenably.

“I suppose you’re right.”

“Even if they are communists there must be someone in charge,” Alaric mused out loud. “Someone coordinating and planning.”

“What? Oh yes, undoubtedly,” admitted Herr Buhler distractedly.

“Is there someone doing that here? At the cement works?” asked von Trelow.

"Oh yes," admitted Buhler, warming to the subject. "Fellow named Glauber. He was a sergeant in the infantry—invalided out. Knows how to lead men though." He seemed sad and bitter, as if the man using his army skills to organise labour against them were a singular and personal betrayal.

"Why doesn't someone arrest him then, if they know he's behind it?" asked von Trelow.

"Oh, we know who he is all right, we just can't do anything about it because he's never personally involved. He gets his communist lackeys to do it for him. If they get caught it's only ever for a small thing, they get away with a fine that the union pays, or they spend a week or two in jail. It's maddening!"

"Never mind, Buhler, each in their time," commented Herr Gephart, with curious, grim cheer.

Herr Buhler did not seem entirely reassured but nodded anyway, then quickly stood up. He took his leave and departed the room.

Herr Gephart pulled himself up too and for a moment von Trelow thought that he also was about to go, but he was simply refilling his plate from the covered dishes on the side. He returned to his seat and began to eat again.

Alaric retrieved Herr Buhler's abandoned newspaper and scanned the headlines, looking for indications of activity at the Front. What there was, was out of date and foolishly optimistic, it bore little relation to the reality he knew. Nevertheless, something had clearly changed, serious enough for the Kaiser to have appointed a new Chancellor. The front page discussed the appointment of Prince Maximilian of Baden to the position of the first minister of state, an aristocrat but with known liberal sensibilities. It didn't hurt that he was the Kaiser's cousin. The editorial wrote expectantly of the new Chancellor deciding upon his cabinet and promising swift action. Von Trelow gave a thin sceptical smile. Prince or not, the man could promise what he wished. If the army refused, he'd be sunk. They were the true government of

Germany, or at least the OHL was, and whilst the war lasted it would remain so.

"Do you know Prince Max?" Alaric asked Herr Gephart conversationally.

The man's eyes swivelled to him over a chunk of sausage poised half-way to his mouth.

"Hmmm? Prince Max?"

"Yes, the new Chancellor. I thought since he's Prince Max of Baden and your company is from Baden, that you might know each other."

Gephart frowned and squirmed in his chair, suddenly uneasy for no obvious cause.

"Uh, yes. We know each other a little. Not well, of course, but we've met." He seemed thoroughly indisposed by the question and quickly changed the subject.

"How have your enquiries been progressing?" he asked directly.

Von Trelow didn't visibly react, he just smiled as best he could with his bruise twisted face and replied, "Well enough."

"Do you still think one of us killed her?" Gephart asked with astonishing bluntness.

Von Trelow shrugged. "Someone did."

It clearly wasn't the answer the businessman had expected. He frowned and tore at a piece of toast.

"I think you're deluded, if you don't mind me saying so."

Von Trelow wondered who wouldn't mind being told as much but didn't reply.

"No one here is about to commit murder, you know," said Gephart. "The worst thing that has happened in this house is a few greased palms to get young Friedrich his position." The businessman slurped his coffee and wiped his mouth with his napkin.

"What does that mean?" asked Alaric in the most disinterested voice he could manage.

Gephart snorted his amusement, his discomfort now passed with the change in topic.

"Nice lad, Friedrich, but not the smartest. Your wife seemed to get all the brains; God rest her. But he's still got himself a plum job at army headquarters—nice and safe. Mummy and daddy made sure of it. Cost them a small fortune. Luckily, they have plenty to spare."

"I hadn't heard," replied von Trelow coldly.

Gephart didn't seem to notice. "Oh yes, but he's paid it back in full, whispered in the right ears and made sure that all the construction contracts from the Front came home to roost." He laughed with obviously genuine amusement.

"And what about you, Herr Gephart?" asked von Trelow. "How has the war been for you?" He thought of the men hanging on the wire, his lost brother officers, all the countless dead.

"Well, it's an ill wind that blows no good," said Gephart pompously, and it was all Alaric could do to stop himself leaping across the table to stab him with a table knife. If he'd been wearing his pistol, he'd probably have shot him. All that blood and suffering, making them rich.

"You make chemicals?" he asked, trying to hide the anger in his voice.

"Hmmm," said Gephart in confirmation. "Dyes for uniforms, ink for the press, all sorts."

"Gas?"

Gephart flinched, setting a ripple in his flesh. "What?" he asked.

“Your company is the Baden Chemical and Gas Company, isn't it? I wondered if you made gas.”

Gephart grabbed his cup and drank from it to buy time, but it didn't seem to help.

“Well, yes, we were a gas company to begin with, domestic coal gas…” he was floundering and von Trelow interrupted him.

“Of course, but what about other gases? Do you make them? For the army for instance.”

Gephart squinted at him, clearly trying to ascertain where the questions were leading, and how to avoid them.

“Some,” he admitted.

“Phosgene?” asked von Trelow.

Herr Gephart was looking rather pale and forced his thick finger into the bulging collar of his shirt to try and make way for air.

“Well, do you make phosgene?” Alaric persisted.

“Yes, actually.” His gaze was fixed on von Trelow, watching what he might do.

He did nothing. He just sipped at the appalling not-quite-coffee and said not a word. The silence drew on, becoming heavy and increasingly painful until Gephart could stand it no longer.

“I didn't kill your wife,” he blurted out desperately.

Von Trelow just sipped more coffee.

“I swear it. I liked her, really, I did. But there was something the matter with her.”

Von Trelow raised his eyebrows curiously.

“She was acting strangely, avoiding people. Said the oddest things—that the boy, your boy, had a monkey's heart, that people lived in the walls and came out at night. Peculiar stuff. Quite disturbing. I admit when I heard about… the tragedy, my first thought was that she might have done it to herself. I'm sorry, not pleasant to hear, but there it is. I didn't say anything before... because, well... not speaking ill of the dead and all that, but since you asked."

"Actually, I didn't," said von Trelow, finally breaking his silence. He folded the paper and placed it beside his empty plate.

"Well... I thought you should know," Gephart said awkwardly.

"Thank you," said Alaric coldly, and left the room.

Alaric found Frau Buhler in the nursery, helping Paul to put on mittens and a coat whilst reciting him his times tables.

"We're going for a walk," she explained, "Down to the lake."

"Looking for ducks?" asked von Trelow, his question directed to Paul.

The boy nodded and glanced at his father nervously. "I like ducks," he murmured with the flicker of a smile, although his eyes still hid beneath his fringe.

"Would you like to come with us?" asked Frau Buhler hopefully.

Von Trelow looked at the boy, remembered all the things he'd never do with Jana, and nodded.

"Yes, I'd like that," he said. "If it's all right with Paul?" He left the question to hang in the air whilst Paul contemplated his feet.

Then the boy nodded.

"Good," said von Trelow, genuinely pleased for the first time since he'd arrived on the train.

The final preparations centred on negotiations over a hat—woollen, with earflaps, and red to match Paul's mittens. Frau Buhler was determined that he should wear it. Paul was equally intransigent that he would not. The trial of strength went on for some minutes as shoes were found, put on and tied, and hair brushed.

"It is a splendid hat," said von Trelow finally. "I wish I had a hat like that. I have this one instead." He showed Paul the peaked officer's cap he'd been carrying tucked beneath his arm.

Paul glanced at it shyly and seemed entranced.

Von Trelow showed him the insignia on the front and cautiously held it out to him.

The boy responded as if it might bite, slowly and carefully extending his hands and ready at a moment to flee. He took hold of it and quickly pulled it away.

"How about if you wear my hat, and I wear yours?" suggested von Trelow.

After a moment's thought Paul nodded enthusiastically.

His father retrieved the red woollen hat from the floor, where it had been dropped at the end of the last unsuccessful debate, and perched it awkwardly and absurdly upon his own head.

"What do you think?" he asked.

Paul glanced at him and giggled.

"Too small," he mumbled.

Von Trelow shrugged, as if he hadn't a care in the world.

"I like it," he insisted.

Paul placed the officers cap on his own head, disappearing down to the eyes, and seemed suitably pleased.

"Excellent," von Trelow assured him, and gave him a best Guards officer salute.

The shy smile became a momentary grin.

"Shall we go for a walk?"

The boy nodded, and seeing that she wasn't needed, Frau Buhler let them go.

Chapter 19

Alaric settled into the leather armchair in the corner of the guest room and opened Jana's diary. He turned to the earlier entries, days he'd previously discounted and not found the time to read.

Thursday, September 4th

The road to town was flooded last night and we are cut off. I'm certain that it will not last and, if need be, it would be simple enough to wade, but it makes for a little excitement. Paul pretended that we were pirates, trapped upon a desert island, and we made an eye patch and a little wooden sword. We buried an old apple box out behind the stables, and he drew an excellent map. It was a very good day.

Friday, September 5th

No more rain, warm again, the ground drying, fog this morning. Mother in one of her moods, apparently because we have guests arriving, not that she needs a reason. She spent most of the day bossing everyone about, to no benefit I could see. Father escaped to the factory, I'm sure he had nothing to do there. He paid the price, some of the workers had laid tacks in the yard and he had to walk home because three of the tyres were punctured. Poor Klosel will have to spend hours patching the punctures.

Friedrich arrived before dinner, how he got leave I don't know, but he is cheerful and well. A Herr and Frau Gephart arrived on the late train. He is in dyes and chemicals and is a bit of a boor. She is lovely, although why she is with him, I cannot imagine. I feel so lucky to have Alaric, even if he is so far away. I shall read his letters again before I sleep.

Saturday, September 6th

Spent much of the day with Louisa Gephart, when not with Paul. She is as I thought, a very pleasant person, although I think she is finding her marriage a bit of a trap. Friedrich made rather a fool of himself with her, but she was very gracious. I'm not sure what he is doing here, it doesn't seem like a leave. He is on the telephone all the time, and when not, spends much of it speaking with father and Herr Gephart. About what I cannot imagine, he never had any interest in, or head for, business.

Dinner was pleasant, with a good-sized party. Dr Meissner joined us from the village and, for once, met his match at cards in Herr Gephart.

Sunday, September 7th

Walked to church in town. A lot of ill feeling and black looks. People wearing red flowers and ribbons, which I'm told is a sign of communism. It seems strange for a communist to be in church, but there they were. More meetings in the house, everyone being very odd, except Louisa, who could not be more congenial. There is something there though that I cannot place. I think she is very unhappy, although she hides it well.

Monday, September 8th

Felt a little unwell again and rose late. Perhaps I should see the doctor, but I am sure I know what it is. It is not the first time I've had this little 'malady'! In any case the doctor is very busy, there is a lot of sickness in the town, and I am otherwise quite well. I will not mention it to anyone yet, not until I'm sure, and then not until I tell Alaric first.

The Gepharts left early, and I missed them. I shall write to Louisa to apologise; I feel that she could be a real friend. Friedrich is also returning to his duty. He was giggling like a schoolboy and very foolish. He is so very different from my Alaric, and I wish he were more like him; it would suit him better. Mother still distracted, although the guests have left. She snapped at Paul for doing nothing but chasing about the hall. He forgot within half an hour; I believe I was more distressed than he was.

The diary spoke of more days in September, when Johanna had played games with Paul, read, walked, arranged collections of old pans for the war effort, folded bandages, attended dinners or church. Normal days, everyday days. Von Trelow read them all, slowly to allow for the code, and to savour them.

Saturday, September 14th

It has been a strange and not altogether pleasant day. Friedrich arrived last night on the late train. I had already finished writing for yesterday, so I add this today. Then this morning Frau Gephart and her odious husband arrived too. I was pleased to see her, as we got on so well last time they visited, although it was a surprise as no one had mentioned that anyone was coming.

All day there have been telephone calls and telegrams. More than usual and quickly snatched away by father. No one will speak of them. Everyone behaves like it is a big secret. It is odd, but nothing beside what happened after dinner.

I had seen Paul to bed and happened to meet Herr Gephart on the upstairs landing. He made advances. Shocking. Disgusting. When I did not scream, he seemed to take it as acceptance of his horrid suggestion and began pawing at me. I slapped him very hard and shoved him, and being extremely fat he almost fell. I shocked him, I know, as he swore angrily, but I was already away, and I locked myself in my room where I am now.

I shall have to write to Alaric, but I will not tell him this, it will make him worry and it is nothing for him to be concerned about. As for Louisa, what am I to say to her? How shall I face her after this?

Sunday, September 15th

I have managed to avoid any unpleasantness after yesterday by being first at church, then on a walk to the lake with Paul, having lunch in the nursery and then spending the afternoon reading, pleading a headache. I feel rather the coward. It's not that I'm afraid of Herr Gephart, only that I will offend his wife, who deserves only praise for putting up with him, or father and mother, as hosts. He and Louisa are leaving early tomorrow anyway, which is a blessing, and I can avoid them until then.

Friedrich is going too, although not until later. He says he has business in Berlin, although who knows what that could be. Friedrich and serious business of any sort are strange bedfellows. Clearly something is going on, he's glowing ready to burst, like he did when he was a boy. I shall write to Alaric and tell him something of this, as I would not have any secrets from him. Nevertheless, I do not wish him to worry. The unpleasantness with Herr Gephart I shall not mention until I see him in person. I am sure that is best.

Von Trelow shut the diary and placed it on the side table, closed his fists over the arms of the chair and squeezed them until his knuckles were white as bone. He remained there, as a statue, until his breathing became calm. All the while the ticking cogs in his mind clicked and whirred. More things made sense, had become clear. Resisting the urge to track Gephart down and thrash him, he instead picked up Johanna's diary again, reopened it at the place he'd reached, and continued to read until he reached the final, missing pages.

It was a little after noon when von Trelow descended the stairs. Lunch had not yet been called, and the house seemed strangely deserted. Only Frau Gephart was to be found, reading alone in the parlour. She seemed pleased when she saw it was him.

"Good afternoon," she said.

"Good afternoon," he replied. "Where is everyone?"

She closed her book on an embroidered fabric bookmark and placed it demurely in her lap.

"I think they're in the study." Von Trelow knew that would make for a close fit in a small room. "There was a telephone call for Herr Buhler just before midday. It must have been good news—even Friedrich seemed cheerful." She seemed a little wistful that his heart, only just broken, could have been so easily salved.

"They all went in there after the telephone call?" asked von Trelow.

She nodded.

Wheels and cogs ticked and whirled.

The bell for luncheon sounded before they could discuss more, and Alaric escorted Frau Gephart to the dining room. They were the first to arrive, and although the others joined them a few minutes later, even that short delay was uncommonly tardy for the precise and punctilious Frau Buhler. In von Trelow's experience it was unprecedented.

Jana had been right; something was obviously going on. Just as clearly, no one was going to speak about it. He would not be the one to do so, not yet. For now, he simply watched.

As Frau Gephart had indicated, the feeling at the table was indeed one of subdued ebullience. The often quiet and thoughtful Herr Buhler was eating heartily, which he rarely did, smiling easily until he caught von Trelow's eye and relapsed into a sombre frown. It didn't last. Gephart, blind to von Trelow's simmering animosity, was as triumphant as he had been at cards, whilst Frau Buhler smiled quietly to herself. That, of anything, left Alaric unexplainably uneasy. Only Friedrich, of their little group, was determinedly unhappy, mooning quite indiscreetly at Louisa Gephart, to her obvious discomfort. Yet even he, from time to time, caught his father's eye and could not stifle a preening smile.

Von Trelow continued to quietly observe until everyone finished their meal and, one by one, they drifted away. Only when it was him alone remaining in the room did he rise and make his way out onto the terrace. He paced it steadily, deliberately counting out ten minutes as he walked up and back, before finally he returned inside and headed quietly upstairs.

Herr Gephart was packing, his suitcase open upon the bed, clothes scattered about. He was sweating lightly from the simple exertion of carrying clothes from the wardrobe to the suitcase. It was a relief to be interrupted from the careful folding of a pair of capacious trousers by a tap upon the door. He finished with the trousers, laid them in the case, and went to answer. He hoped it was his wife so that she might finish his packing for him. He was, in his own opinion, too old and far too rich to pack his own suitcase. He opened the door, drawing breath to speak and received a thunderous blow into the top of his great ovoid belly. All air left his lungs, and he fell hard onto his behind.

Von Trelow stepped into the room, closed the door, and locked it.

"That was for making advances towards my wife," said von Trelow with chilly calm.

Gephart was gulping and gasping for breath. He rolled onto his side, heaving and wheezing, trying to rise to his knees.

Von Trelow patiently waited until he was on all fours, then kicked him savagely in his plentiful girth.

The fat man curled and collapsed, gasping and choking, his face deathly white.

"That was for your pathetic attempt to convince me that she was going mad. You began to worry when you heard about her having a diary. You were concerned what she might have written about you. You were right to be."

Gephart had rolled onto his back, his body an impressive, well-tailored, hillock.

Von Trelow leant down, grasped him by his expensive lapels and dragged him up, ignoring the aches and pains that accompanied lifting such weight.

"And this is for your wife..." He drove his knee up sharply into the older man's groin. He held him upright as his eyes almost leapt from his skull and his mouth gaped, leaving him staring like a landed fish.

Von Trelow dropped him back onto the bed beside the open suitcase, then drew the large American pistol from inside his tunic and pressed it hard into the businessman's stomach. Gephart, unable to catch his breath, gulped and feebly waved his desperate pleadings.

"You don't need to speak, just nod for yes, shake for no. Understand?"

He leant on the Colt and Gephart nodded frantically.

"Good. Did you kill my wife or have her killed?"

Amongst the gasping, Gephart shook his head desperately.

"I didn't think so, you're not the type to get your own hands dirty. What about the phosgene, did it come from you?"

Another shake, wobbling his chins.

"Do you know anything more about her death?"

A third shake, and von Trelow nodded.

"But you're hardly innocent, are you?"

Gephart looked confused and uncertain. He shook his head anyway, just to be sure.

"You wanted an heir at any cost, didn't you?"

The man on the bed had confusion and pain written all over his face, but the pistol being forced into his flesh concentrated his mind. He nodded.

"But you're too lazy, and even with all your money, too odious, to find another woman of your wife's quality. So, you decided to force a good woman into infidelity to provide it."

Gephart gulped a breath and grudgingly nodded.

"You deliberately allowed her to overhear you threatening to replace her if she didn't provide an heir, to panic her, yes?"

Another nod.

"You wanted her to be the 'guilty' party, so she'd be forever beholden to you, yes?"

Gephart slowly nodded again.

"So, you engineered her being here with Friedrich, to give her an easy, suitable opportunity?"

A momentary pause was dealt with by a shove of the pistol and Gephart nodded repeatedly.

"Hence the separate rooms. Your idea I presume?"

A nod.

"You already know that she's pregnant, don't you? You're too smart to have missed the signs."

A slight nod.

"You're never going to tell her or anyone else that you know, are you?"

A moment's thought and a careful but firm shake of the head.

"And you'll treat that child as well... better than any child of your own, yes?"

A firm nod, accompanying the wheezing breaths.

"And from this day forwards you'll treat your wife like a princess, in every possible way."

A longer pause this time. The pistol was sharply withdrawn from deep in the fat gut and jabbed into Gephart's forehead, high between his eyes. He began to nod, small shivering movements so as not to jog the gun.

"Yes," he managed to gasp, "yes!"

Von Trelow left the gun there, just to make his point.

"I will write to your wife from time to time. Who knows, I may even visit. If I even imagine that you are not treating her as she deserves to be treated, we will finish what we have started here, and you will simply disappear. Do you believe me, Herr Gephart?"

The businessman nodded, wide-eyed.

"Yes, yes."

"Good. I knew you were an intelligent man." Calmly, von Trelow tucked the pistol back beneath his tunic and quietly left the room.

Alaric made sure to see Herr and Frau Gephart off. Klosel brought round the Mercedes, its polished sheen already spotted with rain. Von Trelow helped him to load the luggage onto the rack at the rear and cover it with a tarpaulin.

He ignored Gephart, who was doing his best to do the same in return, and instead said his goodbyes to Louisa as he held an umbrella and escorted her to the car.

"It has been my pleasure to meet you, Frau Gephart." He bowed and kissed her hand.

"Likewise, Herr von Trelow." She was pleased and a little confused, she'd stay that way for now.

He handed her into the backseat. "If there is anything I can ever do to be of service to you, I trust you will not hesitate to contact me at once." He said it loud enough to be heard by Gephart, who couldn't help but blanche. Herr Buhler evidently heard too and frowned in confusion. After all, the two of them had hardly seemed like close confederates during her stay. "Please write."

She smiled and nodded, still a little bewildered.

"I would be pleased to, if you would also write to me," she replied graciously.

"On that you may count." He closed the door for her and stepped away, turning towards her husband, who had finished his goodbyes with his host.

"An achievement, Gephart. A great achievement," his father-in-law said proudly.

Gephart himself was hurrying to the car, avoiding von Trelow's gaze. Herr Buhler beamed delightedly and waved from the steps, whilst Frau Buhler scowled at the back of her husband's head. Friedrich, who had made the most cursory of goodbyes, was hanging back in the doorway sulking like a boy deprived of a favourite toy. Von Trelow folded the umbrella and joined him, raising a hand as the big black car clattered into life and eased away. It crunched over the gravel, down the drive, and out of sight down the Retzen road.

He turned and headed inside, leaving the other three to their own thoughts. He'd promised Paul he'd read to him; it was a promise he intended to keep.

Chapter 20

Josef Glauber staggered home through the damp October night, drunk on rough alcohol and spirited Marxist debate. He'd eaten well, drunk better, and spent time amongst men who looked up to him and gave his life purpose. A decent life, if a life that demanded struggle—including, at this moment, walking in a straight line.

He saw the familiar corner lamppost ahead, grasped for its support then moved onto the wall. He followed it with an unsteady hand to the third door. He paused to breathe and check his count; three doors. His door. He fumbled for his keys, finally finding them in his trouser pocket. Coins scattered, jangling across the curb stones. His eyes struggled to focus on their leaping, flashing silver discs. He considered for a long moment and mumbled a curse, deciding that he could not afford to forget them. He slid unsteadily to the step and spent several frustrating minutes, scrabbling to pick them up.

He glanced along the street. He was alone. He resisted the urge to slump back against the door and leave the lock until morning, and climbed, shakily and uncertainly, to his feet. He found the key again and tried to line it up with the lock. It took three attempts, but it finally slid home. He heard the catch slide as he turned it and carefully twisted the handle and pushed open the door.

Von Trelow had listened to the drunken comedy on the doorstep for eight minutes; he'd timed it by his watch. There was no light in the room beside that from the radium painted watch-face and, as the door swung inwards with the mildest creak, the soft light of the gaslights along the street seeped across the threshold. He saw the unsteady silhouette of Glauber step inside, hang his narrow-brimmed bowler hat upon a peg, extract the key from the lock and finally close the door, plunging them back into darkness. The workman's cottage wasn't wired for electricity and von Trelow listened as the drunken Glauber fumbled with matches and lamp.

Finally, light flared with a rasp, faintly illuminating von Trelow's face, his long, crossed legs and the Luger lying upon his knee, but the distracted tenant stood oblivious with his back to him and his attention on the lamp. He carefully lifted the glass and stabbed the match at the wick thrice before he found it. It took light, swelling the glow within the room.

The oily illumination finally revealed a small, cramped parlour reeking of damp and mould. Cracked plaster walls, cheap furniture in its final days, and a door straight to the street. One of a pair of sadly sagging chairs flanking the meagre fireplace harboured the poised and waiting von Trelow. Behind him another door opened into a tight galley of a kitchen barely wide enough to turn around in, and to his left a narrow staircase twisted up to the bedroom and boxroom above. He'd been there long enough to search thoroughly and know the ground.

Glauber, lamp in hand, turned slowly to face the room.

The figure in the chair didn't move other than to level his pistol at the other man's chest. He said nothing and waited to be seen.

Glauber looked blearily about the room, focussing slowly on familiar shapes. He saw the broad, burly figure in the chair but couldn't translate the information he was seeing into a form that made sense. He peered, brow deeply furrowed with confused concentration, until the look changed slowly to surprised understanding, angry outrage, and finally, fearful comprehension.

"Sit down, Feldwebel Glauber," said von Trelow softly. Glauber looked at him, at the familiar black shape of the Luger in his hand and the lamp in his own. "Don't be foolish, I can pull this trigger before you even raise it. In any case you're so drunk you'd probably miss." Glauber seemed to weigh his words, find them sensible, even to his alcohol-fogged mind, and sat down in the other chair as he'd been asked. The lamp he placed on the little mantle ledge above the fireplace, leaving the glow to light their faces and little else.

"What do you want?" he asked.

"Some answers."

"What if I say no?" he said stubbornly.

Von Trelow simply waved the barrel of the pistol.

"You'll shoot me?"

"I will," the calm officer assured him.

Glauber examined the strong, impassive face in the flickering lamplight for some moments and clearly believed him. He shifted in the chair as he rapidly began to sober up.

"What have I done to you?" he asked.

Von Trelow lifted a second pistol from the shadowed table beside him, a small Mauser.

"One round missing from the magazine, and you haven't even bothered to clean it, Feldwebel. That's not the regulation way."

Glauber's features flashed with anger.

"You can fuck regulations, and the army, and all officers. I'm not a Feldwebel anymore."

"No, you're the union boss at the cement plant, aren't you?"

Glauber's attention returned to the gun and his defiance melted. He nodded.

“And you met with Herr Braun two days ago?”

“Yes.”

“Tell me about it.”

Glauber peered at him through eyes bloodshot by cheap booze, smoky lamps and long days working in cement dust.

“What about it?”

Von Trelow leant forwards in his seat, tucked the Luger away and kept Glauber’s own Mauser trained upon him.

“Tell me everything, and you just might see the dawn.”

Glauber, now far less drunk than he had been minutes before, was a man who knew killers, had seen too many not to recognise their eyes. He nodded slowly and clearly then did exactly as he was asked.

“I got a message from Braun, that he was in town and wanted to meet, had to meet.”

“Was that unusual?” asked von Trelow.

Glauber nodded.

“Very, I’d never met the man. Heard of him, of course.”

“Who is he?”

Glauber frowned but if he was surprised by the other man’s ignorance, he sensibly kept it to himself. After all von Trelow had all the cards, and the guns.

“He’s a politician, Social Democrat. A big wheel in the party.” His face scowled in the yellow lamp light.

Von Trelow smiled slightly and nodded. “And they have ties to the union?” he asked.

Glauber nodded again.

"To all the unions. They're for the workers, the common men."

"As are the communists and their ilk?"

Glauber shrugged, a flash of cunning in his eyes.

"If the socialists can't deliver what's needed, there needs to be an alternative."

Von Trelow smiled his understanding.

"So, for men like you, the communists are the stick to keep the moderate men in line, 'back us or we go to the radicals'."

Glauber smirked unpleasantly but didn't reply. He didn't need to; it was all quite clear.

"So, you met him as he asked. What did he have to say?"

Glauber couldn't hide the angry frown.

"Told me that there was a deal being done with Brandenburg Cement, with the bosses, that the strikes and labour agitation had to stop. I told him it wasn't that simple. If they didn't get the men what they wanted the reds would. My men will go along with them, with the socialists, if they deliver, but if they don't... well, look what's happening in Russia."

Von Trelow nodded, he hadn't been to the east for a year, but he'd seen the headlines. It was enough.

"What did he say to that?"

"Said we had to keep it under control. That it was vitally important. Told me they'd done a deal that would give us all everything we wanted, without revolution and blood and chaos. Said we just had to do our part."

"What deal? How?" asked von Trelow.

Glauber shook his head.

"Don't know, wouldn't tell me the details, said it was all secret, but I'd understand when it happened. We just had to keep things calm."

"At the cement plant?" asked von Trelow, confused.

Glauber shook his head and chuckled.

"Not just this plant, I'm senior steward for all the Brandenburg Cement factories, all over the Reich." He said it with pride; it was a power and responsibility hardly reflected in his home. "But it's more than that too," said Glauber, the alcohol making him incautious. He was clearly enjoying revealing how much he knew and how far his influence spread. "It's all the big industrialists, all their union representatives. It's not just Braun; it's the whole damned party machine."

Von Trelow had expected something like it, but to hear it confirmed was still chilling.

"And they'll do it? The other union bosses?"

"Most will," confirmed Glauber. "There are some independents and the Revolutionary Stewards, but for most it's back the majority socialists or go over to the reds. Some may go that way, but most will go along with the SPD."

"So long as Braun and his friends can deliver?"

Glauber nodded, his face twisted with clear anxiety.

"If they don't it will be all our heads on the block. The reds will take it all. It'll be bloody revolution for sure."

It all made sense to von Trelow, it was filling gaps, adding vital cogs to the machine, connections completing the whole ticking mechanism.

"So, who told you to take a shot at me?" he asked with a demonstrative flourish of the offending Mauser.

Glauber watched the pistol with ill-disguised fear.

"Braun," he admitted.

"He told you to kill me?"

Glauber shrugged, then shook his head.

"He's a politician, they never give you a straight answer or a clear instruction. He showed up in a panic, said you'd been digging around, that you knew too much and could mess everything up. He said I had to stop you."

"So, you tried to kill me?" he asked coolly.

Glauber swallowed his nervousness and shook his head.

"Wasn't aiming to kill you, just wing you. Put you out of action for a few days."

Von Trelow observed Glauber's twitching hands. Whether from alcoholism or shellshock, he probably couldn't have hit an arm or leg if he'd tried. The bullet had almost hit him in the head. Deliberate or not, he'd probably never get an honest answer, and in the end it didn't matter.

"Did you have a drink to keep you warm while you were waiting?" It had been a cold night.

Glauber paused but nodded a yes. More than one, von Trelow suspected. He'd found dozens of drained bottles of cheap booze around the cottage. Glauber drank to forget the trenches, that night had been no exception. Perhaps he'd been drunk enough to miss, certainly drunk enough to be staggering as he'd fled, leaving stumbling, unsteady tracks. The ticking mechanism in Alaric's mind was almost complete.

"When that didn't work, you sent some of your union friends?"

The union man nodded with a grimace.

"Didn't expect you to beat them half to death," he complained.

"Only half."

Von Trelow slowly lifted himself from the slack confines of the chair and rose to his feet. He had to stoop beneath the low ceiling, but he kept Glauber's little gun levelled. He dropped the magazine into his other hand and flicked out the small gleaming 7.65mm rounds with his thumb, letting them drop and chime against the bare floorboards. When he was done, he cleared the slide, leaving the Mauser as dangerous as a paperweight. He dropped it onto the table and put the magazine on the mantlepiece.

"If I see you again in anything other than the most mundane and social setting, I'll assume you're there to kill me. Clear?" he asked.

Glauber nodded, looking faintly sick, just beginning to think that he might survive the interview.

"Clear," he confirmed.

Von Trelow backed into the tiny kitchen, keeping his eyes on the cautiously still former soldier, quietly opened the back door, then stepped out into the night and disappeared.

*

The forest was dense, deep, and fresh, the sunlight shimmering in slanting golden beams through the layered canopy above. Wide spreading oaks, pale ash, maple, beech, wide-fingered sycamores, dark pines, reaching linden and sprawling willow spread a patchwork before them. The myriad hued greens: near black like the deep ocean, pale as new Hock, vibrant as Ottoman emeralds, dazzled and delighted. The grey men smiled as they moved, the weight of cares lifting. Some laughed, breathing deep of wildflowers and pine. It was unearthly, like stepping into a world where war had never been dreamt of.

He found him curled beneath a spreading oak, lying still and quiet, his head pillowed on soft deep moss. The boy was no more than eighteen. His face as pale as milk, his lips full and his lashes as long as a pretty girl's. He had cut his hair terribly short, to make himself look older or more manly and he'd tried to grow a moustache, but it was a shadow, nothing more. His tight belted tunic was a deep green-brown, like the bark of a tree, with broad epaulettes at his shoulders. His breeches were a deeper, duller shade, his leather boots muddy, scuffed from running, but now quite still. There was a holster at his hip, but it was empty, and a canvas map case draped about him by a corded strap. Von Trelow crouched beside him and carefully lifted the cord, trying to ease it from under him. He was slow and gentle, like a father trying not to wake a child, but it wouldn't move, stubborn and intransigent. He reached over and slid his hand beneath the boy's head. He cradled it delicately as he lifted him lightly from the moss, leaving small flecks of black and green speckling the pale cheek. The boy's shoulder began to rise, his arm hanging loose across the sward, gradually making space between him and the ground through which to draw the strap. Alaric began to pull, felt it hold and tugged.

The dried blood tore with a harsh whisper and ruby-black entrail coils fell lurching; a looping, slithering, sliding, bilious disgorge, cold and fetid, spreading towards him across the dark fertile earth. The cord strap sprung free, and he staggered up and away—dropping the young corpse back to its bed—heaving and snorting to purge the mortal stench. Alaric shook his head to clear it, glanced at the maps in the youthful Russian officer's case and stepped away from the widening puddle of guts.

The boy had made it almost three kilometres from their broken lines. Three kilometres towards Lemberg, towards safety, towards home. Three kilometres after a bullet or shrapnel shard had torn him open and killed him. Death had simply taken his time to catch up.

*

Alaric woke, still smelling the flowers and the filth and cleared his head with a shake. It was an old dream, an easy one to forget. He sighed, rolled over, closed his eyes, and waited for the next.

Chapter 21

Von Trelow breakfasted alone, late after his nocturnal wanderings. He made his way through the morning papers, sipping tea and eating sparingly. The war news was as bland as the censors could make it, telling him nothing new. He felt painfully out of touch, the call of duty pulling at him like a hauled line. He was looking for one final fragment. He found it on an inside page.

The last, ink-stained piece of the machine clicked into place and finally, everything ran smoothly. He smiled, without joy, but with a certain completist contentment, then took his time, it was a luxury he could now afford. After breakfast he went up to the nursery and played with Paul until he heard the car returning.

"I'll be back soon, Paul. I just need to speak with grandfather," he told his son. Paul nodded and allowed him a rare shy smile, before returning to the important business of balancing brightly painted wooden blocks. "See if you can get twelve by the time I get back," suggested his father, and the boy set about the task with a familiar determination.

Herr Buhler was in the drawing room, pouring himself a pre-lunch aperitif. Friedrich already held one in his hand.

"Good morning," said von Trelow.

They almost seemed surprised to see him.

"Good morning, Alaric." They were suppressing the smiles that had been on their faces as he'd walked in, cautious of his mood.

He let himself fall into an armchair and smiled broadly.

"Congratulations. You must be very pleased."

Friedrich affected to look confused, but it was a poor performance, his father merely looked a little surprised.

"Whatever are you referring to?" he asked as he replaced the stopper in the decanter and returned it to the Tantalus.

Von Trelow leant back calmly, crossed a long leg over his knee, took a deep breath and began.

"I saw in the newspaper that Prince Max has named his cabinet. A lot of Social Democrats in high positions, key positions."

Buhler lifted the crystal glass to his lips and sipped, his eyebrow slightly raised but otherwise doing nothing to recognise von Trelow's words.

"I found that interesting, considering Herr Braun's presence here over the past few weeks. I expect he will receive a plum position somewhere as well?"

Herr Buhler didn't speak, but Alaric's eyes fell on Friedrich in his scarlet-gilded staff uniform.

"The Prussian state cabinet," the younger man replied with a shrug, ignoring his father's scowl.

Von Trelow's smile broadened as his mind's complex machinery smoothly whirred.

"Of course. And these new socialist cabinet members are immediately speaking of peace, telling the press that the war is lost, and an armistice must be sought at all costs. That's going to come as quite a shock to a lot of people, after four years of relentlessly banging the drum."

He saw Buhler's frown behind the glass shielding his lips.

“Not that I disagree, the Spring Offensive was our last chance, everyone with any sense knew it, I just wasn’t sure that included the OHL.”

Friedrich looked a little uncomfortable but said nothing.

“There are men there who would gladly drive us through the gates of hell to preserve their honour. You knew that, you and your friends. You saw what was coming, defeat, famine, and revolution. So, you did what you do, as businessmen. You made a deal.”

Herr Buhler put down the small, slim sherry glass, still unfinished and picked up a brandy bowl instead, which he filled with a decent measure. No one spoke. He turned back to the room and toasted von Trelow with an arrogant smile.

“Well done, my boy, very clever. I thought we’d been quite careful, clearly not careful enough. Who talked?”

“Braun,” said Alaric, even if it were largely a lie.

Buhler nodded.

“Typical politician, can’t keep their mouths shut. How much do you know?”

Von Trelow shrugged.

“More than enough, I may lack some of the details but most of it is quite clear.”

“Then you understand,” said Buhler confidently. “It was the only course of action that made sense. You’re right of course, the war is lost, all that matters now is what comes next. Someone had to take charge, otherwise it will be like Russia, only worse. So yes, some gentlemen of my acquaintance agreed that we needed to act.”

“Rich industrialists—steel, concrete, chemicals?”

“Amongst others.”

“And they chose you because Friedrich was on the Staff at OHL, all carefully paid for in advance. And Gephart because he knew

Prince Max—a liberal cousin of the Kaiser who could be an acceptable figurehead."

Buhler didn't like that and shook his head.

"The Prince is a patriot, doing his duty for Germany. He also happens to believe that we need a liberal democracy, not monarchic autarky. It's what needs to happen for now."

"But he'll toe the line? Follow the plan?" said Alaric, and Herr Buhler grudgingly nodded. "So, the socialist politicians get to take over government, without needing a revolution that they can't control, without the risk of the communists taking it from them like in Russia?"

Another nod over a sip of brandy.

"And you and your friends get what? To keep your factories and fortunes, no seizures on behalf of the state in Germany?"

"That's right, property to remain inviolable," said his father-in-law.

"All property?" Von Trelow received a cunning smile in reply.

"Well, land may not be quite so inviolable as other types of property," Buhler admitted.

Von Trelow felt the jolt but showed nothing. "So, the old Prussian Junker landowners will pay the price. Sacrifice the Junkers to placate the socialists, giving you and your friends even more power?"

"Someone has to lose out, and they're not the only ones who'll pay, Alaric. We've paid plenty, the SPD and their allies need funding if they're to hold power, and we have provided. Money buys newspaper columns, buys rallies, buys turnout, it buys elections. The old days are gone, the war, and the revolution in Russia have seen to that. But it doesn't have to be like that in Germany. It could be different, the 'English model', you must understand that. You're half English."

Von Trelow scowled, thinking of the great concrete bunkers of the Hindenburg Line, from the Alps to the coast, the vast dumps of munitions, and endless batteries of arms. All manufactured by industrialists like the Buhlers, all paid for by the state.

"Funded by money you've made from the war, Heinrich? How much will you pay them, will it amount to a full one percent, or just a rounding error?"

An angry sneer flashed for a moment across Buhler's features but was gone almost as soon as it appeared: Whatever they'd paid, it was a pittance.

"And in addition, they'll ensure that the strikes stop—or at least will be kept under control?" asked von Trelow.

Buhler took his brandy to a chair and sat down too, with every sign of beginning to enjoy himself.

"Correct."

"Which only leaves the army," said von Trelow. "They're hardly going to give up complete mastery of the state and their Götterdämmerung just because you ask them to, or was that where you did have to pay a truly monstrous bribe?"

"The generals?" Buhler laughed. "Do you think that type care about money? Power and honour are their gods. They'll die before they give them up, and take us with them, you're right about that."

"Then how—?"

"We offered them one to give up the other." He paused, quite smug and self-satisfied whilst Friedrich fidgeted nervously.

Von Trelow's mind whirred. "They won't take the blame for having to surrender," he said slowly. "They keep their honour."

Buhler laughed, as delighted as if watching a cunning card trick.

"Very good! Johanna always said that you were clever, too clever by half by the looks of it."

Alaric inclined his head, coldly accepting the compliment.

"Yes, the socialists will negotiate the armistice and peace, and the army will be able to distance themselves from the whole pathetic, sorry event.

"Even though General Headquarters has been in charge for years, that it's been a military dictatorship in all but name? All of this is their doing," von Trelow said accusingly as the faces of the countless dead rose in his mind.

"But that's the ingenious part," said Friedrich, finally finding his voice and pacing the floor. "They've controlled all the newspapers too. No matter how bad things have been people have never been told. Things may be tough at home, but they've always been told that the war is going well. Today's papers are the first time they've been told that the war can't be won, and it's the democrats telling them." His face was flushed with the cleverness of it. Alaric had never wanted to punch him so badly. "The army will survive," Friedrich continued triumphantly. "It will retreat and let the politicians negotiate with the Allies."

"The French refuse to deal with the Generals anyway," said Buhler, breaking in. "Good, let them argue with the socialists instead. If it gets Germany a more lenient peace, so be it. If not, the politicians can take the blame."

"Your politicians," said Alaric.

There was a slight noise from the doorway as Frau Buhler walked in.

"No, Alaric," she said smoothly. "The people's politicians, the left's politicians."

"So, it's all lies, all to protect your money and your power?" he asked, his voice betraying an anger he could no longer entirely disguise.

"Not just us; Germany," she said reverentially.

He didn't bother to reply, to point out their hypocrisy, that it was only their kind, the rich, they were protecting. It was only them she cared about anyway.

"What about the Kaiser?" he asked, the weight of his oath bearing on him.

Frau Buhler now made herself a drink too, offering one to Friedrich who refused.

"The Royal Family will be retained if they can be," she said with little concern, "but the Kaiser will probably have to go. The Allies want a scapegoat. But at least they'll all live, there won't be slaughter like in Russia. We've saved Germany from that." She sipped her drink like it were a victor's cup.

"Perhaps you have, but at what cost?" asked Alaric coldly.

Friedrich looked uneasy, like a naughty child waiting for punishment, Heinrich looked bored, but Frau Buhler simply smiled.

"Whatever it is, we'll pay it later," she said.

Von Trelow nodded. It was all complete, every moving part. There was just one more thing he needed to know.

"And Jana found out," he said, not bothering to make it a question.

"Yes," confirmed her mother, "somehow she overheard Heinrich and Friedrich speaking with Gephart and Braun."

"She was walking on the terrace," said Alaric with disciplined calm.

Frau Buhler nodded.

"That explains it." She turned on her husband. "I told you to keep the outside door closed."

"It was stuffy," he complained childishly.

"Is that why she had to die?" Alaric asked coldly, expressing no emotion; that could come later once he had an answer.

Frau Buhler had no such control—she spun about and hurled the glass with all her force, shrieking in fury. The glass was as poorly aimed as it was forcefully thrown and exploded harmlessly against the wall behind him.

"You're a fool!" she yelled. "No one killed Johanna. We loved Johanna. She was too curious, too clever, but we'd never have hurt her. Never!"

She subsided into angry sobs, her outburst so stunning to Buhler and Friedrich that they simply stared in silent shock until she recovered. Her composure was quickly regained.

"I found her diary the following day, after they'd taken her away. I could read it, of course. I was the one who taught her about codes as a child, so we could send each other little messages." For a second, she was wistfully elsewhere, with a young Johanna. Then she was back, hard and remorseless. "The code in her diary was dreadfully simple. Anyone with half a mind would have been able to decipher it, and it told all about the plan, about what was going to happen. It couldn't come out, not yet, so I tore out the pages and burned them in the grate."

"There were other parts of the diary in another code, a numeric code," Alaric reminded her.

She scowled bitterly.

"Yes, she started using that when she was fifteen, for all the little secrets she wanted to keep from me. I expect there's plenty in there about you. If she'd written in that I'd never have known, but then neither would anyone else. I've never been able to find the key. Did you?"

"No," said Alaric honestly. So, the other code was to stop her mother reading it, not him. It was a scant consolation, but he accepted it and silently apologised to Jana's shade for having doubted her. "So, her death was just a coincidence?" he asked disbelievingly. “A coincidence that she died that very night having overheard your plan, in a manner precisely like phosgene poisoning, when you have a man who manufactures phosgene staying in your home?”

Her eyes narrowed.

“Yes, of course it’s a coincidence. If enough people die, then some of those deaths will be coincidental with other things happening. Millions of people have died: it’s not murder it’s mathematics!” Her voice had risen once again to a shriek, her eyes blazing and furious.

She took a breath, smoothing her skirts, her composure settling like armour.

Von Trelow nodded and quietly stood up.

“That’s what it all is, isn’t it, Marla? Mathematics. You’ve always loved your numbers and your puzzles. And that’s what this is, isn’t it? Even the war is just a puzzle to solve, and you solved it. How to protect the family, the company your father founded, your world. You came up with a plan. It wasn’t the other industrialists coming to you, you went to them.”

Her angry eyes narrowed shrewdly.

“Yes. It was my plan,” she snapped, straightening with her rising pride. “But they won’t listen to a woman, they never have. I needed Heinrich to speak for me, just as I’ve always done!”

Behind her Herr Buhler looked sullenly cowed and von Trelow wondered how he’d ever mistaken him for a man of force.

“He took the idea to them,” she snapped, “not that they needed much persuading, they know a good deal when they hear it. Faced with the alternative of Bolshevik revolution, they fell over themselves to agree.”

“And Friedrich was already in the OHL,” von Trelow added.

She nodded curtly.

"It cost a small fortune over the years to get him there and keep him there, but I knew when the war began that at some point it would be worth it, and we had a very large fortune to spend."

The distant sound of Paul's laughter drifted down from the nursery. Frau Buhler paused, her expression flickering for a moment, then it was gone.

"Friedrich approached General Groener for us and the realists on the General Staff grabbed at the chance like drowning men at straws. The die-hards will be forced out; they don't even know they've lost."

Across the room, Friedrich blanched.

It was all quite brilliant. Johanna had said she'd got her brains from her mother. He'd replied at the time that since she certainly got her looks from her too, what did she get from her father? She'd said her heart. She was right; Buhler looked sick, pale with the strain of contemplating what had been done and what it would mean. His wife had no such scruples. She was clear, resolute, and entirely ruthless.

"And the politicians?" he asked, just to be complete. "Contacts via the unions?"

She smirked and shook her head.

"They came to us." She moved to the window, gazing out with satisfaction. "They begged for our support, trying to scare us into backing them rather than the communists taking over." She turned back, her voice dripping with disdain. "I expect they still think it was their idea."

"You were always the smart one, Marla. Jana always said that."

Frau Buhler nodded,

"You should have listened. I told you when you arrived to just look after Paul. There was nothing to find here, nothing you needed to see." She moved closer, her voice now so low it was barely a whisper. "You should have stayed out of things." It sounded like a threat.

"So, what happens to me now?" he asked.

"Nothing happens," Frau Buhler snapped irritably. "There's nothing you can do—it's done. Who can you tell? Who'd believe you? No one would print it. Your own commanders would order you to shut up." She paused, allowing the truth to sink in.

"Go home, Alaric. Spend time with your son whilst you can."

Von Trelow said nothing.

"Johanna was a very rich woman—my father left her a fortune in company stock and investments. It's yours now." She smiled coldly. "Do what you want with it. Save your family's estate if you like, live like an old Prussian Junker."

She paused, allowing the weight of her words to settle.

"Do what you wish—just keep out of the way."

Alaric, hollow as an empty drum, cheated of revenge, stymied of any form of justice, simply nodded, rose, and went to see his son.

Chapter 22

Days of rain had left the ground soft beneath his feet, but today the sky was clear and blue and bitterly cold. He dropped a handful of earth onto the coffin in the grave. It scattered over the wreath of tissue paper roses and pattered off the polished wood. He stepped back, brushing the remains from his gloves to stand with his son. His veiled mother held Paul's other hand and hung on the arm of Alaric's tall and impassive father. She was crying softly and muttering an English prayer. Across the grave Herr and Frau Buhler and Friedrich stared blankly at the ground, no one meeting his eye. He had no words for them. He turned away.

"I'll be back in few minutes," he whispered to his mother. She nodded and held the little boy close. Von Trelow stepped through the silent crowd of mourners and on through the gravestones, leaving the sad gathering behind, until he reached the road outside. Lise was waiting, all in black.

"You didn't have to come," he said, "you could have sent a telegram."

"I know," she replied, "but then I couldn't stop you doing something truly stupid."

"I thought you didn't care." His voice was tight, but he tried to hide it.

"I don't, but Erich did," she explained. "Besides, if anyone's going to kill you..."

"I know, it's going to be you."

"That's right," she agreed. She was still bitter, still in pain, but perhaps the edge was not as sharp as it had been.

He turned and walked slowly along the pavement, unable to bear standing still. She fell in alongside him, her swift steps matching his even stride.

"You said it could take five days," he reminded her.

"I said at least three, and that's what it took."

"So, what was it?" he asked heavily. "Was it phosgene or influenza?" He closed his eyes already anticipating her answer.

"Why?" asked Lise. "If it's phosgene what will that mean? You can't bring her back."

He scowled. "Do you think I don't know that? But at least it will confirm who killed her."

Dr Lise Freisinger sighed but had to ask.

"Who?"

"Her mother," said von Trelow sadly. "She was the only one it could be. Johanna died sometime between a quarter past eleven and three o'clock. Her father, brother, Braun, and Gephart were all together until four. No one else had a motive. I know that the maid was busy, and Johanna was in her room and then walking on the terrace, which meant Frau Buhler was looking after Paul for most of that time. From the nursery she could have easily seen Johanna run back inside. She could have guessed what she'd heard, she knew what the men were discussing after all. Maybe she even went to speak to her. They may have argued, they did all the time, but perhaps this time Johanna wasn't going to ignore what was happening. She was a good woman; I don't believe she'd have just let it be. Her mother is her father's daughter, cold and hard, she always believes that she knows best. I'm not sure where she got the poison, from Gephart I assume, but when it comes to it, she's the only one it could be." He glanced at her as she walked alongside him.

"It's not her," she said firmly.

"What?" he wasn't sure he'd heard right.

"It's not her," Lise repeated, "It wasn't phosgene, von Trelow. It really was influenza. Meissner was right."

A relentless pounding hammered in his head, making him stop and close his eyes until it eased.

"I've been reading what I could find these past three days. This new strain is cruel, it's sweeping through Spain, and probably France and England as well. It's worse than we've ever seen."

"But like this?"

"Yes. In some cases, the symptoms are exactly like your wife's. Quick, severe and with the highest mortality amongst the otherwise young and healthy. Death comes in hours."

He heard her words, they all made sense, he just had to wait until he could believe them.

"You're certain?" he asked, grasping for straws.

She nodded firmly.

"The cultures produced substantial growths of Pfieffer's Baclllus, and there were no indications of burns amongst the tissue samples I took. I'm sure."

He nodded, finally beginning to accept.

"So, she just died? She simply died?"

The serious young woman frowned beneath the brim of her hat and nodded once.

"Yes. I'm sorry. There was no conspiracy, no crime, just a loss, another pointless, tragic loss." Her hand twitched, as if she'd thought to reach out to comfort him and instantly decided not to.

He smiled at that and her words, the absurd, mistaken falsehood in her words.

"Oh no," he said firmly, "there was a conspiracy, Lise, and crime; treason, fraud, corruption, on a scale we'll probably never really understand. It just happens that Jana's death wasn't involved. She simply died, like all the other poor bystanders of this war."

They stood for a while, saying nothing as the clouds of their breaths drifted and merged.

"What will you do?" she asked finally.

He shrugged his broad shoulders beneath the uniform greatcoat.

"Nothing," he admitted. "Anything I could do would probably only make things worse. One way or another this damned war will end soon. It must; we've nothing left to give. Perhaps then we can start again and try to forget."

Down the road the figure of his mother appeared through the cemetery gate, leading Paul by the hand. The child was so tightly wrapped he waddled. Alaric smiled.

"And until then?" asked Lise.

He looked away from the approaching figures and caught her eye. It surprised her and she flinched, glancing down at his shining boots.

"Until then," he said, "back to the division, to the men." There was nothing more to say. He took her gently by the shoulders, feeling her start with surprise, and kissed her on one cool cheek. He left her and walked away towards his mother and son.

Twenty metres later Paul tottered to a stop, his mittened hand held high in his grandmother's. Alaric dropped to his haunches, looked into the nervous, curious face with Jana's round blue eyes and attempted a smile.

"Hello, Paul. Are you warm enough?"

The small boy nodded silently, without any sign of tears.

"Good. Do you know, I met your mother on a day like this?"

The late afternoon sun was hovering above the horizon, shimmering through the frosty mist that rose gently from the lake. The vaporous tendrils were reaching across the cropped grass, weaving between the stark trunks of the willows and the legs of an ornamental bench. Friedrich was pacing, making his uneven way up and back along the lakeside, turning and returning, sometimes shorter, sometimes longer. Every now and then he would stop, pull a folded note from his pocket, and read it feverishly, as if he hadn't already done so twenty times. Then he thrust it back into his pocket and began pacing again. He stopped, looked around, saw no one and nothing but the lake, the trees, the bench, the grass, and the mist, and pulled the note out once more. It read:

"Friedrich,

Must see you alone. Have grave news about truth regarding Johanna. Meet me by the willow walk at half past four. Very important you come alone and tell no one. Bring this note.

Alaric."

It still made no sense to him, but that was not an unusual experience and so he'd done as the note asked. He put it back into his pocket and looked up again. An unmistakable greatcoated figure was striding through the knee-deep fog towards him. He breathed a sigh of relief and waited to greet him.

"Alaric."

"Friedrich."

"What's all this about?" he asked urgently.

Von Trelow held up a placating hand, "In a moment. Were you followed?"

The question worried Friedrich, but he'd been bothered enough by the note to check.

"No," he told him.

"You're certain?" asked Alaric.

Friedrich nodded assuredly.

"Yes."

"And you told no one you were coming or meeting me?" he asked suspiciously.

Friedrich was now increasingly concerned, but anxious to appease.

"I promise you; I told nobody."

Alaric nodded, clearly pleased.

"That's good. Do you have the note?" he asked, holding out his hand for it.

Friedrich at once pulled it from his pocket and handed it to him, watching in astonishment as his brother-in-law pulled a trench lighter from his pocket, sparked it, and lit the corner of the paper. Holding it carefully in his gloved fingers he twisted it about until every scrap of it was burned. He let the ashes fall to the mist-shrouded grass and ground them into the mud with his boot.

"What in heaven's name is going on?" Friedrich asked in confusion.

Von Trelow dropped the lighter back into his pocket and instead removed a large Colt pistol. He levelled it at Friedrich.

For a moment Friedrich was so stunned that he was convinced that it was meant for someone else. He looked frantically about, expecting to see lurking assassins or vengeful Bolsheviks. Finding neither, his eyes inexorably returned to the handgun and to von Trelow.

"What's happening?" he asked again, his voice tightening with fear.

"It was you, Friedrich. You killed Jana," von Trelow said coldly.

It was such an absurd suggestion that Friedrich, despite the terror crawling up his spine, laughed.

"Never, Alaric, I'd never," he pleaded.

"But you did, Friedrich, as surely as if you'd used phosgene, or this gun. You were sick when you came home that day. You'd been sick for several days, hadn't you? So sick you hadn't been able to travel when you were meant to and had to come when you'd recovered a little. That's why you had to use your OHL credentials to get the late-night express to stop, because you'd missed the last stopping train."

Friedrich couldn't speak. He was mesmerised by the gaping black mouth of the gun-barrel.

"You arrived home and immediately retired with a hot toddy to help you recover, didn't you? But not before hugging and kissing your sister. Your father would never do more than shake your hand, and your mother's not the hugging type, but Jana, Jana did, didn't she?"

Friedrich looked up at him in panicked disbelief.

"Didn't she, Friedrich?" von Trelow repeated menacingly.

"What?" said Friedrich, "Yes, I suppose. Yes, we hugged, we always did."

Von Trelow nodded, sadly.

"That's when you killed her, Friedrich. You had influenza, the new, bad strain that kills the young and the strong, like Johanna. You gave it to her, and she was dead, she just didn't know it yet."

Friedrich, the words slowly beginning to make it through to his understanding, went pale.

He began to gabble, "No, no, that's absurd, I was fine. It was just a cold, a bad cold..."

"No, Friedrich, it wasn't."

Desperately Friedrich sought an escape.

"But I had no choice, my orders."

Von Trelow shook his head, heavy with regret.

"No, Friedrich. Your mission had been completed weeks before. You already had the agreement of General Groener and the General Staff, otherwise your father and his friends would never have dared be in discussion with a Socialist politician like Braun. It would have been treason. They'd have been shot for fomenting a coup. Which is exactly what they've done, except they've done it with the agreement of the army—and their agreement was obtained long before that weekend."

Friedrich looked around for a way out and, finding nothing, settled for pleading,

"Alaric, please!"

"No, Friedrich. You could have stayed away, should have done. The influenza has been laying waste to troops and civilians for months. You knew that; you had to. Being on the General Staff, you must have seen the intelligence. You were sick and there was no good reason for you to be here. You came because of your tawdry little affair with Louisa Gephart and because you wanted to be part of the action. It wasn't even your plan; it was your mother's. You were just the messenger boy, but you wanted to feel important, so you had to come." He stepped closer; the pistol still levelled.

"You're going to kill me, for that? For being sick? I didn't mean to hurt her, Alaric, she was my sister! It was an accident!"

"I promised her I'd find out who killed her, and I'd make them pay. So here we are," said von Trelow.

As his words penetrated Friedrich's fear-addled mind the frightened young major saw a sliver of hope and grasped at it.

"You won't do it!" he gasped on the edge of hysteria. "You're an honourable man, Alaric von Trelow und Ehlinger, an officer, and a Prussian Junker. I don't believe you'll kill an unarmed man. You won't do it!" He laughed now, seeing the bright dawn of his salvation.

Von Trelow ignored him, stepped past him to the wooden bench, where he'd proposed to Johanna back on a chill autumn day three years before, and laid the Colt on the seat. He stepped back, unbuttoned the leather holster at his hip, drew the comfortable shape of his Luger and pulled the toggle to cock it. The clack of the mechanism shocked Friedrich back to reality. He stared at von Trelow, the Luger, and the Colt lying on the bench.

"Pick it up, Friedrich," said Alaric.

Friedrich gaped at the big American automatic and shook his head.

"No, if I touch it, you'll shoot me," he stammered.

Alaric snapped up his pistol and pointed it at his head.

"I said, pick it up. I don't want to gun you down, Friedrich. You'll get the chance you never gave her. We're going to do this the old way, the honourable way. Twenty paces between us, then we turn and fire. If you want to live, pick it up!"

"You're insane!" gasped Friedrich.

"I've been at war for over four years, Friedrich, would that be such a surprise? Now I'm giving you a chance, but if you don't take it, I will shoot you anyway. Now pick it up!" he barked.

Friedrich did so, snatching at the pistol and holding it in a wildly shaking hand.

"Now we're going to turn and walk, ten paces each..."

"I can't..." Friedrich whined pitifully.

"Then we turn and fire. If you run, I'll shoot you. I won't run. You have seven shots in that pistol, use them all if you want, I'll only fire once."

He was so calm, so cold.

Friedrich showed nothing but icy terror.

"I can't..." he begged again.

Von Trelow looked at him, saw his shaking hands and unsteady legs and decided that he was probably right. He probably couldn't walk ten paces.

"I'll walk twenty paces; I'll count as I go. On twenty we turn and fire." The sun was on the amber horizon, the light the spectral softness of dusk, there would be just enough time.

Friedrich made no reply.

Von Trelow turned and began to walk away along the bank, counting out loud.

"One, two, three, four..."

He heard a clack as Friedrich checked the chamber, but he knew there was a round ready.

"Five, six, seven, eight..."

He wondered if Friedrich would do the smart thing, as his mother would have done. Marla Buhler would have fired already, but no shot rang out across the lake.

"Nine, ten, eleven, twelve..."

Surely now, he'd had time to compose himself, to swallow his fear, find the safety catch and aim.

"Thirteen, fourteen, fifteen, sixteen..."

Von Trelow closed his eyes and waited for the shot he'd never hear and to see Jana again.

"Seventeen, eighteen, nineteen, twenty."

He opened his eyes with a heart swollen with an agony of loss and turned. The Luger rose in his hand, an extension of his body and intent, and came to rest on target.

Friedrich was standing motionless, mist swathing him to his knees, the pistol loose at his side and his head slumped, as his shoulders shook with sobbing. Von Trelow's trigger finger gently squeezed, taking up the tension, finding the firing point with long-honed practice.

A breath, so gentle, stroked his cold cheek and a gossamer touch lay soft upon his hand. He smelt rose otto. Slowly he lowered the gun.

"I'm sorry, I'm sorry, I'm so sorry..." Friedrich was rambling over and over.

Von Trelow watched for a moment, then carefully holstered the Luger and buttoned it down.

"I'll leave you the pistol, Friedrich," he called across the twilight lakeside, "for when you find your honour."

When Friedrich, alive and disbelieving, finally raised his tear-streaked face, the daylight and von Trelow were gone.

Glossary

Adjutant	Assistant to a senior officer
Argonne	Forest in France, scene of savage fighting in late 1918, where the American forces fought some of their first battles
Bursche	The equivalent of the British 'batman', an officer's personal servant and orderly
Communication Trench	A trench running between the lateral lines of trenches to allow movement between them without being seen or shot
Ersatz-Coffee	Fake coffee, made from roasted acorns, often with chiccory. Bitter and typically disliked. The only type of coffee available to most Germans due to the British naval blockade
Feldgrau Bluse	Field-Grey Blouse, a soldier's tunic, typically worn in the field instead of the Waffenrock, having a flap to cover the buttons

Feldwebel	A senior sergeant, the highest rank of non-commissioned officer in the Imperial German Army
Firing Step	A step inside a trench, facing the enemy allowing the soldiers to stand up on it to fire
Guardsman/Guards	Elite units in the Imperial German Army. Footguards were recruited for their size, strength and discipline. All had to be at least 5'10"
Hauptmann	Captain. A junior commissioned officer. Typically, responsible for leading a Company (c.120 men) or a staff role including Adjutant
Junker	Class of Prussian aristocrats, mainly landowners from traditional feudal families who dominated the officer class of Imperial Germany
Kaiser	The German Emperor. In 1918 this was Wilhelm II, who was half British, his mother having been Queen Victoria's daughter
K-Brot	Short for Krieg-Brot, literally 'war-bread'. Bread made of potato flour and rye, a cheap alternative to wheat bread, given originally to the poor, but increasingly to everyone. Other variations included turnip bread
Landgendarmerie	Prussian armed police, a paramilitary force responsible for policing outside of the cities in the small towns and rural areas. The largest police force in Germany

Leutnant	Lieutenant. A junior commissioned officer, either assigned to lead a platoon of around 30-36 men, or to assist a more senior officer
Luger (P.08)	The standard sidearm of the Imperial German army. Fires a 9mm Parabellum round. One of the first semi-automatic pistols. Known for its quality, accuracy and power, but prone to malfunctioning if dirty
Major	Major. A mid-level commissioned officer. Typically, responsible for a Company (c.120 men), or second in command of a Battalion, or supporting a General officer as staff or Adjutant
Maxim Gun	Colloquial name for the MG.08, standard German machine gun. Water-cooled and fired from a tripod, sometimes called a 'Spandau' after the fortress outside Berlin
No-Man's Land	The area between enemy trench systems, belonging to neither side. The area fought over. Consistently full of obstacles and mines. Regarded as lethal to enter
NCO	Non-commissioned officer. A soldier promoted from the ranks for his experience, like a sergeant
Oberste-Heeresleitung	Abbreviated as OHL. The General Headquarters of the Imperial German Army, in late 1918 based at Spa in Belgium

Oberstleutnant	Lieutenant Colonel. A mid to senior-level commissioned officer, above a Major but below a Colonel. Typically, either responsible for leading a Battalion (c.400 men) or for a senior staff role at divisional level. Often referred to in conversation as Oberst/Colonel
Oberst	Colonel. A senior commissioned officer, below a General officer. Typically commands a Regiment (c.800 men) or has a senior staff role at Army level
Parados	The back wall of a trench
Parapet	The front wall of a trench, often used to refer specifically to the raised sandbags at the top
Phosgene	One of several commonly used poison gases used by both sides in the Great War, and typically the most lethal. Caused rapid death by asphyxiation, leading to cyanosis (blue skin, particularly the face) and rictus (violent spasming in the limbs and extremities
Potsdam	Town to the south-west of Berlin, famed for its military facilities, particularly as home to the Prussian Guards
Pour le Mérite	Known colloquially as the 'Blue Max', the highest honour in Imperial Germany, reserved for the most important civil contributions or most valorous military exploits
Prussia	The largest state in Imperial Germany, with lands from the Rhineland in the

	west to the Russian border in the east. Traditionally highly militarist and making up the majority of the Imperial Army. The King of Prussia was also the Kaiser of Germany
Rose Otto	An early, popular perfume with a flowery fragrance, very popular amongst polite society of the period. The alternative, eau de cologne, being seen as rather racier
Stahlhelm	Steel helmet typical of the Imperial German Army by 1918, replaced the earlier spike topped Pickelhaub which was made of hardened leather
Vice-Wachtmeister	Deputy Sergeant Major. A senior NCO in the artillery and other technical units, also used in the Prussian police
Waffenrock	A military tunic with buttons down the front, typically worn without a belt

Historical Context

This story is set in the final weeks of the Great War, later to be known as the First World War, or World War One. Whilst not the first war to span the globe—the Napoleonic Wars, Seven Years War, or the War of Spanish Succession have earlier claims to that title—it was the first global industrial war. The powers that fought it entered it expecting a nineteenth century conflict of short engagements and cavalry dash, some still marched in bright coloured uniforms with officers in white gloves. Instead, it became an industrialised slaughter where machine guns, barbed wire, artillery and, eventually, poison gas, reigned supreme. Millions died as generals on all sides sought ways to break an impossible deadlock.

Scouts (Späher)

With the Western Front fixed and immobile from the Alps to the North Sea, specialist troops—scouts or Späher—were sent into no-man's land to gather information, to reconnoitre, to take prisoners, and to map minefields, wire barriers and enemy positions. These varied from skilled and daring individuals, often former poachers, gamekeepers, or hunters, through to well-armed raiding parties. By stealth and cunning, they moved amongst the terrible and lethal territory between the enemy lines. Encounters with their counterparts often led to savage hand-to-hand battles in shell-holes and mud, invariably in silence for fear of the artillery and machine guns of both sides.

The character of Alaric von Trelow is based upon the exploits of these men, and though remarkable, his behaviour and deeds are not unprecedented. Some men did seem to lead charmed lives, lasting the entire war in even the most dangerous of roles. Most were not so fortunate—reconnaissance casualties were amongst the highest of any military specialty. Alaric is amongst the fortunate survivors, one of Frau Buhler's mathematical anomalies, although the war has certainly taken its toll.

Shellshock

In 1918, what we now recognize as PTSD was termed "shell shock" and woefully misunderstood. Military and medical authorities largely viewed it as a failure of character—cowardice disguised as illness. The British Army alone executed 306 soldiers for cowardice or desertion, many of whom were almost certainly suffering from what we would now diagnose as severe psychological trauma.

Treatment, when offered at all, was primitive and often brutal. "Shell-shocked" soldiers might be subjected to electric shock therapy, cold baths, or simply told to "pull themselves together." The few progressive doctors who recognized it as genuine medical condition had no effective treatments to offer.

Even those who understood that psychological breakdown was real believed it primarily affected men of "weak character" or inferior breeding. Officers like Alaric—from the right social class who had previously demonstrated courage—were more likely to be quietly invalided out or given extended leave, their symptoms attributed to "neurasthenia" or "nervous exhaustion" rather than the stigmatizing label of shell shock.

The result was that vast numbers of former soldiers returned to civilian life carrying invisible wounds that no one understood or could treat. Many, like Alaric, learned to function despite recurring nightmares, flashbacks, and hypervigilance, their trauma becoming a private burden to be endured rather than healed.

The War by 1918

By late 1918 new weapons and tactics meant that breakthroughs, though terrifyingly costly in lives, were possible. In 1917 Russia had collapsed into revolution and been forced out of the war, freeing up hundreds of thousands of German soldiers for use in the west. The resultant Spring Offensive of 1918 broke the Allied lines and almost drove them back to Paris, but it failed, being too little, too late. The Allies recovered and rebuilt in a way the German forces could not and were boosted by a newly arrived and fresh American army, the US having entered the war in 1917. The Hundred Days Offensive by the Allies began on the 8th August and drove the Germans back to their early 1918 positions and beyond. Despite dogged German resistance there would be no recovery.

By late September all but the most fanatical German militarists understood that the war was lost, and many were looking for a way to bring the conflict to a close. Many looked to the moderate Fourteen Points proposed by US President Woodrow Wilson as a potential model for peace.

The Home Front

In Germany, four years of blockade by the British Royal Navy had brought deprivation and near famine, driving the population to desperation and the brink of revolution. The winter of 1916-17 had been so bad that it became known as the "Turnip Winter" since turnips were the only food most could get, for many the following year had been even worse. In autumn 1918 the German people looked forward to the coming winter with anticipatory horror. At the same time, and exacerbated by poor nutrition, numerous diseases also took a terrible toll; cholera, typhus, typhoid, and tuberculosis all affected far higher numbers than had previously been the case, not only in the trenches but also at home.

Spanish Flu

During the spring of 1918 a particularly virulent strain of influenza also appeared, first in America, but spreading rapidly to Europe and worldwide. Because most of the countries initially hit were belligerents in the war, and therefore subject to censorship, news of the epidemic was suppressed. Uncensored reports of the disease from neutral Spain led to it being named the “Spanish Flu”, or “Spanish Lady”.

The first wave had passed by late June, but a second wave, with a more lethal strain, began to appear in August. This strain was unprecedented in its effects, striking particularly at healthy young adults and in some cases proving lethal within hours of the first symptoms. No one had ever seen a disease like it.

Death was typically due to a cytokine storm which ravaged the immune system, flooding the victim’s lungs with fluid, causing death by asphyxiation, leaving them cyanotic (blue) and in a rictus state (twisted extremities). By a peculiar coincidence these were precisely the same symptoms as death by phosgene poisoning, the most lethal of the poison gases used on the battlefields of 1918. In these circumstances I hope you will be able to forgive von Trelow’s error, he was not alone.

Medical Understanding in 1918

Although we now know that influenza, in all its forms, is caused by a virus, in 1918 this was not understood, and it was believed to be caused by some kind of bacteria. The presence of a particular bacterium, “Pfeiffer’s Bacillus”, was taken to be indicative. It is now regarded as entirely coincidental, but at the time was taken to be a clear proof. When Lise Freisinger, one of the new breed of female doctors graduating for the first time in this decade from universities like Heidelberg and Freiberg, grows cultures to look for Pfeiffer’s Bacillus, she is following the latest medical practice, wrong as we may now know it to be.

Political Upheaval

By 1918 the German General Staff, the OHL, had been effectively ruling Germany for three years, the Kaiser rubber stamping their decrees and orders. With the war heading towards defeat, certain senior generals sought a way for the military to escape blame for the national disaster. At the same time the democratic politicians were calling for a true democratic government.

The largest political group were the social democrats, with their party the majority SPD. They feared their more radical communist colleagues would push Germany towards an extremist revolution, as had happened in Russia. In the event they saw the opportunity to take control, for themselves and their moderate allies, just as the army wished to relinquish power, and stepped in. This gave them the political ascendency they sought, but at the cost of being seen as national traitors who had 'stabbed the army in the back,' as it was they who were left to explain and negotiate the defeat.

Contrary to expectations, the SPD and their allies kept to very moderate demands for economic redistribution, hoping to ensure national unity. They focussed their reforming attention on the traditional Prussian Junker landowners who had formed the core of the Imperial ruling and military class. Industrialists were not touched, largely for fear of appearing to favour the workers unduly, thereby strengthening the communists.

The alliance of industry and labour would be openly formalised on the 15th November by the signing of the Stinnes-Legien Agreement between the major industrialists and the unions, whilst the SPD politicians and army had formalised their alliance through the Ebert-Groener pact five days earlier. The alliance of army, industry and socialist politicians would shape the new Germany, but it would ultimately seed its doom.

Historical Speculation

This story postulates the idea that this was all more than just coincidence and fortune. Certainly, there were many conversations being had between disparate groups and odd fellow travellers in those desperate days of late September and early October, as various people sought a way out of an unwinnable war without plunging into a Bolshevik-style revolution. Could things have happened as the story suggests? I think they could have done. Did they? Who can say?

Legacy

In the end there was peace, but it would be a far harsher peace than the American Fourteen Points had suggested, and the German politicians and people had hoped for. It included the removal of the Kaiser and the monarchy in favour of the democratic Weimar Republic, the acceptance of blame for the war, the loss of colonies and huge European territories, the reduction of the proud German military to a shameful rump, and the payment of vast reparations.

The anger and sense of injustice this caused, in a nation where many believed that their mighty army had never lost but had been betrayed, would go on to fatally direct the future of Germany and the world. When Frau Buhler says that whatever the cost, they will pay it later, she is right, everyone would pay.

Author's Note and Bio

Hello, and thank you for reading *'Prussian Blue'*. If you've skipped to the end, please go back and have a read. It was tremendous fun to write, and readers tell me it's a lot of fun to read—I certainly smile every time I reread it.

I grew up in the UK in the idyllic, but rather quiet and staid county of Cornwall, at a time when the veterans of the Great War were still, just, amongst us—grandfathers and great-grandfathers. Their stories were there to be heard if we wanted to listen. I did. Even more accessible were tales of the days that came after and would culminate in the Second World War. I listened. I read. I became a lover of history.

Like many who learned of that period, I initially gravitated to the two cataclysmic conflicts that defined the early twentieth century. Yet increasingly it was that odd period between them—what Ferdinand Foch called the "armistice for twenty years"—that captured my imagination.

I was immensely fortunate in being able to indulge this interest for several years at the University of Oxford, before life intervened and it became a mere interest and hobby. But it was one that never left me and often occupied more of my mental time than my career did.

On New Year's Day 2023, I began to write. I wrote about the end of the Great War, not from the perspective of the victors, but that of the losers. I wanted to write about what happened in Germany after the Great War ended, and before the monochrome good and evil of the Nazi regime. In that brief period from 1918 to 1933 a brief flower bloomed. Weimar Germany was wondrous, frenetic, chaotic, often violent, sometimes bizarrely strange, and yet strangely familiar and modern. These were the stories I decided I wanted to tell, and I wanted to tell them through the eyes of someone as bewildered, confused and as surprised as we would be.

Enter Alaric von Trelow: a Junker soldier, a war hero, a living embodiment of the former regime, thrust into a new and transformed world. He was to be wealthy, so that we could see the wonders of this time, not get dragged down by the grit and grime and the needs of surviving day to day. I've given him a familiar literary burden—the untimely death of a beloved wife. This was, I promise, a deliberate choice. So much of his world will be strange and confusing, this at least we can understand. It is important to add that von Trelow is not perfect, he is a product of his experiences, as we all are, and he fails as often as he succeeds. He is certainly no apologist for militarism or, worse, fascism, he would abhor both, and will, as we shall see.

I have been fortunate to travel to many of the places that will appear in these stories, to have had certain experiences that, through the ever more dramatic lens of fiction, can be reframed. Most of all, I have continued my love of history. As well as every new published work on or around the period, I have sought out obscure texts, journals, diaries, period guidebooks, magazines, ordered odd periodicals sent from small bookshops overseas. I've used Google Translate to understand documents my mediocre German could never have managed. I've sat in libraries and museums, listened to the music, watched the cinema, walked the streets, eaten the food, handled the objects and worn the clothes. I have literally walked a mile in von Trelow's shoes, and in his coat. In short, I have immersed myself in Weimar Germany, to the point where I feel like I know the streets of 1920s Berlin better than those of my home city.

During this research I have constantly found the odd, the unusual and the forgotten in its pages. There are so many tales, events, places and machines we should remember, but lie forgotten. They are marvels and delights, and I have tried in writing these stories to bring them, if only for a moment, back into the light for us to look at one more time and be amazed, astonished, perhaps horrified, and be better for it. I chose the mystery format to explore these marvels because detection requires careful observation, a focus on details, an eye open at all times. As von Trelow investigates and discovers truths, we travel beside him and discover his world. There's a lot to see between 1918 and 1933, and von Trelow keeps busy—from political conspiracies to jewel heists, cocaine rings to communist risings, Polish prisons to African valleys. We'll meet princes, prostitutes, revolutionaries, millionaire industrialists, jazz singers, exotic dancers, movie stars, gangsters, heroes, villains, and, of course, a few Nazis.

This is the beginning of von Trelow's journey through one of history's most vibrant eras. It's going to be a long, winding, and exciting road—I hope you'll join us for the ride.

Jason Collings, 2025

BEROLINA
BOOKS

Printed in Dunstable, United Kingdom

70721419R00147